A CYCLE PATH MYSTERY

W9-AVT-233

GEARED FOR THE GRAVE

DUFFY BROWN

WHEELER PUBLISHING
A part of Gale, Cengage Learning

GALE
CENGAGE Learning·

Farmington Hills, Mich • San Francisco • New York • Waterville, Maine
Meriden, Conn • Mason, Ohio • Chicago

GALE
CENGAGE Learning®

Copyright © 2014 by Duffy Brown.
A Cycle Path Mystery.
Wheeler Publishing, a part of Gale, Cengage Learning.

ALL RIGHTS RESERVED
This is a work of fiction. Names, characters, places, and incidents either are the product of the author's imagination or are used fictitiously, and any resemblance to actual persons, living or dead, business establishments, events, or locales is entirely coincidental.
The publisher does not have any control over and does not assume any responsibility for author or third-party websites or their content.
Wheeler Publishing Large Print Cozy Mystery.
The text of this Large Print edition is unabridged.
Other aspects of the book may vary from the original edition.
Set in 16 pt. Plantin.

LIBRARY OF CONGRESS CATALOGING-IN-PUBLICATION DATA

Names: Brown, Duffy, author.
Title: Geared for the grave / by Duffy Brown.
Description: Large print edition. | Waterville, Maine : Wheeler Publishing, 2016. | Series: A cycle path mystery | Series: Wheeler Publishing large print cozy mystery
Identifiers: LCCN 2016037399| ISBN 9781410495006 (softcover) | ISBN 1410495000 (softcover)
Subjects: LCSH: Murder—Investigation—Fiction. | Mackinac Island (Mich.)—Fiction. | Large type books. | GSAFD: Mystery fiction.
Classification: LCC PS3602.R6958 G43 2016 | DDC 813/.6—dc23
LC record available at https://lccn.loc.gov/2016037399

Published in 2016 by arrangement with The Berkley Publishing Group, an imprint of Penguin Publishing Group, a division of Penguin Random House LLC

Printed in the United States of America
1 2 3 4 5 6 7 20 19 18 17 16

*To the great folks on Mackinac Island . . .
a little taste of heaven. To Pam and
Kristen at the Market Street Inn where I
stayed. Thanks for the great island stories
and a glimpse of how the island operates.
Thanks to Jared and Dave at the
Mustang Lounge, the Stang. Your fried
green beans are the best. Thanks to Neil
at the Woods for the drinks; thanks to
Mary Patay and Neeko, the island cruise
directors. Thanks to Tamera and Mary
Jane at the Island Bookstore for the
warm welcome.*

*Thanks to daughter Ann Marie
Kruetzkamp for going with me to
discover Mackinac Island.
Mother-daughter memories are the best.*

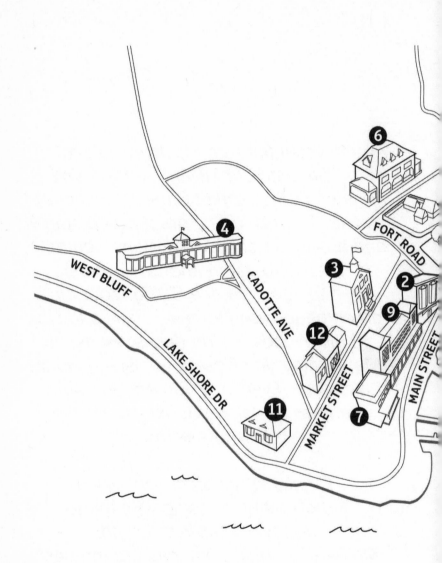

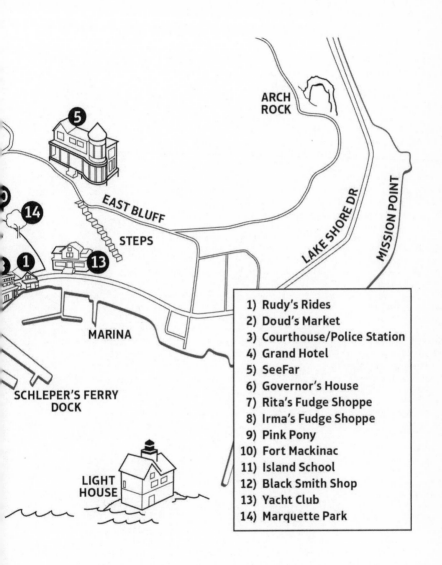

ARCH ROCK

EAST BLUFF

STEPS

LAKE SHORE DR

MISSION POINT

MARINA

SCHLEPER'S FERRY DOCK

LIGHT HOUSE

1) Rudy's Rides
2) Doud's Market
3) Courthouse/Police Station
4) Grand Hotel
5) SeeFar
6) Governor's House
7) Rita's Fudge Shoppe
8) Irma's Fudge Shoppe
9) Pink Pony
10) Fort Mackinac
11) Island School
12) Black Smith Shop
13) Yacht Club
14) Marquette Park

1

While cowering in the back of a ferryboat, head over railing and losing my lunch in Lake Huron, it occurred to me that no matter how old I am, I want to impress my parents. Deep inside I'm just a kid yelling, *Mom, look at me! No hands!* Granted, this wasn't exactly a *look at me* moment, but it's what got me into this mess.

"Hey, lady. Where should I put these paint cans?" a man in a neon yellow vest asked as I staggered off the last ferry of the day. After a ten-hour drive plastered with orange construction barrels followed by the boat trip from hell, I so wanted to tell this guy where to put those cans. Instead I handed him a twenty and said, "Get a taxi and put them in the trunk."

"First-time fudgie?"

I was thirty-four, had been around the Chicago block a few times and ten months ago got left standing at the altar thanks to a sports-aholic fiancé and the seduction of last-minute game three World Series tickets. I wasn't a *first-time* anything. "Fudgie?"

"Yeah, good luck with that trunk."

And for that smart-ass crack I'd forked over twenty bucks. I zipped my fleece against the lake chill, grabbed a paint can and my duffel and trudged up the dock with the rest of the tourists to Main Street, lined with twinkle-lights and cute shops shutting down for the night, the whole place smelling kind of . . . earthy?

"Can you get me a taxi to Rudy's Rides?" I asked a college kid as he tossed luggage onto a horse cart. He nodded to a two-horse-power red and yellow wagon with people merrily climbing on board.

I dangled the can. "A car taxi, like as in fast transportation weaving in and out of traffic scaring everyone. It's been a long day."

"Lady, this is as fast as we get around here." College guy added another bag to the cart, and people and luggage carts clip-clopped off past meandering pedestrians and bikes, with no traffic lights or roar of internal combustion engines anywhere. A poster in the window of Fred's Deli announced a Dirty Pony Wash. Not a car wash? Where the heck was I?

I yanked out Sheldon, my BFF iPhone. *OhthankGod* he had bars. I hadn't slipped into some time-warp thing, and there on the screen right below the Mackinac Island ferry schedule was the no-car statement. *You got to be kidding.* This was Michigan; Motown; the birthplace of hydrocarbons and gas-guzzling engines and ozone central.

I followed Sheldon's directions past the Lilac Hotel, Doud's Market and one, two, make that seven fudge shops just within the two blocks I could see. My guess was that fudgies were tourists, and dentists and Weight Watchers owned the biggest houses on the island. Rudy's Rides sat next to Irma's Fudge Emporium. Why couldn't it be the broccoli emporium? I could resist broccoli ten feet from where I'd spend the next week.

Propped-open, weathered double doors marked the entrance to Rudy's, where a shiny new yellow three-wheeler sat at the curb next to a horse and buggy. I stepped inside the shop only to find rental bikes from the Ronald Reagan years. Dusty handlebars and pedals lined the wall next to a spotless trophy shelf, and tools littered the workbench. A pool table sat in back with a stained-glass light suspended overhead. Mark Twain said, *Rumors of my death have*

11

been greatly exaggerated, and here he was in a white crumpled suit, wild gray hair, cigar balanced across a whiskey glass and his left leg in a cast.

The Twain look-alike, whom I took to be Rudy, aimed at the nine ball as a girl about my age in a purple sequined paperboy hat with a pencil stuck in the band hustled inside scribbling in a notebook. A knobby-kneed granny in electric pink biker shorts brought up the rear.

"I took a good look around this place," Knees huffed at Rudy. "It's a dump, just like I thought. Town council meets tomorrow night, and I'm getting on the agenda and recommending they shut you down."

Knees turned to the sequined-hat girl. "But whatever you do, Fiona, don't put that in the *Town Crier.* You're just getting the hang of being the editor now that your mom and dad headed off for Arizona and the sun and left us in the lurch. This isn't that *Inside Scoop* rag where we tell all. You need to say something like *Rudy's Rides is closing for remodeling.* Fudgies pay for Norman Rockwell around here, so we give them Norman Rockwell." She swiped her finger across a dusty bike fender. "This is *Beverly Hillbillies.*"

Fiona scribbled more notes. "It's late and

I'm tired and cranky and getting a lot crankier the longer this takes. I'm doing an article on bicycle shops like you want, Bunny, and right now Rudy's Rides is open for business, period, end of discussion."

Rudy sent the nine ball across the green felt, missing the left pocket by a mile. "Geeze Louise." He jabbed his cigar at Bunny. "I know what you're trying to pull, and it's not going to work. That snotty historical committee of yours up there on the bluffs has three votes on the council — just three. The business owners down here in town trying to make a buck got the other three, and I'm one of 'em. Our shops would go belly-up with rules about original windows, pine floors and the other half-baked ideas that pop into your little pea-brain 'cause you got nothing else to do. You wanna shut me down to get me out of your hair."

Bunny stuck her prune face inches from Rudy's. "The only thing up to snuff in this joint are your euchre trophies and that pool table. Start packing, Rudy boy, you're history."

Bunny tromped through the bike maze and climbed on her three-wheeler as Rudy raised his whiskey glass. "Here's to the old bat going, and that's a heck of a lot better than the old bat coming."

Fiona closed her notebook. "Bunny thinks she's hot stuff around here because her family's been on the island longer than dirt and she lives in a big house. Rudy's Rides is staying in my article." Fiona gave Rudy a kiss on the cheek, then hurried out, her departure followed by the sound of horse hooves on pavement fading down the street.

"Take any bike that suits you," Rudy said to me as he lined up his next shot. "I keep them all running good even if they are a little rough around the edges. Put the money in the coffee can on the workbench — no charge for local drama. It's free, and there's a lot of it these days."

"I'm Evie Bloomfield from Chicago. I'm here to help you."

"The only help I need is with sinking the dang nine ball. Haven't made a decent shot all day."

I dropped my duffel and purse, snagged a cue, aimed for the far pocket and sent the yellow-striped ball sailing across the felt, till Rudy plucked it right off the table. "Hey, why'd you do that? I nailed it."

Rudy scooped his hand into the pocket, dragging out a sleepy black-and-white kitten. "Bambino hangs out there; left pocket's off-limits." Rudy balanced on one crutch —

he was a one-crutch kind of guy. "So, Chicago, what brings a pool shark to my doorstep this time of night? From the way things are going, it can't be anything good."

I did the innocent look and got the *don't mess with me* look in reply. "Pool's the only thing I could do better than my brother, and the doorstep part is that I work for your daughter." Though one look at Rudy's Rides and it was hard to see any connection to a daughter with dollar signs on her license plate. "Abigail's tied up with a business deal at the ad agency, so I'm here in her place to lend you a hand."

"Or a leg." Rudy took a piece of kibble from his pocket for Bambino. "What juicy carrot did my daughter dangle to get you out of Chicagoland to an eight-mile island without a shopping mall or car in sight?"

"Just trying to be useful." I plastered my best perky *please the nice client* smile on my face.

"Twain says, *Don't tell fish stories where they know the fish.* I know my daughter. There's a carrot."

My perky died. It was late; I was tired. Rudy had me, and he knew it. I plopped down on my gallon can of beach-baby blue paint. "Bloomfields are lawyers — really successful lawyers except for me — and my apartment's the size of your pool table, except the table's nicer. I'm thirty-four, Thanksgiving's the next great family gathering and I need a promotion — some bragging rights for a change." I tapped the can I was sitting on. "Hauled nine of these all the way out here so I could spruce up the place. So, what do you think?"

"I think you're kissing up to the boss."

"Being of assistance sounds better. Abigail sort of takes me for granted."

"Abigail takes everyone for granted unless they're a client." Rudy sipped the whiskey. "I'll get caught up around here once the cast comes off." He rapped his knuckles against the white plaster. "Planned on making repairs this spring till I got busy with this town council feud and maybe a euchre tournament or two. How'd Abigail find out that I broke my dang leg in the first place? I sure didn't tell her."

"That would be my doing," a man said, making his way through the shop. He was about the same age as Rudy and balding, and had the words *Euchre Dude* embroidered across his shirt pocket.

"You'd think your only offspring would show up," the guy said, giving me the head-to-toe disapproving glare. "I came to check on the bikes I ordered last week and I heard

16

you had a visitor from Chicago. Never thought Abigail would send in a pinch hitter who —"

"Look," I interrupted, acing out another *go away* speech. "There aren't any ferries till morning, so unless you want me to doggie paddle it back to Mackinaw City with paint cans strapped to my ankles . . ."

Rudy took a sip of whiskey. "Guess there's no harm in you waiting around for my last rentals while Ed and I play a few hands of euchre down at the Stang." Rudy brightened. "Sounds pretty good, actually. The tournament's on, and I got room for a new trophy up there on the shelf."

"I can do whatever," I said in a rush. I had no idea how to play euchre or what the Stang was, but I could park a bike and I'd have time to figure out how to make Operation Brownnose a potential success instead of a looming failure. Ed snuffed the cigar in a crackled flowerpot. "Don't know why anyone smokes these things. I'll get our lucky deck from my place. Can't believe Abigail isn't here. Kids — they grow up and only come around when they're the ones needing something."

Ed sauntered off, and Rudy tucked Bambino back in the left pocket on the pool table. He pointed his crutch at the front door. "All you gotta do is pull it shut. It sticks, so you gotta give it a tug. Then turn off the lights. There's one little lock that don't 'mount to much, but it keeps the drunks at the Pink Pony from taking my bikes and pedaling themselves straight off a dang cliff and into the lake. This isn't the big city; nothing happens around here. Kitchen's in the back, cold pizza in the fridge, extra bedrooms upstairs, make yourself at home for the night. Just one night."

Rudy thump-stepped his way down Main Street, and I saw my promotion thump-stepping into oblivion. Bunny was dead-on about the place being a dump, and if I didn't think of something fast, I'd be on the first ferry back to the real world by morning and eating turkey at the little kids' table by Thanksgiving.

I parked the late rentals inside as the phone on the workbench rang — a customer needing two bikes delivered to a house called RestMore by morning to get an early start and catch the sunrise at six. Must be one heck of a sunrise.

The phone went dead before I got an address, and I had no idea where or how to deliver bikes around here. I found a pencil on the workbench and scribbled RestMore on a can of red primer as the words "Yoo-hoo, Rudy, me darling man, how ye be doing this fine night?" singsonged through front door.

"But you not be Rudy, now are ye, dearie," the woman said, an Irish lilt in her voice. "I suspect ye be that Chicago fudgie girl with a bunch of paint cans we've been hearing about all night long. You kind of stand out, ye do."

Before I could answer, two handlebars fell off the wall, crashing to the ground, an owl hooted three times, the lights blinked on and off, and a rooster crowed somewhere in the distance. The woman clutched the gold shamrock around her neck, her eyes big as goose eggs. "Great day in the morning and blessed be Saint Patrick!" She kissed the shamrock. "How can it be you're still alive?"

"Hey, Chicago isn't *that* bad."

" 'Tis not the geography that's the worry, me dear, but a big black cloud that's hanging right over ye." She gazed around me. "Bad signs these are," she said in a low voice. "Bad indeed, and all happening at once! Saints preserve us. I be Irish Donna and I know these things. I got the gift, I do." She lowered her voice even more. "Ye should be making up a will; the sooner the better, if you be asking me."

Irish Donna was on the upward side of sixty, with curly red hair, and she scared the heck out of me, but the dark cloud theory explained a lot about my life lately. I said to Donna, "Rudy and Ed are at the Stang, and a customer needs bikes delivered. Got any ideas where RestMore is? And just how big is this cloud anyway?"

Ten minutes later Irish Donna and I did the slow . . . really, really slow . . . clip-clop up a steep hill in her one-horse carriage. We'd wedged two bikes in the back, and after Donna patted the Saint Christopher medal where a cup-holder should be, we took off.

A nearly full moon lit the street, which had huge Victorians standing guard on one side and the town stretching out below the cliff on the other, and me contemplating the fact that they should make Pampers for horses. Amazing what you think about when dead tired, the minutes ticking away like hours and the business end of a large animal swaying in front of you. I was suffering from car withdrawal. "What do you do on the island?" I asked Donna, to keep awake and get my mind off giant-size Pampers.

"Shamus and I run the Blarney Scone over there on Market Street, and I be helping answering the phones with Fiona at the

Town Crier on occasion. It gives me dear husband and myself a break from each other and we don't end up in screaming matches over how much butter to put in the pastries and what to charge for Earl Grey. I'm working my way up to reporter. Lucky for you, Paddy here and me were out delivering the newspapers and could lend a hand with the bikes.

"You know," Irish Donna went on. "While we're riding along like we are, ye can be telling me all about your lovely self so I can be working on your obituary for when things take a turn for the bad as I figure they might anytime now. A touch of autumn in the air, did ye notice, just a touch."

I was with her till *obituary.* Donna nodded up ahead. "Well fancy that, will ye, it be Bunny's yellow bike all by itself. On her way to the euchre tournament be my guess." Donna pulled the reins and our four-legged engine shifted into neutral beside the yellow three-wheeler. "And will ye look at this." Donna clutched her shamrock. "The front's all mashed in, the light's busted out and the handlebar's twisted up like a giant pretzel, it is. Yoo-hoo," Donna called out. "Bunny me dear. Are ye in need of a wee bit of assistance this fine evening?"

"There," I said, seeing the moonlight hitting Bunny's electric pink shorts. "She's sitting by those two trees."

"More a'leaning if you ask me," Donna said on a quick intake of breath. She gave a nudge. "Go have a look-see?"

"Me?"

"I need to be minding Paddy here."

Right. Paddy was a thousand years old and asleep where he stood, and after the hill he had just climbed I couldn't blame him. I stepped down from the carriage, the sound of crickets and night stuff I didn't know everywhere. I crawled between the wood fence slats, hoping that something with wiggling antennae didn't land on me. "Bunny?"

Heart rattling around in my chest, I crept through the bushes. Leaves crunched underfoot, moonlight weaved between the overhead branches and I tried to remember to breathe. Maybe Bunny had fallen asleep on her perch and didn't hear Donna calling, or maybe she was just enjoying the view.

Bunny's eyes were wide open all right, but they weren't taking in the view. They weren't taking in anything. They were cold; vacant; dead.

My legs went to jelly and I crumpled to the ground. I'd lived all my life in Chicago and had never come across a dead person.

A few bar fights when the Bulls lost or shoving matches at a Bloomingdale's sale, but that was it. Yet here I was in the middle of freaking nowhere sitting next to a corpse named Bunny. Next time I wanted to impress my parents I'd buy them theater tickets.

2

"Well?" Donna called to me through the dark.

Yelling *dead as a doornail* seemed a little insensitive. Instead I punched up 911 and some dude answered, happy noises in the background.

"What?"

"Dead person on hill," I said, my brain in acute meltdown.

He disconnected.

I stared at the phone. What the heck! Since when did 911 disconnect! Pissed-off Chicago Evie elbowed scared-spitless Evie out of the way and repunched the numbers. "Look, you jackass," I growled into the phone. "There's a dead woman on Huron Road by some steps, so put down the brewski, drag your sorry self off your bar stool and get your big fat island butt up here now." I was from Chicago. I knew a bar when I heard one. I disconnected.

"Glory be," Irish Donna gasped from behind. "That someone would be a putting a well-aimed bullet in the old biddy at a council meeting wouldn't have surprised me. Never dreamed she'd be having herself an accident on a road she traveled all her life. Looks to me like she crashed herself head-on into the fence, then went airborne, wedging her bony body between the trees. Bet she was tearing down the hill like a bat out of hell to get up that much speed."

"I take it Bunny wasn't one of your favorite people."

"Slept with me husband, she did." Irish Donna slapped her hand over her mouth, her eyes huge. "That was twenty years ago and I never told that to another living soul, not a one."

"Your secret's safe with me. Is this the turn for the bad you mentioned?"

"Bunny would be thinking so."

Rustling sounded in the bushes. "Holy crap, there really is a body," came a deep male I-just-ran-the-steps huffing and puffing voice.

"Duh." I glared up at a guy, fortyish, tall, dark and handsome, not that looks mattered, especially at that age. I had the younger version of TD&H once, and once was enough. At present I belonged to the

Single and Loving It Club and intended to be president.

TD&H hunkered down beside me, favoring one knee, absently rubbing the other one. There was an official-looking police patch on the sleeve of his black Windbreaker and a slight bulge underneath. Either he was packing a gun even here in the land of make-believe or he'd brought along his brewski. A thin scar crossed his jawline, his left eyelid drooped slightly and his nose was less than perfect. The man hadn't spent all his life sitting at a bar on Mackinac Island.

He closed Bunny's eyes like someone who'd performed the ritual more than once. "Figured you were drunk-dialing," he said without looking at me. "It happens around here. What doesn't happen is dead in the bushes."

"Hey, Nate? Are you back there?" It was Fiona coming our way. The bushes rustled and I could see the purple sequins in the moonlight. "What's going on? You ran out of the Stang without finishing your beer, and that never happens, so I knew something important was up and — yikes!"

"It looks to me like Bunny hit the fence," Irish Donna said to Fiona. " 'Course, the trees stopped her from winding up downtown." Donna peered over the edge of the

26

cliff. "A few feet more to the right and she'd have made it all the way to Saint Ann's down below. Hard to tell for sure. Would have saved us a bit of transport time, it would."

We all stared at Donna, and she gave a little shrug. "Just making a friendly observation."

I wobbled to my feet and TD&H stood, pulling out his phone. "I'll call Doc Evers to meet us at his office, then get the ambulance up here to take the body and —"

Fiona yanked the phone right out of his hand. "No way. You can't do that. Not that I care the nasty old bat's dead and finally quiet for once, but we all know that dragging out an ambulance and a body bag is bad for business, and Labor Day is a week away. People are already pouring in and having a good time. The town merchants will string you up by your toenails if you mess with that, and with the late spring it's already been a lean year."

"Fine. What should I do, Fiona?" TD&H asked. "Take Bunny piggyback down the hill?"

"That would probably be the most exciting thing to happen to her in ages, dead or alive, but what if we use Donna's carriage to take Bunny to the medical center and

27

then in the morning we airlift her off to Mourning Meadows Mortuary on Saint Ignace? We need to keep this on the downlow, and I'll keep it out of the paper. Any hint of dead will kill the fun around here for sure."

Fiona smirked at her *kill* crack, and TD&H rolled his eyes as Donna added, "She's right as rain, she is. Fudgies are a touchy lot. The least bad thing a'brewing is like a curse from the Great Beyond. They'll all be a'scurrying off to Canada, spending their money there and not be a'coming here like they planned to partake of our life of peace, tranquility and days gone by. Now if Bunny could have bought the farm in the wintertime or early spring, the news would get itself buried and out of the way by summer when the crowds come and all would be well. The old meddling blabbermouth never did consider anyone but herself."

TD&H rubbed the back of his neck, muttering something about the effects of a full moon, and added, "Fine. I'll take Bunny in the buggy so the business district doesn't blow a gasket, but someone has to tell Dwight that his mother's not coming home tonight, or any other night. Bet he'll throw a party."

"I be knowing Dwight Harrington the

Third well enough," Donna huffed. "Not that he cares what Bunny does as long as she pays his bills."

TD&H looked at me with midnight blue eyes, putting my *single and loving it* status in serious jeopardy. "Well, Chicago, what's it going to be? A ride with the corpse into town, or delivering the news?"

Twenty minutes later Irish Donna and I watched the cop, Fiona and Bunny — wrapped in a blanket and strapped in the backseat of the buggy — trot off. We pushed the bikes the rest of the way up the hill to a big Colonial Revival; least that was my best guess, since I mostly slept through art history class. We parked the bikes that had been ordered at the back door, then continued on, the clouds skating across the moon. If the Headless Horseman galloped by, I wouldn't have been surprised.

"There's Bunny's cottage, pretty as ye please," Irish Donna said to me in a normal voice, as if we'd only walked a few feet on flat ground instead of hiking up a blasted mountain. We stood in front of a grand white Victorian that looked out over the lake, two lighthouses blinking in the distance.

"Where I come from," I huffed and puffed, bent over at the waist to catch my breath. "A cottage is where Red Riding Hood visited Grandma. This is more where the Rockefellers swill brandy with their cronies."

"It's the rich and their ways. They understate everything and be all snooty about it to boot." Donna glanced to the second floor. "Well, there be no lights a'blazing at Bunny's place this night, so it be my guess Dwight's not at home, but we'll give it a try."

Leaves tumbled across our path as we squeaked opened the rusting wrought iron gate and took the steps to the weathered front porch. A plaque with *SeeFar* stenciled in faded yellow hung next to the door. Donna rang the bell and rapped down the heavy brass lion's-head knocker, the only other sound the breeze whistling through the pines. How did people live with so much quiet? It was . . . deafening.

"Dwight's off-island and hiding out just like I thought," Donna said after one more rap. "The Seniority is a scary lot from what I hear. I'd be hiding myself out too if they were hot on my heels."

We started down Huron and I glanced back to the cottage. Was that a curtain closing in an upstairs window? "What's the Seniority?"

"A bunch of trouble from what I hear. Dwight's been nipped by the good life, he has: fast cars, fast boats and lots of fast women. The word is he swindled some old folks with serious connections out of money to pay for his fun and now they be coming after him. He probably didn't know about the connections part or he would have picked some other oldsters to swindle. The island's a good place to lie low for a bit, but he can't do that forever now, can he?"

We reached the lit wood staircase leading to town, my gaze taking in the bazillion steps in front of me. Next time I saw my little blue Honda Civic I'd kiss it. We started down, our footfalls the only sound, a damp fog circling in the trees and around our ankles. Irish Donna gave me a sideways glance when we reached the bottom. "Been a strange night it has."

"Because of the black cloud?"

"First ferry be leaving at seven."

Sheldon's alarm of "Penny." *Knock, knock, knock.* "Penny." *Knock, knock, knock.* "Penny." *Knock, knock, knock,* jarred me awake, sun slipping through the window. I bolted upright to the sound of clip-clopping outside. Now what? The frat boys next to my apartment swiped somebody's mascot again? Last time it was a monkey; it fit right in with the frat boys, except the monkey was cleaner.

The aroma of bacon and coffee drifted into the room, caffeine vapors rousing memories of a ferry ride, fudge shops, horses and a dead Bunny. I suddenly had a new appreciation for the frat boys. I pulled on shorts and a sweatshirt, tied back my hair and ran a toothbrush around my mouth. Any day that started off with shorts and bare feet instead of heels and a skirt had to be a good one, right? I followed my nose down the narrow stairway to the kitchen, a low fire crackling in the small hearth chasing off the morning chill. A tabby lounged on a wide windowsill that overlooked a lazy harbor with sailboats, cruisers, blue water and a bright blue sky. *Definitely* not my apartment in Chicago.

Rudy had on a crumpled shirt and pants slit up to his thigh to accommodate the cast. His hair stuck out in Twain tufts as he sat at a blue Formica table older than me, devouring bacon and eggs. He nodded to a plate of the same across the table.

"Eat this stuff and you die," I said, plopping a chunk of eggs into my mouth.

"So far I just broke a leg. Heard you had yourself quite a night. Thought I'd let you sleep in before you got that ferry out of here."

I sank into a chair and picked up a strip of bacon as Rudy passed me a mug of coffee. "I think I killed Bunny. Irish Donna says I have a black cloud. Maybe I should wear garlic or find some eye of newt or toe of frog."

"Ever since the old battle-ax got those biker-babe shorts she's been riding around here like a maniac thinking she's sweet sixteen. Twain says, *In all lies there is wheat among the chaff.* That Bunny is dead as a duck and never been sweet a day in her life is a pure fact. That some cloud had anything to do with her present situation is a big bucket-load of horse manure. You can take that to the bank."

I wanted to believe Rudy, I really did, but something was sure messing up my life. I chomped the bacon. "So why Twain? Why not Washington? You could ride around on a horse and you'd have money with your own picture. That's kind of cool."

"We already had a George Washington when I came here five years ago. This whole island is eighteen hundreds — God, mother and apple pie — and we have lots of parades and demonstrations and events for the tourists to go along with the theme. It's kind of a time warp here, and we play to it by each of us assuming important historical figures to add to the fun. Up at the fort there're soldiers in uniforms with muskets and cannons. We even got a blacksmith with his own forge. Some gal with a spinning wheel weaves cloth, and the coach drivers for the Big House dress in top hats and tails and act all snooty."

"Big House as in jail?"

"Big House as in the Grand Hotel up there on the hill. I got to be Twain, including the cats, since Twain spent some time here." Rudy nodded to the windowsill. "That there's Cleveland, and you met Bambino. Our Betsy Ross ran off to Lauderdale last year after a particularly bad winter. Her arthritis just couldn't take the cold anymore. I hear she's been arrested twice down there in Naples for prancing around in her birthday suit saying she needs her vitamin D after years of deprivation."

"Maybe I could do Betsy in the parade?" I said, trying to think of a reason to keep me around. "Thread, needle, up-down-up-down. I've got good credentials. I did a sheep once in a nativity play. What do you say?"

"I say you should go back to drawing pretty pictures in Chicago."

34

A knock came from the back door. "Well, if it isn't Nate Sutter," Rudy said around a mouthful of egg. Sutter had on a black T-shirt, the same police jacket as last night and soft jeans molded over sexy, lean hips and other fine male body parts.

"Help yourself to coffee," Rudy offered as Sutter came in. "Hard stuff's in the cabinet — you could stand a good belt after chauffeuring a dead body around town in a buggy. Bet that was some sight. Dang shame I missed it."

Sutter shoved his hands in his pockets, standing on one foot, then the other, favoring the other. "We got a problem, Rudy. Bunny's bike was tampered with, the brake cable cut. I found a red paint smear on the wire, and you're painting bikes red. Mind if I take a look around?"

Rudy sloshed his coffee and stared, bug-eyed. Finally he managed, "You think Bunny died on purpose and that I —"

"Got a warrant?" The words just popped right out of my mouth. All that legal blah-blah-blah stuff over family dinners that made me crazy had had more of an impact than I thought and finally did me some good. I pointed to Rudy. "Don't say anything."

"But Nate can look around if he needs

to," Rudy said, innocent as a lamb to the slaughter. "Bunny and I had our differences, to be sure, and might have said we wanted each other dead and buried and out of the way and that I hoped she rotted in the depths of hell, but we —"

"Not now, Rudy," I hissed in a listen-to-me voice, wagging my head back and forth to get his attention. Granted I'd just met Rudy and didn't know him that well, but he let me sleep in, fixed me bacon and eggs and took my side in the black-cloud situation, and I was still hoping for the Betsy Ross position.

Sutter pulled a warrant from his jacket pocket and dropped it on the table. "You're not helping things, Chicago," he grumbled at me, then headed for the front of the shop.

"Depends what side of *help* you're on," I grumbled back while following him into the shop. He flipped on the light, the can of primer red right there on top of the work-bench where I wrote the info for the bikes. Drat!

"You really think I'd do something like cut Bunny's brakes?" Rudy took Bambino from the pocket in the pool table and stroked his little sleepy head.

Sutter searched the workbench and the tools hanging above it, my gut tying into knots over what he might find. The problem was that Rudy would have lost his business if Bunny had gotten her way with shutting him down, and where I came from people killed for way less than that. Rudy had motive, lots of it. Sutter heaved a toolbox from below the workbench, rifled through it, tools clanking together, then slid it back where it belonged. He stood, his mouth pulling into a defeated frown.

"See, no cutters, nothing here," Rudy said. His wiry mustache tipped in a smile. "I'm sure not the only one on this island with red paint, and there's a list a mile long of people who wanted the old bird dead."

"And truer words were never spoken, me dear man," Irish Donna called in from the kitchen. "Came to see how you're getting on," she added, her voice muffled as cabinet doors opened and closed. "Pleased as punch you must be. Bet you'll be doing a jig at Bunny's wake, crutch and all."

Irish Donna sauntered into the shop, coffee mug in one hand and a pair of red-paint-splattered wire cutters in the other. Holy freaking heck!

" 'Morning to you, Nate," Donna said. "And see what I found when helping myself to a bit of the cinnamon for the coffee," Donna went on. "Hiding there behind the spice rack, it was. Bet Rudy'd be looking himself blind when he went to fix up his bicycles. How'd these things wind up in the kitchen of all places?"

Rudy stumbled, and I smacked my hand flat against my forehead. Sutter took a plastic bag thing from his jacket and snagged the cutters right out of Donna's fingers. "Rudy Randolph, you're under arrest for the murder of Bunny Harrington."

"Jumping Jehoshaphat!" Donna gasped, clutching her shamrock, her mug crashing to the concrete floor and splattering coffee everywhere. "Nate Sutter, have ye gone daft in the head? Why would you arrest Rudy of all people for doing in Bunny?"

Sutter slid the bag in his pocket. "My guess is these wire cutters are the ones that were used on Bunny's brake cables, and we'll find out soon enough when we examine the sever marks. Everyone knows Bunny was here last night raising hell. That gave Rudy the perfect opportunity to cut her brake cables."

Irish Donna's eyes went squinty. "Rubbish, nothing but rubbish! Rudy wouldn't be doing in Bunny now when he's held his temper all those many times in the town council meeting when he wanted nothing more than to strangle Bunny dead right there on the spot."

I gave Donna the *finger to the lips* gesture to try and get her to stop talking.

"I used to babysit for ye, Nate Sutter," Donna continued, not paying one bit of attention to me. She tapped her foot like Principal Lancaster had when I adorned my fourth grade math homework with Daffy Duck images. "Wait till I tell your ma what you're up to this morning. She's not going to be pleased one wee bit about you doing this, you know."

Oh boy, and there was another person not being pleased one wee bit about all this. Abigail! Having her dad wind up the prime suspect in a murder less than twenty-four hours after I got here would not get me a promotion. It would get me instantly fired if she found out.

"You . . . You can't arrest Rudy," I blurted, my brain scrambling for some legal reason I'd heard over Thanksgiving turkey or opening Christmas presents. Bloomfield attorneys had a one-track mind no matter the occasion.

"Because . . . because of Labor Day." I waved my hand toward Main Street. "If a dead person in the bushes is bad for business, what will a full-fledged, out-in-the-open murder do? This island will be a ghost town. All the stores will be empty, shop owners will bitch and complain and you'll never get elected police chief again."

"I didn't get elected *this* time. I'm filling in for the chief of police 'cause he had back surgery last month over in Traverse City and is laid up for a while till he can get back on his feet."

"That's even worse!" I pushed on. "The island will go right down the toilet on your watch. Some legacy you'll leave behind. All you have to do is wait till after the holiday to make the arrest."

Sutter gave me the *you're out of your flipping mind* look. "I uphold the law, Chicago. That means arrest the criminal when he commits the crime."

"*Suspected* criminal," I tossed in. "No eyewitnesses. No one saw anything. All speculation."

"I have the smoking gun."

"That be wire cutters, dearie," Donna tossed in. "And we're just saying you need to be delaying things a bit for the good of the island. What can another week matter? Bunny's got all the time in heaven . . . or the other place, if truth be told. Believe me, the old girl doesn't care if we be putting things off for a few days."

"And you can put Rudy under island arrest," I said, feeling instantly brilliant.

Sutter rubbed his forehead. "All right, sure, I'll bite. What the heck's island arrest?" His eyes started to cross.

"House arrest, but bigger. Like eight miles bigger. Just tell the ferry operators and the airport that Rudy can't leave, and he sure can't climb on a boat with that cast up to his thigh, so he's stuck here. That gives the fudgies time to spend their money and it gives us time to find the real killer."

"I have the real killer," Sutter said.

Rudy looked pained, and I added, "Come on. You gotta see that Rudy wouldn't hide the murder weapon in his own kitchen and that someone's out to frame him."

A devilish glint lit Donna's green eyes. "Since there's no refrigeration at the medical center, we'll put body-bag Bunny in the freezer over there at Doud's Market to keep her fresh as a daisy. She'll be wrapped up nice and tight and not going anywhere and we can have a funeral later. We sure can't have it this week — talk about killing a mood and bad for business. We'll wedge Bonny Bunny behind the stacks of pizzas and ice cream Doud's keeps on hand. Andrew will go along with the idea; his market will be suffering as much as anyone's if this murder thing gets out."

Rudy nodded in agreement and Sutter let out a long breath as he stared at the floor. "This was supposed to be a cushy temp job for four or five months," he said, mostly to himself. "I take some time off, help Bernie while he's on the mend, mind his house, water his philodendron, do some fishing, sail, drink beer and leave the crazies back in Detroit. But they migrated."

Irish Donna patted his cheek. " 'Tis the black cloud hanging over our Chicago girl here, is all. She brought it with her when she came across the lake, and it can't be helped now and we need to be making the best of it."

Irish Donna picked up the phone on the workbench. "I'll give Andrew a jingle and tell him to be a'sending his dray over there to the medical center to pick up Bunny."

She turned back to Sutter. "Don't be so down in the mouth, me boy. Nothing to be gained by moping about like a redheaded stepchild. You best call Doc and tell him not to put Bunny on the ten o'clock flight but ship her carcass straight over to Doud's. The back entrance be best if you ask me. Maybe you should be lending him a hand to make sure it's done proper and take Chicago here with you, since she brought this on."

"Me?"

" 'Tis your cloud, dearie."

Rudy shook his head. "Chicago doesn't belong here."

"She's here now and seems to be on your side, and it's looking like you need all the help you can get, my dear man." Irish Donna hooked her arm through Rudy's. "Well, now that we got that straightened out, it's setting out to be a lovely day on the island, lovely indeed, just like it always is. Our job is making sure it stays that way, even with Bunny laying over in Doud's freezer taking up space like a giant pink popsicle."

3

"Whatever you're doing here, go do it somewhere else," Sutter said to me as we crossed Main Street, heading for Doud's Market on the opposite corner.

"I came here to help Rudy."

"And how's that working out for you?"

" 'Bout the same as being the local cop is working out for you." We turned onto Fort Street, which led up, way up, to what looked like a fort plus country club, complete with yellow umbrellas flapping in the breeze, pristine clapboard houses and a white stockade fence. Lewis and Clark would have killed for a fort like this. We ducked into a back alley between Doud's and Nadia's Fashion Shop as a dray clip-clopped in behind us, a lone wood box in the middle of the flatbed wagon. A balding man in a faded blue polo sat next to the driver in a baseball cap looking as if dropping off bodies at the local market was an everyday occurrence. Polo Shirt climbed off his perch and parked his hands on his hips. He scowled at Sutter. "We could go to jail for this."

"Around here I'm jail, and it's either the freezer or getting lynched by the island's Better Business Bureau." Sutter nodded my way. "Doc Evers, meet Evie Bloomfield from Chicago. She's here to help Rudy."

He gave me a half-smile. "You're off to a bang-up start, Chicago. Heard there's something about a black cloud you got going on."

"You believe in that stuff?"

"Lived here for forty years, life in the middle of a lake, everyone believes that stuff."

I was so screwed. I held open the beat-up door with *Doud's Market* stenciled in faded red, and the three men slid the box off the dray, carried it up the steps and through the door. A shiver snaked across my shoulders at the thought of Bunny inside in her little pink biker shorts and matching gym shoes.

"Shove her in the corner," a man in a green Doud's apron said, pointing to the open freezer in the back of the storage room. "If this gets out, I'll be stuck with a gazillion cases of pizzas, fish sticks and tater tots. Fudgies really got a thing for tater tots."

"Any idea who did this?" I asked, hoping for a lead.

"Rudy," all four of them answered in unison.

So much for a lead, but camouflaging Bunny with stacks of frozen carbs didn't seem like the best time to refute that statement. The men turned to leave, but I stood in the doorway blocking their path. "Don't you think we should say a few words?"

Doc folded his hands and bowed his head. "Bunny, I should have told you this years ago, and I'm mighty sorry I didn't. Let the doorknob hit ya where the good Lord split ya. Amen." Doc looked up and found all of us staring at him wide-eyed.

"What?" Doc asked. "Bunny was a first-class pain in *my* butt for all the years I've been here. I said *amen,* didn't I? What more do you want?"

"Dear Lord," I started again, hoping we didn't all get struck dead for the last comment, "Grant peace to Bunny in her temporary resting place."

"And don't let anyone find her sorry ass till after next weekend so Andrew can sell all his tater tots and fish sticks," the dray driver added.

It wasn't exactly high Mass at the Vatican, but it was better than the doorknob.

The dray and horses trotted back down the alley, and Doc trotted off to the Stang, my guess was to meet up with his good friend Jim Beam after our burial-at-freezer.

"You got a worried look, Chicago. What kind of trouble are you cooking up now?" Sutter asked as we stood alone in the alley.

"I need to find the real killer. So, besides Rudy, who has the most to gain with Bunny out of the way?"

"Why get involved in this?"

I wasn't about to toss out the *I'll get fired* motive. That was a whole other conversation. For the moment I went with, "Rudy's a good guy and he's innocent and you're dead-set on finding him guilty and he's not."

Sutter raked his fingers through his hair and muttered a few colorful phrases. "All I'm doing is following the evidence and you're going to stir up a bunch of trouble for nothing and everyone's going to be pissed. You're right that Rudy's a great guy, but Bunny threatened his business and he snapped, end of story. Go back home."

"What about the other bicycle shops on the island? With Rudy out of the picture, they get his business and —"

"You saw his shop. What business?"

"— and if Bunny's pushing up daisies, or in this case sleeping with the fish sticks, there're no regulations on their shops. Seems to me it's a win-win for them, and they know all about wire cutters and brakes. Rudy's not the only one with motive to do in Bunny."

"This isn't the inner city, it's the land of milk and honey, and people don't kill and frame someone over money and historical accuracy. The best thing you can do is help Rudy get his shop fixed up so he can sell it. He'll need cash for the attorneys."

"Holy cow, the paint. I have nine cans of beach-baby blue sitting on the docks to spruce up Rudy's place."

"Well, there it is. You can haul the cans in one of the bikes with the oversize baskets. You're big enough to handle it. Then you can get painting and make yourself useful."

Big enough — gee, just what every girl wants to hear. Then again, at five-ten I'd left petite somewhere back in the fourth grade. Sutter took off for places unknown and I headed for Rudy's. The basket idea would work except for the fact that I didn't know how to ride a bike, a little something I'd kept from Abigail and saw no reason to 'fess up to now. My plan was to stay on the island, find the killer, save Rudy and save my job.

Sheldon buzzed my butt and I picked up

a text from my older sister Lindsey. It read: Made partner. Celebrate tomorrow Travelle @ 8.

I did a quick reply of: On Mackinac for work. Major congrats. Well done. Catch up later. Lindsey was brilliant and beautiful and deserved the promotion. If there was a poster child for most perfect daughter, Lindsey was it. I ordered her flowers online, figuring I'd pay for them with my new promotion when this all worked out, right?

Five minutes later, after snagging one of Rudy's bikes, I was pushing the oxidized heap of brown metal down Main Street, dodging horses, wagons and tourists staring at my scraped and bloody knees.

"Well, my goodness, are you okay?" asked a woman in a white apron and flowered skirt as she hustled out of Irma's Fudge Emporium. "I saw you take a tumble while I was making up a batch of chocolate-nut. If you haven't ridden a bike in a while, it takes some practice to get the hang of it again. Just off the ferry, are you?"

"Came in last night. I'm helping Rudy fix up his shop, since he has a bum leg." I swiped a trickle of red from my leg. "If I live that long."

The woman pushed her glasses back up the bridge of her nose. "Why, I know who you are. You're that fudgie girl from Chicago we've been hearing about. Come on inside and I'll find the Band-Aids and patch you up. Can't have you bleeding, it gives the island a bad name."

She dropped her voice. "I'm Irma, and none of us here in town thinks Rudy's responsible for the Bunny Festival. That's code for Bunny's little mishap last night so the fudgies don't pick up on what we're talking about. Since we've already got the Lilac Festival, the Fudge Festival, the Horse Festival and the Jazz Festival, a bunch of us doing breakfast down at the VI, that's what we call Village Inn, decided the Bunny Festival fits in nice to what goes on around here. Personally I wanted to call it the Dust Bunny considering dust fits Bunny's present set of circumstances, but I got outvoted."

"Any idea who the grand marshal of the Bunny Festival might be?" I limped inside the empty emporium to find a decor of English pub meets Martha Stewart, with dark oak on one side and three long marble-top tables on the other. Wads of paper and cardboard littered the floor.

"There's a list of folks wanting her out of the way."

I sank down into a chair. "Always thought

small towns were chicken soup, borrowing a cup of sugar and marrying the boy next door, not sending someone off a cliff."

"There's the soup side and then there's the sending side. Last year when Big Ray won the Great Chili Cook-off we have every year, John from over at the VI objected and there was talk of a duel. Ray's been walking with a limp ever since. People get feisty no matter where they live."

So much for Sutter's milk-and-honey theory. Irma headed for the old display case with enough fudge to give me a visual sugar high. "If you want my opinion on who gets top billing for doing in Bunny," Irma said to me, "Dwight gets my vote. SeeFar has been their family cottage for over a hundred years and is worth a bundle. Dwight's a screwup and always looking for a payday. He's got a sister, but she married some gazillionaire in Florida. My guess, Dwight inherited the house all by himself and is happy as a clam right about now."

"Think he'd talk to me?" I picked gravel out of my knee.

"If you dress like a Dallas Cowboy cheerleader and shake your pompoms — and I'm not talking about the ones at football games." Irma made a gagging sound at the shaking part and handed me a box of Band-

Aids and a wet towel.

I patted my knees. "What's with all the paper on the floor? Redecorating?"

"My last batch of fudge was a total bust, just like every other batch I make, so I'm giving up, burning the place to the ground and collecting the insurance."

Okay, Irma didn't look crazy. No twitches, no evil glint in the eyes, no dagger strapped to her hip or snake tattooed on her forehead. She looked like someone who should have *Grandma* in front of her name. "All that over bad fudge?"

"Because I'm having a dreadful time making good fudge — any kind of good fudge." Irma sat, shoulders sagging. "Dutchy swiped my husband's fudge recipes and is now cohabiting with that two-bit Delong tramp on the next block, do you believe that? They opened Rita's Fudge Shoppe and are getting rich off of what's mine. I suppose they had this planned all along. My dear departed husband made the best fudge on the island. Then Dutchy made goo-goo eyes at me, the lonely widow, and I fell for it hook, line and sinker."

"What about dropping your prices, running an ad and giving Rita and Dutchy some competition."

"My dear husband did all the cooking,

and so did Dutchy. Heaving those pots and flipping fudge takes lots of muscle. I took care of the customers and the books and now there isn't any of either one."

Irma waved her hand over the store, then pulled a box of matches from her apron. "So how much more paper do you think I need to get a nice hefty blaze going in here? And don't worry about being a witness or tattling on me. You're a fudgie, so no one will pay any attention."

"But you can just sell the place."

"There will be more gossip and I'll feel stupid because I can't get it right." She nodded to a five-foot loaf of something chocolate on one of the marble tables. "Looks real good, doesn't it? Tastes like roadkill with nuts. Takes years to perfect a big-batch recipe."

Irma nibbled her bottom lip, glasses sliding down her nose. I knew this feeling of being double-crossed by a piece-of-dung guy and having your job in the toilet. My pocket buzzed and I yanked out Sheldon to find a text from Abigail. Call me! What was I going to say? *Hey, boss, your dad's accused of murder and his shop could be a pile of cinders by noon thanks to the crazy lady next door starting a fire?*

"Let's go see this Dwight guy," I blurted.

I needed answers to the Bunny Festival and had to start somewhere, and a change of scenery might help Irma stay off the island's most-wanted list.

"I wasn't kidding about the pompoms."

"I'm Evie Bloomfield from Chicago. I can handle anything Dwight the Third has to offer, and fresh air will make you feel better."

"So will a match."

Ten minutes later, Irma and I climbed the same steps I had come down the night before. In the light of day I could read the sign: *Crow's Nest Trail.* The steps zigzagged up the hillside, leading from downtown up to Huron Street, and by the time we got to the top my lungs were on fire, and Irma not breaking a sweat. We could have taken Huron all the way around to Truscott Street, like Irish Donna and I did last night in the buggy, but it added twenty minutes to the commute. There were two directions on the island, up and down, and one was a heck of a lot easier than the other.

"These houses have some view," I wheezed, staring out at Mackinac Bridge, boats bobbing at their moorings and rooster-plumes of spray behind the ferries whizzing fudgies to the mainland under a bright blue sky.

"And they sure pay dearly for it, I can tell you that." We continued on up the road, one massive cottage bigger and grander than the next, with wide verandas, curved porches and flowers galore. We passed a cluster of concrete planters, purple and white petunias spilling over the top like a waterfall. We stopped in front of SeeFar, Fiona and her horse cart pulling up right beside us.

Fiona was a skinny Tina Fey, minus makeup. She leaned down from her perch, the sunlight bouncing off the purple sequins, a healthy blush to her cheeks — an obvious perk of driving a convertible around town and hunting island stories.

"If you're calling on Dwight," Fiona said, "I was up at the Grand doing a piece on *Condé Nast Traveler* naming the hotel one of the five top resorts in the US and I saw His Sleaziness shoveling breakfast like he was King Tut on a throne. The man's already zonked and told the waiter he intends to spend the whole day celebrating. If you want my opinion, I think Dwight's a little too overjoyed about the Bunny Festival. He's got a finger or toe in this somehow, I just know it."

Fiona nodded to Irma. "Hey, I know," she continued. "Since there's a good chance he orchestrated the Bunny Festival, maybe you can get him to orchestrate Dutchy. After the way that jerk double-crossed you, he's due a festival of his own." Fiona stared at my Band-Aids. "New fashion statement? How about a lift back into town?"

Thank you, Jesus! I started to climb on board, and Irma yanked me back. "We could use the exercise."

At this rate I was going to die of exercise. Fiona gave a little wave and flicked the reins, and hooves plodded off down the hill. "But . . . But we had a ride," I said to Irma, trying really hard not to whine.

Irma sat on the steps in front of SeeFar, staring blankly out at the water. She pushed her glasses up her nose. "They all know about Dutchy. I'm the laughingstock of the island. I'm like one of those people on *Judge Judy* that you want to slap silly because they're so brainless. I've made some bad decisions, and there's no way to fix things now. I'm just going to burn down the emporium and be done with the place."

I parked beside Irma. I'd had similar thoughts about Abigail's ad agency until Grandpa Frank, my own personal cheer-leader since I was old enough to hold a crayon, gave me a pep talk on not caving in when times got tough. It was my turn to pep. "Light the match and Dutchy wins. You don't want him to win, do you? You've got to be strong. So what if you can't make fudge? There are already a bunch of fudge shops here. Do something that people will notice, and then they'll forget about Dutchy. Something new and different — like maybe open a bookstore. That's it, everyone loves bookstores, and there's no cooking."

I could almost see little gears churning behind Irma's intent gray eyes, a slow grin rippling across her face. "I think you're right."

"I am?"

"Bunny winding up in the bushes is new and different around here, even better than the chili duel. Rudy's not guilty of the Bunny Festival, but someone sure the heck is, so I'll find out who." Irma gazed skyward and folded her hands. "I feel so much better now; better than I have in months. I can help a friend, a really, really good friend who I haven't been all that nice to, and do something exciting for a change." She gave me a hug. "Thank you; you saved me."

"Can't you get saved with a bookstore?"

"We already have the Island Bookstore." Irma took my arm and hauled me to my feet. "We've got to step on it while Dwight's off getting drunk as a skunk. We all know he owes people money, so he might have it written down somewhere. If it's a lot of money, that's motive for him wanting this house to sell off." Irma lowered her voice. "I think he did the old girl in; now we just need proof."

I stopped in the middle of the sidewalk and held my hands out like a school crossing guard. "Waitaminute. *We* cannot break into someone's house."

Irma waved her hand in the air and grinned. "You are such a city girl. There's no locked doors around here, and we're simply making an unannounced neighborly visit to see how Dwight's getting on since his mamma's gone to that great town council meeting in the sky and isn't it too bad Dwight's not home and we'll just have a look around to see if we can help." Irma ducked under my arm and hustled toward the back door before I could stop her.

"It's locked! There must be something really juicy inside." She pointed to an open window on the second floor. "I'm wearing this skirt. You climb the trellis and take a look. Easy as pie. We don't have to worry about neighbors ratting on us. I have a get-out-of-jail-free card. My son's the police chief around here, least for a few months." Irma sighed, a proud twinkle in her eyes.

"He's such a handsome boy, and so polite. I taught him that."

Of course her son was the police chief. What did I expect? My black cloud must be the size of Texas. Detroit cops did not have *polite* in their job descriptions, and sonny boy didn't get those scars from writing parking tickets. Plus I was already on his poop list for standing up for Rudy. "If something goes wrong, it'll be my butt in the slammer. An island can never have too many bookstores."

Irma harrumphed. "Isn't it the code of the universe that if you save someone you owe them whatever they want?"

"I think it's the other way around."

"Well, close enough." Irma squared her shoulders, bunched up her long skirt into her waistband and stomped toward the rickety-looking trellis.

4

"All right, all right, I'll do it. I came to help Rudy, and this is a good place to start." And I really had to save my job. "You're on lookout. Throw a rock at the window if there's trouble." I grabbed the first rung of the trellis and glanced back to Irma. "So what am I looking for?"

"Something suspicious."

"That would be us."

At least thorny roses weren't growing up the trellis, but some leafy plant instead, and it was the only thing holding the slats to the house. One plank gave way under my foot, then another, splinters floating to the ground, me holding on by my fingertips.

"This is so much fun," Irma stage-whispered. "I never do things like this."

"It's not exactly a night on the town where I come from either," I whispered back. I grabbed the edge of the gutter and shim-mied onto the roof. I crawled on scraped knees, thinking *ouch, ouch, ouch* every inch of the way. I stuck my head in a window to find an unmade bed, an overflowing ashtray and a half-finished bottle of Jose Cuervo tequila on an antique dresser next to a copy of *Playboy.* Miss August smiled up at me in all her natural glory with *G. Winslow* and a phone number scribbled across her boobs. Next to it was Tiffany 1-800-HotBabe. When I got back to the cycle shop, I would be scrubbing my eyeballs.

"Well?" Irma called from below.

"Dwight's a horny slob." I swung a leg around, lost my balance and tumbled inside, landing in a pile of dirty laundry. If Rudy *was* guilty after all this, I'd draw and quarter the man myself. A large unopened envelope from *The Seniority,* whatever that was, sat next to the *Playboy* along with a black one-hundred-dollar chip from Caesars Palace. I pulled out Sheldon and added Winslow's number. Tiffany's digits were branded in my brain for all eternity.

I yanked out dresser drawers full of neatly folded clothes thanks to mamma Bunny — I sure couldn't see Dwight folding anything. There were more unopened envelopes with *Urgent* stamped across the front. The guy needed a master course in fiscal responsibility, sometimes referred to in the real world as *a job.*

Four other bedrooms were bare, two freshly painted, and Bunny's bedroom was at the end of the hall with Queen Anne style furniture and old photos giving me the evil eye of *what are you doing here.* If I could find canceled checks that would prove Bunny was paying for Dwight's lifestyle, that would help explain the motive of why he wanted her —

A door closed downstairs, an off-key whistling of "We're in the Money" drifting up to the second floor from below, making Irma the worst lookout on the planet. I crept back down the hall toward Dwight's room and the open window, the floorboards creaking under my right foot.

All movement and whistling from below stopped. A beat passed, then footsteps sounded on the stairs, the top of a bleached blond, bad comb-over popping into view. I took another step with another creak as a hand closed over my mouth, propelling me backward into a closet. A shaft of light slicing through the crack between the door and the jamb cut across a man: fiftyish, fedora, cunning eyes, wearing a leather jacket. He made the *shhh* sign with his finger to his lips, and we sank deep into the shadows of mothballs and coats.

Footsteps got closer to the closet. I tried to come up with some story as to why I was in here with a guy in a fedora when I heard a loud pounding out at the front door.

"Dwight?" came Irma's muffled voice. "Are you there, sweetie? I saw you coming up the walk. Dwight? I'm here to comfort you in your hour of need. That's what neighbors do around here. Let me in."

Slurred four-letter words filled the hallway, followed by retreating footfalls. I let out a lungful of air and turned to my fedora-wearing rescuer, but . . . but he wasn't there. Gone? How could he be gone? This was a freaking closet. I pawed through winter clothes. A ghost? Ghosts didn't smell like cigars and a touch of mint, did they? Secret passage? I bet this old house had a lot of secrets.

I eased out of the closet and tiptoed to the open window, keeping close to the side of the room, hoping for more solid construction where floor met wall. I took Sheldon from my back pocket so as not to crush him, then butt-scooted across the roof through gravel that had never made it to the window, rock-throwing not being Irma's strong suit. I climbed/fell down the trellis, skulked through the neighbors' backyards, and met up with Irma on the sidewalk by the giant flowerpots with the purple petunias.

"Let me tell you," Irma groused as we headed for the steps leading to town, "Dwight is nasty and rude and practically threw me out of the house. Can you believe that? I was there to comfort him."

"You were there to break into his house."

"That's beside the point, and he sure didn't know about it. The only thing that boy cares about at the Bunny Festival is winning the jackpot, and what he deserves is nothing but the booby prize."

And he had that sitting right there on his dresser. "Do you know a guy with a fedora and a leather jacket?"

"Jason Bourne. He lives two doors up in the green and yellow cottage."

"Jason Bourne, like in *The Bourne Identity*? I don't think so. This guy was more Robin Williams."

"We all just gave him the name and it sort of stuck. When he goes off island, he always has his silver briefcase handcuffed to his wrist and wears a leather jacket. Sometimes he even wears a wig and fake mustache." Irma dropped her voice. "He's a hit man. He leaves the island and is gone for a few days, then comes back. He always has money and doesn't do any work and gets a mean look in his eyes if you ask what he's got going on."

"A hit man? Really?"

"Irish Donna delivers him scones every Tuesday and Friday. Once he had to take a call and she got a chance to nose around and saw that silver briefcase right there in the hall. About peed her pants."

"Well, Mr. Bourne was inside Bunny's house hiding in the closet with me."

Irma stopped, her eyes huge. "Get out of town."

Oh, if only I could. "If he is a hit man, maybe someone paid him to orchestrate the Bunny Festival. But why was he in her closet hiding out? And surely a hit man could come up with something a whole lot better than cutting a bike cable." I held up Sheldon so Irma could see the screen. "I found this number on Dwight's dresser."

"Two three one is a Mackinaw City area code. Probably another sleazebag; they all hang together like on that *Breaking Bad* show." Irma grinned. "I never said sleazebag before, and it's thanks to you."

And your son's going to hang me up by my thumbs. "Since Dwight had the number written down, my guess is it's new to him, not a friend's number."

"Cell phone reception around here is the pits, but give it a try anyway. Maybe we're in one of those hot spots fudgies are always looking for. Yesterday I saw a guy hanging off Arnold's ferry dock looking for bars, and I'm not talking the drinking kind."

I punched in the 231 number and hit *speaker.* A sweet voice on the other end answered, "Hollister and Winslow, Attorneys at Law."

I disconnected. "An attorney? The Bunny Festival happening and Dwight doing the happy dance and him contacting an attorney aren't coincidences. If we start poking around the Bunny Festival, Dwight could *festival* us. There's money and murder, and things could get ugly. This is serious stuff we're dealing with here."

Irma's eyes widened to cover half her face. "I hadn't bargained on that." We started down the steps to town.

"So you're rethinking the bookstore?"

"I'm thinking I should call Winslow and ask a bunch of nosy, irritating questions about Bunny's estate and Dwight's finances."

I stopped Irma on the first landing and put my hands on her shoulders. "Because you have a sudden death wish?"

A smile hung at the corners of her mouth, and she patted my cheek. "Because I'm going to tell Mr. Winslow, Attorney at Law, that I'm Rita Delong and own a fudge shop right here on Mackinac Island and that Dwight owes me a ton of money and I want it now that he's getting SeeFar and that I know everything."

"Dwight will blow a gasket."

"And he and his attorney will come looking for Round-heeled Rita and Dutchy," Irma said, hiking up her dress and doing a little jig right there on the landing. "Those two thought they could mess over me and I'd roll over and play dead. I almost set my shop on fire, of all things. Well, I'm not dead anymore, and a little grief is just what Rita and Dutchy deserve. I'm so clever I scare myself."

5

"There's a little glitch, oh Scary One," I said to Irma as we tackled the next flight of steps. "You have to make the call from Rita's Fudge Shoppe. Chances are good Winslow has caller ID."

"So *you* go buy a pound of fudge and borrow the phone and make the call," Irma said to me when we got to the bottom of the steps. "Easy as pie."

"I just did pie and nearly broke my neck."

Irma waved her hand, shooing off my objection. "All you do is ask Winslow how much SeeFar is worth and say you're Rita and that you're getting tired of waiting for your money and intend to take legal action of your own to get it. Winslow tells Dwight someone's after his money, and Dwight goes after Rita and Dutchy."

"Winslow will show up all right. The one thing a lawyer hates more than anything is the threat of another lawyer on his turf," I said as we cut across a grassy park, where a big bronze statue of Father Marquette was looking out at the harbor. "I need to get Rudy off the hook, and you want to sic Dwight on Dutchy and Rita. I guess it's worth a shot."

"Now you're talking. It's another gift from above."

"Meaning God works in mysterious ways?"

"Meaning I'm from Minnesota and God helps those who help themselves."

A thundering *boom* rocketed over our heads, my heart jumped out of my chest and I dove under a white concrete bench by the Father Marquette statue and waited for the Canadians to attack. I peeked up at Irma. "I think that's God saying we should forget this."

Irma turned toward the fort perched up on the hill and put her hand over her heart as a bugle played *I hate to get up, I hate to get up, I hate to get up in the morning* — least that's what we sang to the tune at Camp Wichicaca when I was in junior high.

"It's ten o'clock and the Boy Scouts are raising the flag like they always do at this time," Irma said as I left my bunker. "Three o'clock is a busy time at the fudge shops with all the day tourists buying fudge to take back home. It's a perfect time to get to the phone and call Winslow."

"Rita or Dutchy will overhear what I'm saying. The shop can't be that big."

Irma swaggered toward the emporium. "Not to worry, dearie," she called over her shoulder. "That *those who help themselves* part I mentioned involves planning a little distraction to take care of things. All you have to think about is making that phone call."

This is why people run off to the wilds of Alaska, I decided as I pushed the bike down the street to finally retrieve the paint cans I had left at the dock. They didn't have to run after killers to keep their jobs, share closets with hit men and deal with lawyers.

Rita's Fudge Shoppe sat at the next corner pimped out in pinks and chocolate-brown with a matching striped awning across the porch. A big front window let tourists watch a burly guy flipping fudge on one of those marble-top tables. Dutchy? He looked like Irma's Dutchy, with his bad hairpiece, fake suave manner and smile that didn't reach his eyes. How could Irma fall for this guy? Then again, how could I fall for Tim the superjock? That he slept on NFL sheets and our honeymoon — which I assume he went on himself after dumping me unceremoniously on our wedding day — involved taking in two Chicago Bears football games should have been a dead giveaway I was not his top priority.

I wanted to find fault with Irma's plan of getting Winslow on the island, but Dwight was a prime candidate for the Bunny Festival, and with a little luck this would bring his motive for murder front and center. Least it was a start to finding the real killer. To pull off *easy as pie* part two I should case Rita's shop to see where the phone was, if I would be overheard and, the most important part, whether Rita gave out free samples.

I parked the bike, then blended into a group of tourists close to the plate glass window watching Dutchy toss in handfuls of nuts and chocolate chips to the long loaf of chocolate fudge on the table. He flipped the gooey concoction onto itself, making it smaller and smaller as it cooled on the marble surface. Behind the counter a woman with a phone trapped between ear and shoulder waited on customers.

Aha! There was a phone with one of those curly cords — a landline to prevent dropped calls from the less-than-terrific island service. I opened the door to Rita's Fudge

Shoppe as a woman barreled out without looking up, her scarf-covered head bowed low. She collided right into me and I grabbed her arm to keep both of us upright. She had one of those *deer in the headlights* looks on her face when our eyes met. "Fiona?"

"Chicago? What are you doing here? Drat! Look, you can't tell Irma you saw me," she blurted, hiding the pink and brown bag behind her back and scooting me off to the side of the wood porch so customers could get by us.

"Irma's been friends with the family for years, but since Big and Ugly inside here ran off with her recipes," Fiona went on, "Irma's fudge has tasted like nut-covered hockey pucks, or worse, if there is worse. My niece just loves peanut butter fudge and I send her some once a month as a special treat. You won't say a word to Irma, will you? Promise?"

I did the *zip across my lips* routine and gave her a wink as I started off. But before I could, Fiona grabbed my arm to hold me back. She whipped out a book with the words *My Little Princess* scripted in pink across the front. Oh for joy, I knew what this was all about — it was the proud-grandma ritual, which was obviously now also the proud-aunt ritual. It was the displaying of the cute little kid pictures and the expected oohs and aahs from the peanut gallery, meaning me. I'd seen more than my share of brag books at work and beyond. Take me out and shoot me.

"Here's Kimberly on her fifth birthday," Fiona said with a big smile as she flipped open the book. "Isn't she cute?"

"Ooh."

"This one's on her new Disney princess bicycle that I sent."

"Aah."

"Kimberly's in Florida thanks to Bunny and her mouth. If she hadn't interfered, Smithy and Constance would still be married and Kimberly would be here on this very island with her daddy, where she belongs, riding her cute little bicycle."

Okay, don't shoot me just yet. What was this all about? "Smithy and Constance?"

"Smithy is my brother, and he married Bunny's daughter, Constance." Fiona's eyes narrowed to slits. "Bunny never thought Smithy was good enough for Constance. Kept telling Constance she could do better, and then what do you think happened? Two years ago Constance divorced Smithy for some real estate tycoon vacationing here. Smithy hasn't been the same since, so quiet and keeping to himself. Everyone can tell he's upset, even the horses."

"He's a vet?"

"Blacksmith. He's been the historic interpreter and blacksmith over at the blacksmith barn since he got out of high school. His herb garden is the only thing saving him. I keep telling him to put his place on the island garden tour, but he won't have any of it. He's shy and sweet and sometimes just a big kid at heart. I think that's why dad gave me the *Town Crier* when he retired, so Smithy would have family around. That and Mother probably talked him into it hoping I'd find a husband from the tourist trade. She's desperate. I'm thirty-five and wear a purple hat, and mother sees cats and crocheting in my future."

"From my brief but painful experience with almost-marriage, cats and crocheting is the way to go."

And that was true enough, but the part about Constance, Smithy and Bunny was news — big news. Not of the *Town Crier* variety, but good old island gossip that gave me another candidate for my *I hate Bunny* list. Smithy had no use for the woman, with her ruining his marriage.

Fiona headed off to interview performers for the jazz festival and it occurred to me that if Smithy or Dwight could have done in Bunny, what about the others who had it in for her? And there had to be others; the woman was a pain in the butt, just like Doc said. But I was a fudgie, an outsider, so the locals wouldn't talk to me about anything more than what time the ferry left.

"And what bear did you tangle with?" Rudy asked, staring at my knees as I parked the bike piled with paint cans, some dangling off the handlebars. Both doors to Rudy's Rides were wide open this morning to let customers and sun inside — not that there were any customers.

"Holy crap! Forget my knees, what's with the red smear across your chest. Should I call nine-one-one?"

"Primer. Knocked the dang can with my cast and scared the heck out of poor Bambino. He landed in the paint and then on me." Rudy pulled the black cat with red whiskers, tail and paws from the side pocket of the pool table. Snarling and hissing, Bambino stuck his tongue out at Rudy; I swear, he really did. Rudy said, "After six treats I'm still in the doghouse . . . make that the cathouse."

"And you'll be lucky if you can afford that," some slick-looking spandex guy said as he pedaled up to the storefront on a racing bike. An entourage followed, all in matching black and poison green spandex suits and helmets. "I'm going to redo this whole place when I take it over," he pontificated, as much to the crowd as Rudy. "Or maybe I'll just level the place and start over with a building with a lot of chrome and windows that look out onto the harbor. This place has some view — the only thing it's got going for it."

"That view's mine," Rudy said, as Bambino leaped onto the pool table.

The guy sat back on his skinny seat, designed to give a permanent wedgie. He parked his hands on his scrawny hips, the rest of his gang assuming the same attitude. "You got problems, big problems. You'll sell, you'll have to." He gazed around like he already owned the place. "I'm starting the Speed Maslow Challenge, a three-day race along the Michigan coast, and this will make a perfect Speed Maslow training camp to talk strategy and nutrition. I'll make it my headquarters."

"In your dreams," a girl in short-shorts said, weaving her blue bike to the curb. She was tall and lean, with thighs of steel and a perfect peach-shaped butt. Wow, I so needed to get my flabby apple butt on a bike . . .

even though I might kill myself in the process.

"You're not buying Rudy's Rides, I am," she said. "I'm calling it Huffy's Hut — my coffeehouse where cyclers on the island can chill. I'm putting a massage clinic in the back and we'll do yoga overlooking the harbor. A place to decompress and get away from the big city."

Speed curled his lip at the basket strapped to the front of Huffy's bike. "Your bikes are second-rate and your place has been losing money since I moved here last year; everybody knows it. You can't afford another shop. What are you going to do, have Daddy buy it for you?"

"And all those fancy steeds at your shop are putting you in the poorhouse," Huffy scoffed.

Huffy jabbed Speed in the chest with her index finger, and Rudy jabbed his crutch between Speed and Huffy. "Take a breath, you two, this is my bike shop, and it's staying my bike shop."

Speed gripped his handlebars, his knuckles blanching white, the vein in his neck throbbing. "You'll come begging me to buy this place, Rudy, and I might not be so generous then. You got medical bills, and there'll be attorney bills." Speed pedaled off with his army in tow, the long black and green line snaking its way up Main Street.

Huffy gave Rudy a mean-girl look. "Too bad for you that Bunny got herself festivaled, but the rest of us here in town are glad it happened. And just so you know, I don't need my father's money to buy you out. I'm doing just fine on my own now. Your shop is as good as mine, Rudy — get used to it."

"Don't listen to either of them," I said to Rudy as Huffy propelled herself down the street. "This is an eight-mile island. We'll find the chairman of the Bunny Festival. In fact, I'd say those two are prime candidates. And how in the world does someone get the name *Huffy*?"

"It was her first bike, and word has it she used to park it in her bedroom every night."

That seemed like a really stupid thing to do, but then, superjock parked in my bedroom for almost a year. Huffy made a better choice.

"Speed and Huffy are harmless," Rudy added. "They're all talk. That's what people do around here, Evie: talk a lot."

And Rudy was a teddy bear in a cast who thought the best of everyone. Maybe Abigail was adopted. "Why don't you take a few hours off and go to the Stang? You could do with a break, and you might find out who had an interest in our local furry little mammal presently on ice. Bars have a way of making people loosen up and say stuff they normally wouldn't. Keep your ears open, see what you can find out and I'll hold down the fort for a while here."

"Twain says, *The best way to cheer yourself is to try to cheer somebody else up,* so maybe you're right. I'll call Ed. He's always ready for a game of euchre, and he's been worrying about his son. The guy's not exactly Mr. Industrious, and Ed still owns a chunk of the ad business. I tell you, with kids you're always worrying about something."

"You worry about Abigail? Trust me, she's doing great."

"On the outside maybe, but the girl's got her priorities all muddled up. You work to live, not live to work, like she's doing." Rudy hoisted himself up, balanced then paused, giving me a long look. "Okay, Chicago, level with me. Why are you hanging around here? You could jump on a boat and hightail it back to the city where you belong. There's got to be an easier way of getting a promotion from my daughter than hunting for a killer. Buy Abigail some chocolate. She's a real sucker for dark chocolate."

The Abigail I knew wasn't a sucker for

anything, but it was time to level with Rudy. "I talked Abigail into letting me come here, and you wind up a murder suspect. Not a great situation for either of us. Abigail will fire me in a Chicago minute if she finds out what's going on. She'll think I should have been looking out for you and I screwed it up big-time, and a Bloomfield hasn't been fired since March twelfth, nineteen forty-four. Some kids memorize *In fourteen ninety-two, Columbus sailed the ocean blue.* In our family it's *In nineteen forty-four, Uncle Lamoure got kicked out the door.*"

"You're kidding."

"They buried him some place in Georgia. It's the land of the fried, big hair, *y'all* and *ain't she precious.* How could they do such a thing?"

I started to sweat, and Rudy paled at the description. "You're *not* kidding," he said. "I'll go make like a sitting duck over at the Stang and see who comes hunting. This red shirt will get people talking. The South, huh? That's really harsh." Rudy shook his head in disbelief, then thumped his way out of the shop.

I snagged a paintbrush and eyed the primer on the floor. Seemed a crime to throw it away with so many bikes in need. By two o'clock I'd only rented out four bikes, but I did have a nice line of dent-free, rust-free, primed cycles parked outside in the sun to dry. Visions of the last piece of pizza in the fridge danced in front of my eyes and I headed for the *home sweet home* part of Rudy's Rides.

I went into the kitchen, patted Bambino and Cleveland and came face-to-face with Speed Maslow coming in the back door.

6

He was taller than I had thought, had more muscles than I remembered and looked threatening in black jeans and T-shirt, not giving a rat's behind that he didn't knock and had just barged in like he owned the place. Cleveland arched his back and hissed, and I pretty much felt the same way.

"Saw Rudy down at the Stang." Speed folded his arms across his solid chest and gave me the *cool-jock to stupid-chick* stare. "He's going to need money to get him out of this Bunny mess, and the doctor bills are eating him alive. Get the old fart to sell to me and there's an easy grand in it for you. Rudy says you work for his daughter in Chicago and you're here to make brownie points and get a promotion. This is quick money staring you right in the face."

Personally I thought it was the island jackass staring me in the face. "Cycling's big out West or in Europe. Why are you setting up shop on an eight-mile chunk of land in the middle of a lake?"

Like throwing a switch, Speed morphed into Lance Armstrong, the better years. "Michigan is virgin territory. There are no major cycling events in the state, and I can make a difference here. I can bring the fun and competition of cycling to Michigan."

I gave Speed the *smart-chick to stupid-jock* stare. "The perfect sound bite for press and investors everywhere. How's that ad campaign working out? Any takers?"

"Yeah, I got takers. Lots of 'em." Speed took a step closer, his lips thin and eyes cold, hot breath across my face, trying to get me to back up. Fat chance. "I've got plans," Speed growled. "And you're not screwing them up just 'cause you're from the big city and think you know it all. Bunny tried to mess with me, and look where she ended up. Get me this shop, and no one gets hurt."

Speed slammed the door as he left, the panes rattling in their frames. I yanked out Sheldon, who really did know it all — that's why I named my iPhone Sheldon — and Googled *Speed Maslow jerk*. Okay, I left off the *jerk* part, but I was thinking it.

Speed won some minor race last year and came in second in a few more and snagged a couple of endorsements along the way. He had his very own patented Speed On-The-Go water bottle in black or poison green, but that was about it — nothing blockbuster in the last two years. Four years ago he won the Tour of Texas, and since there was a list of Google references for that, I figured this was a big deal, except that it was four years ago.

My guess was Mr. Speed planned to cash in on his name while he still had one that people recognized. Okay, so how did Bunny figure into this or was Speed just shooting his mouth off to scare the dumb city girl?

"Cripes almighty," Rudy said, hobbling his way in the door between the shop and the kitchen. He did the thinking man's pace back and forth across the kitchen, Cleveland and Bambino watching like it was a slow-motion Ping-Pong match.

"Everybody in town here thinks I'm innocent, the snobs on the hill think I'm guilty, and to top it all off, I wasn't at the Stang more than five minutes and Huffy comes in and shoves a paper at me to sign agreeing to sell her Rudy's Rides. Said she'd have the cash in a month and would add a ten percent bonus, and that her dad had nothing to do with it and this was all her doing."

"Well, guess what. Speed stopped in and wants me to sweet-talk you into selling him the place. Said if I got in his way I'd wind up like Bunny. Does anyone get along around here? So far we know that Dwight wants his mother's money 'cause he's in debt, and from what Fiona said, her brother, Smithy, had good motive for sending Bunny over a cliff for screwing up his marriage, but neither of them has a reason to frame you. Then we got Speed and Huffy, who want your shop really bad, probably frame you without batting an eye, but why would they kill Bunny? Did you find out anything else?"

"Jason Bourne's off to the mainland. Saw him heading for the ferry with a black trench coat slung over his shoulder, briefcase handcuffed to his wrist and sporting a glued-on mustache. Wonder who he's got in his crosshairs this time around?"

Bourne, or whatever his real name was, obviously didn't want anyone to know he'd been at Dwight's house, or he wouldn't have been hiding in a closet. "Do you really think he's a hit man?"

"Do you glue on facial hair and handcuff your luggage? Bet he has one of those put-together guns in there with a silencer like you see on TV. I saw Irma walking down the street when I came in," Rudy added. "She had on a big pink hat with a feather, had a wild look in her eyes and was carrying a plate of fudge. Wonder what that's all about?"

"Holy cow! Did you smell smoke? I gotta go." I took the back door that faced the picture-perfect harbor and tripped over a busted wood step with a crack clear through the middle. No wonder Rudy broke his leg.

I turned onto Main Street, which was crowded with horses, bikes and tourists moving so slow I wanted to yell, *Get out of the way!* I spotted Irma's hat in the crowd then her pink and chocolate vest. She ambled her way toward Rita's Fudge Shoppe, holding her tray high like a grand prize.

"Come and get some terrific fudge right here," Irma sang out, her voice carrying over the street din. "See for yourself how Rita's Fudge Shoppe makes the best fudge in town. Get some to take home for friends and family. They'll thank you for it."

Irma spotted me and gave a big impish grin. She hitched her head toward Rita's shop. "Free samples of what you'll find inside," she sang out again as she stepped onto the porch.

Tourists crowded close, snagging the little

white tissue cups and popping the delicious-looking morsels in their mouths. Smiles turned to frowns with fits of choking and gagging, along with bulging eyes, sour faces and some actual spitting on the ground. People pushed and shoved to get to the free fudge, then pushed and shoved to escape.

The crowd on Rita's porch scattered, the word going viral and spreading to the customers waiting their turn inside. In a flash, the thriving Tuesday afternoon business at Rita's Fudge Shoppe morphed into impending bankruptcy. Eyes glaring, Rita and Dutchy stormed their way out of the shop, heading straight for Irma.

So this was the Mackinac version of God helping those who helped themselves. With all attention focused on Irma, I slid inside the empty store and past the cute pink and white ice-cream parlor chairs and tables, then slunk behind the glass display counter piled high with really yummy-looking fudge. I snagged a piece along the way, popped it in my mouth and yanked the wall phone off the cradle.

Holy freaking cow! The fudge was maple walnut and was creamy and mind-blowingly delicious. I couldn't see a thing or even feel my toes and fingers. My brain refused to function, every ounce of my being savoring the orgasmic taste. All this from fudge? Yeah, most definitely, all this from fudge!

Get a grip, Evie. I tried, I really did, but there was no gripping. Instead I ate two more pieces! I didn't think my mouth was that big, but it was! I needed fudge therapy; a twelve-step program. When a bit of sanity returned, I punched in Winslow's number.

"Is somebody there?" asked the receptionist.

My mouth was too full to talk. I sucked in a breath around the candy. "Mithr Winow?"

"Pervert." The line went dead.

I swallowed and tried to convince myself I was a rotten human for eating fudge and not concentrating on the task at hand, except my heart wasn't in it — the fudge was just too awesome to contemplate remorse.

"What are you doing?" a voice said from behind me.

The only reason I didn't scream was that my mouth was full of fudge. I swallowed the whole glob in one gulp.

"Fiona?" I coughed as I spun around. "You scared me to death . . . almost literally." I coughed again.

"I need to make a phone call and I have to hurry. Irma's got an idea how to get even with Dutchy and Rita for doing her wrong."

A huge smile skated across Fiona's face, her green eyes dancing. "Revenge! You bet-cha'. I'm in, do it."

Fiona was my kind of gal.

I repunched the numbers. "Mr. Winslow, please. This is Rita Delong calling from Mackinac Island. I need to speak to him, it's an emergency."

Fiona stifled a giggle and I licked a stray glob of fudge off my thumb as I waited for Winslow to come on the line. I could see Rita and Dutchy arguing with Irma on the porch, their heads close, faces red, words like *slut, thief, old biddy* and *granny* drifting our way.

"The tourists are snapping pictures as if this were the local zoo," Fiona said.

"From what I can see, they aren't too far off the mark."

Fiona backed us and the curly corded phone into the kitchen, which had copper pots stacked on a table, big bags of sugar on the counter, a king-size stove and a mixer. "Avoiding fudge temptation," she said, plopping a piece of vanilla fudge in her mouth. "And keeping us out of sight. How long could a fudge-fight last?"

We peeked around the corner as Rita threw a piece of fudge at Irma and Irma hurled a chunk at Dutchy, resulting in the whole tray going airborne and everyone backing away from the toxic pieces. "Pretty darn long," I said. "Who would have thought?"

"Winslow here," came the voice on the phone. "How can I help you?"

"This is Rita Delong. Dwight Harrington owes me money, a lot of money. Since you're Dwight's attorney, I'm assuming you know his mother bit the big one, and now that he's inheriting his mother's house, I want my cash, and I want it now."

Fiona gave me a thumbs-up.

"Who is this?" Winslow growled.

"Rita Delong. I own a fudge shop here on Mackinac Island and I want my money. Don't forget to tell Dwight Harrington that I called."

The phone went dead and Dutchy rounded the corner, plowing straight into me and knocking me against the giant mixer. "Thought I heard . . ." He looked from me to Fiona. "What are you two doing back here? You're fudge thieves. I'm calling the cops."

Dutchy grabbed for the phone and Fiona beat him to it, clutching it in her hand. "You can't do that 'cause we were doing you a favor. The phone rang, no one was around, so we took the order."

Dutchy towered over me, backing me toward the wall, a scowl creasing his forehead. "I heard you talking. What does Dwight have to do with this? And what don't you want him to forget?"

"Dwight's the one who made the call," I said, lying my little fudge-stained heart out as best I could. "He wants five pounds of chocolate-pecan delivered, and I told him I wouldn't forget to tell you."

"Dwight?"

"Says he's your biggest fan. Just add it to his bill."

"What bill?"

"Drop it off at SeeFar tomorrow. Put it on the back porch. He's on a sugar high," Fiona said.

"That's a nice order." Dutchy looked confused, and Fiona and I seized the moment of Dutchy contemplating his bank account to duck under his arm and hustle out of the shop, not stopping till we got to the street,

"I think he bought it," Fiona gushed as we blended in with the foot traffic.

"Now maybe, but when five pounds of fudge gets dropped off and Dwight calls Rita's Fudge Shoppe wanting to know what's going on, we're toast. My grandpa Frank talked me out of being a lawyer because I suck at lying. He said things never got better when I opened my mouth; just a lot more complicated."

Fiona gave me a friendly shoulder bump. "Maybe he's right, maybe he's wrong, but at least this time your mouth was filled with really good fudge."

7

The sun sank into Lake Huron, a big ball of fire against the gray blue of deep, cold water. I hadn't seen Irma since the great fudge encounter of the unbelievable kind, so I couldn't tell her I contacted Winslow. That I'd gotten myself into a holy mess with the phony fudge order was something I intended to keep to myself, since it involved stuffing my mouth with maple-nut from her stolen recipes. But right now the big question was, where the heck was Irma?

I added another paint-primed bike to the thirteen others as Rudy scooped Bambino from the left pocket of the pool table and plopped down in the wicker rocker. He eased a straightened coat hanger between his thigh and the plaster cast, a look of relief on his face as he maneuvered the wire to a certain spot.

"Dang cast is so blasted itchy, it's driving me nuts," Rudy said. "Only good thing is that it takes my mind off the fact that we've only rented out eight bikes the whole blessed day. At this rate I'll be bankrupt by Thanksgiving. When I bought the shop four years ago, I thought of it as vintage bikes on a vintage island. Now my bikes are just old, really old."

"Old can be good."

"If it's Scotch and wine."

"We need a gimmick. A saying."

" 'Geezers a go-go'?"

"I was thinking more like chocolate candy that melts in your mouth and not in your hand, or cereal that goes snap, crackle and pop."

Rudy thought for a minute then let out a long sigh. "I got nothing. I'll hobble on over to Doud's and get a few groceries. Least I can do is feed you for all your work. The bikes you painted look good — a lot better than they did before — but they're still just old."

"A word of warning: Skip the tater tots and pizza," I offered as Rudy strapped a shopping tote to his crutch. "You never know what or who those things have been sitting next to in the freezer, if you get my drift."

Rudy gave me a smile and a two-finger salute. "Got it."

Rudy fed Bambino and Cleveland a treat each, then stomped off. I scratched my chin and my neck, probably in sympathy to Rudy and his itchy cast. A family of four strolled by the shop, took one look at the red-primed bikes and kept on going. Okay, this was just what I needed: a local focus group. If I got some feedback, maybe I'd find out there was something I could do to fix the bikes that wouldn't cost an arm and a leg.

"Excuse me," I called, rushing out onto the sidewalk. I slapped on my best *please the customer* smile. "What would it take for you to rent these bikes for your family to explore the island?"

The dad was a young exec type with a big income and the ego to match — just the kind of client I loved dealing with in Chicago, always so cooperative.

"A miracle," he said with a sneer as he studied the front of the shop. "This place is a dump."

"What about lakeside rustic?"

"Dump."

Mom flipped back her long blonde hair. "In the fourth grade I had a pink Sweet Thunder bike with a banana seat and purple streamers and a doll carrier. 'Course it was new, not like these. I'd never let my children on these; probably get some disease."

The smaller boy folded his arms. "I have a Batman mountain bike, special edition."

The bigger kid sneered like dad. "I play basketball, that's all I care about. These bikes suck." I got the snotty-kid eye roll, and the family pranced on down Main.

So this was my target audience? They weren't out for a bargain rental; they wanted flashy, new and different, something to brag about to family and friends. They were after something that made for great vacation pictures on Facebook and Twitter or got pinned on Pinterest. They wanted a red Ferrari on two wheels. Rudy was right — this wasn't going to work, and I had no idea how to fix the problem.

"Well now don't these bicycles look darlin'," Irish Donna said as she tugged Paddy to a stop by the curb. "Just darlin' indeed. Rudy is lucky to be having you around even if you are sporting a big black cloud."

"How would you like to do me a favor and rent one of these darlin' bicycles?" I said, a wave of desperation washing over me. I needed a bit of good news to save Rudy's day. "You could ride around tomorrow and give Paddy here a well-deserved rest. Bet he's one pooped horse, and you'd get some great exercise; wouldn't that be nice?" I rubbed my hands together to stop the itching. Grandpa Frank once said that an itchy palm meant money was coming. I hoped this was it.

"Well that's not a bad idea a'tall," Donna said, a big smile on her face. "I suppose I can be helping out my old pal Rudy by renting a bike. My guess is that sales are pitiful and you're fighting to save the sinking ship. I can cheer him up on this fine night and be making you a good deal too now that I'm taking the bike off your hands."

Donna reached down beside her and pulled out a wiggly furball of tan and white. "Our Miss Blueberry snuck out one night and went and got herself in a family way before me and Shamus had the good sense to ship her off to the vet and get her saucy female desires adjusted."

"It's a cat."

"Well now, ye must be one of those brainy college graduates."

"Rudy already has two cats."

"And I be a horse person and have Paddy here to be taking me around the island in grand style and I'm in no need to be a renting a bike, yet I'm getting one stashed away in my caboose. Fair is fair now, don't you think?"

"A cat for a bike? One lasts a day, the other for a whole lot of years — and there's the litter box and dead mice by the bed and cat puke in your favorite gym shoe when you go to put it on in the morning. What about you rent two bikes for one cat?" I tried to barter.

Donna reached down again and retrieved another butterscotch kitten with four white paws. "I'm thinking fair is two for two."

Rudy wasn't the only one screwed. "One for one is the best I can do," I agreed, scratching my nose and forehead, my hands itching more than ever, and knowing I'd just been had. "What am I going to do with a cat in my apartment?"

Donna held up the cat and studied his paws. "I'd be getting myself a bigger apartment."

I hoisted the bike into the back of the carriage, where we'd parked Bunny the night before. Irish Donna forked over the rental money and the kitten about the size of my hand. "Gee, he's really little."

"Enjoy the moment." Donna and Paddy ambled off and I sequestered Little-bit in my room with food and litter till I could think of a way to introduce the new kid on the block to the rest of the gang.

Rudy returned with a sack of groceries, plus chips from Horn's bar and fried green beans that had to be the best vegetables ever and things called pasties from Millie's. Back in Chicagoland pasties were not delicious flaky crusts covering meat and veggies. Pasties covered something else entirely — and not something from the food pyramid.

The next morning I woke up at six thirty to the sounds of Sheldon knocking on Penny's door emanating from my phone, a feline motor humming on my chest and the moan of foghorns out in the harbor. My legs, arms and face itched like mad. Not only did I have my very own cat — I had my very own cat allergy. I pulled on jeans and a sweatshirt between scratching and more itching, slid my credit card and Sheldon in my back jean pockets then did the good cat-mommy thing and tucked Little-bit under the covers.

I tiptoed down the steps so as not to wake Rudy and have to spill my guts on what I was up to — stealing fudge off Dwight's porch — and why I was doing it. Instead I left a *little white lie* note about taking an early-morning run, figuring Rudy hadn't known me long enough to realize what a crock the note was.

Stepping out onto the sidewalk, I had five-foot visibility at best, with the whole island cocooned in a wad of wispy cotton. I heard horse hooves way before I saw the horses, and considering their Budweiser dimensions, that was going some. I turned for the steps that led up to the bluffs and smacked right into Irma coming the other way — least, I thought it was Irma.

"Well, there you are," Irma said to me. "Just the person I want to see. But I didn't think you'd be out and about at this hour. How did the call to Winslow go?"

"You're blonde . . . and where are your glasses? And what color lipstick is that?"

"I'm now officially a Pink Coquette girl; that's what the package of lipstick said I'd be if I bought this stuff." Irma puckered up and kissed the air. "I needed some coquette in my life and everybody knows blondes have more fun and men don't make passes at girls who wear glasses."

"You're looking for passes?"

"You betcha." Irma held out her arms and did the *look at me* twirl. "I went off-island and got modernized. I got contacts, baby blue ones, and those jeans that hold your stomach and butt in so you look skinny." She gave her backside a swat. "Now I got a pretty nice rump for a gal my age. And I got Top-Siders like all the boat people wear around here. I'm part of the in crowd."

"What brought this on? You were fine before, you know." I itched my neck, then rubbed my arms.

Irma's lower lip dropped into a pout. "Rita the Bimbo called me a granny and Dutchy said I was an old biddy. I decided if I'm going to find the instigator of the Bunny Festival I need to get in the groove, change things up — think outside the fudge box, right?"

"Like as in Jessica Fletcher?"

"Like as in *CSI.* I just got back from the Lucky Bean," Irma went on. "Took my new threads out for a test-drive and got a wolf-whistle from Smithy heading over to his blacksmith barn. He's always so relaxed, a pleasure to be around. He gave me a Little Debbie Cosmic Brownie to go with my coffee. So what's the scoop with Winslow — is he coming to the island to harass Dutchy and Rita or what?"

A kid on a bike with pink and chocolate brown boxes piled in the front basket for a bunch of deliveries zoomed by, nearly running us over. "There's a problem," I said in a rush to Irma, feeling the need to get a move on before the kid headed up the hill toward Dwight's house. "I made the call but Dutchy caught me using his phone at the fudge shop. I needed an excuse, so I said I was taking an order and Dwight wanted five pounds of fudge delivered this morning. Dutchy saw dollar signs and ignored the logic of Dwight never ordering fudge, but now I've got to get that order before —"

"Before Dwight and Dutchy realize you're up to something and start wondering what's going on," Irma said, grabbing my hand and trotting off for the steps with me in tow. "We got to get Dwight's fudge before he does is what you're saying. Looks like that kid has a lot of deliveries; we can make it."

"You don't have to go." I started off, guilt riding me hard, knowing if I hadn't stuffed my cheeks with maple-nut I wouldn't be in this mess. "I can do this on my own."

"But I got outfits for just this sort of thing. More jeans, a cute denim blouse. Right now I'm all decked out and ready for action. Maybe I should get pepper spray."

I am never eating fudge again.

The bluff was socked in just like town, the weird sensation of Irma and me being the only people on the island closing in around us. We hung a left onto Huron and crossed the street to the sidewalk. The big Victorians were completely hidden in the clouds and my scalp itched like the invasion of a million ants.

"We can hide here and wait for the kid on the bike," Irma said when we passed the concrete pots with purple and white petunias spilling over the edge. "Dwight's house is right next door, and he's more of a party-hearty, late-night kind of guy than an early riser. We can snatch the fudge and no one will see us in this fog and —"

A door opened somewhere in the haze and I put my fingers over Irma's mouth. She pointed to SeeFar and I nodded in agreement. Low, sweet-talking voices and seductive giggles drifted our way from Dwight's front porch, followed by footsteps coming down the walkway heading right for us. Irma ducked behind the big flowerpots, pulling me with her, the two of us hip-to-hip, and the urge to scratch driving me nuts.

The wrought iron gate squeaked open just as the shadowy outline of a bicycle and rider headed up the street from the other direction. Dwight's early-morning visitor . . . or more than likely overnight playmate . . . jumped behind the pots. Huffy's left foot now squashed my right one, her nose flattened Irma's and three pairs of eyes rounded to the size of baseballs in *what are you doing here* fashion as we all stared at each other. I bit back an *Ouch*.

None of us moved a muscle as the kid put down the kickstand on the bike, opened the gate and ambled up the walkway, my pink and brown fudge package tucked under his arm. In a flash, Huffy flipped us the bird of the non-feather variety, then scurried off down the street, fading into the swirling froth with *CSI* Irma right behind her. Go, Irma.

I scratched and itched everything I could reach till the delivery kid took off to complete the rest of his deliveries. I then hoisted my leg over the gate, avoiding the squeaky hinge alarm system, and made my way to the back porch, keeping below the window-panes, which revealed lights on inside. Picking up the fudge, I then chanced a peek into the kitchen, and there, right in front of me, was Dwight. If he weren't so caught up in a phone conversation, he would have seen me for sure. A cigarette dangled from the corner of his mouth, with two more smoldering in an ashtray, taking chain-smoking to the master class level.

As part of my lawyer-infested upbringing, I knew that seven AM nicotine-enhanced phone calls came in two varieties: business that's gone down the drain or someone who was dead. With a little luck this was both, involving Bunny croaking and Winslow delivering bad news, but there was no way of knowing for sure. Itching that little space between my eyes and then the one between my nose and lips, I clam-crawled my way to the front, keeping close to the house and out of sight.

Pea soup still engulfed the bluffs as I scrambled back over the gate onto the sidewalk, landing right in front of a man whose chin had not connected with a razor in days — maybe weeks. He wore a crumpled navy captain's hat, a ragged Green Bay Packers sweatshirt and a knife with a well-used handle strapped to his belt.

8

"Who the heck are you?" captain guy grumbled, eyeing my fudge package. "You're Dwight's newest squeeze? Sweets for his new sweetie?"

I shuddered so hard at the thought of me with Dwight together that I stopped itching for a full minute.

Captain guy took a step closer, his barrel chest nearly touching my mostly flat one, for once making me grateful for 32-A's. "Stay away from Dwight if you know what's good for you. He's taken, and don't forget it. Mind your own business around here."

The left corner of the captain's lip arched in a sneer, exposing teeth the color of chewing tobacco and black coffee, then he strolled down the hill, disappearing into the mist. Since I'd seen 1-800-HotBabe on Dwight's dresser and just witnessed his secret rendezvous with Huffy, it was a pretty fair assumption that Captain Yellow-teeth's interest in Dwight was not of a personal romantic nature.

So why was he warning me off Dwight and why was he standing here in the fog staring at SeeFar and just how big was that knife he was packing? Was he casing the place out? Planning a burglary and not wanting me to burgle it first — is that what he meant by saying Dwight was taken?

Scratching my arms while making sure to keep away from the edge of the cliff and the express route to town, I located the steps. When I reached the bottom, I cut through Marquette Park, giving the Father a little good-morning salute, then passed the big Dutch Elm at the corner and crossed Main Street.

Okay, I should dump the fudge in the trash out of respect for Irma and her recipe plight, and I sure didn't need five pounds of butter and sugar clogging up my arteries and adhering itself to my behind. But in the world of Evie Bloomfield, dumping fudge was never going to happen, so I dropped it off at Doud's Market for them to share with their customers. I snagged a piece for myself because the devil made me do it, then crossed the street and banged on the back door of Irma's shop.

Inside I could see her hustling around the

kitchen, which was piled with bags of sugar, chocolate, maple caramel, shelves of nuts, a rainbow of candies — all the good things in life. Using a Goliath-size spoon, Irma stirred a massive copper pot simmering on the stove, ribbons of steam curling over the edge. Irma was the poster gal for the *if at first you don't succeed* philosophy of life. Here she was giving fudge yet another try . . . God save us all.

"Did you catch up with Huffy?" I asked Irma when she let me in and poured coffee.

She did another stir while kicking out her left foot for me to see. "Top-Siders are the bomb — that's what the kids say these days, *the bomb.* I guess 'cool' is back to being about the weather. These shoes don't make a sound, and I scared the bejeezus out of Huffy when I caught up to her on her porch. She told me to mind my own business if I knew what was good for me."

"That phrase seems to be making the rounds this morning. So what's with Huffy and Dwight anyway? I got the feeling this was more than a one-night fling." I pulled my socks down and scratched my ankles.

Irma gave the brew another swish, then sat across from me at a little wood table by the window. The fog was starting to burn off the harbor, letting in patches of sun and blue sky. "Everyone around here knows those two always had the hots for each other," Irma said to me. "But Bunny put the kibosh on it from the get-go, just like she didn't want her daughter to get involved with Smithy. Huffy's dad runs the delivery system on the island; he ferries in all the stuff we need from the mainland."

"He sounds like a respectable enough guy — so why didn't Buffy approve?"

"Oh, he's got money to be sure, and Huffy's his pride and joy, but a shower, shave and clean shirt don't exactly top his priority list. Bunny used to say that she was related to the Rockefellers, and she told Huffy right to her face and in front of half the town she must be related to Kentucky moonshiners. Dwight wouldn't cross Bunny, since she paid for his lifestyle, but now that Mother Moneybags is between Rocky Road and Cookies 'n' Cream, Dwight and Huffy can do what they want."

"But that's just it, they're not — they're slinking around like love-struck teenagers. And there's something else going on with Huffy — she also wants to buy out Rudy and take over the bike shop. She said she'd have the money in a month and it was her money, not her dad's. She sure didn't get that kind of cash from her own shop.

Where's it coming from? And I think I saw her dad outside SeeFar when I was rescuing the fudge off the back porch. What's that all about?"

"That the captain was up there doesn't surprise me a bit," Irma said over the rim of her mug. "Now that Bunny's at the big town council meeting in the sky and driving them all nuts, the captain wants to make sure his little girl gets what she's always wanted . . . Dwight!"

A little smile played at the corner of Irma's mouth as she went back to the stove, turning down the flame under the pot. "I know where this is leading; I'm getting good at detective stuff. I think it's the clothes I'm wearing. Gives me good snooping vibes. I never had vibes of any kind before."

"We're not detectives. We're just concerned citizens trying to help Rudy."

Irma added cocoa to the cooking mixture, the aroma of rich chocolate filling the kitchen. "I bought a fingerprint kit at Walmart yesterday, so that makes us detectives — it says so right there on the back of the box — and I think that you think that Huffy joined up with Dwight and they got rid of Bunny for the money and maybe a little payback for keeping them apart all these years. That's where that buyout money's coming from, I bet."

Irma held up her big spoon in triumph, dripping chocolate on the floor. "And that explains why they don't want to be seen together. They knock off Bunny and frame Rudy."

"Fingerprint kit?"

"I was thinking about getting a stun gun too; Tasers are too expensive. We really need a stun gun."

Nate Sutter was going to kill me dead.

"And we need a plan." Irma put down the spoon and whipped open double cabinet doors to reveal pictures of Bunny taped on one side and Huffy and Dwight on the other. "It's a murder board like they use on those TV shows, except this is really a murder cupboard. We have the victim and suspects. I got the pictures out of my *Town Crier* recycle pile. Pretty slick, huh?"

"How'd we get from bookstore to murder cupboard?"

"What bookstore? I'm sorry to say my son's convinced Rudy's the killer, and that leaves finding him innocent up to you and me. So what do you think?"

"I think we're looking at five to ten in a Michigan state prison for obstruction of justice."

"So we won't obstruct; we'll just divert."

Irma turned down the boiling fudge, then looked back at me. "I don't want Rudy to go to jail. I'll do whatever it takes to keep him out." There was a hitch in Irma's voice that I hadn't heard before.

"Whoa — you like Rudy."

"Everybody likes Rudy; least everyone in town here."

"You *really* like Rudy. That's what this is all about, isn't it?"

Irma faced me, nibbling at her lower lip. "That dumb widow thing I told you about before with Dutchy . . . well, I sort of chose Dutchy over Rudy. Talk about stupid on steroids — that would be me. I hurt Rudy's feelings something terrible. If I can help find the real killer, it might make things right between us and we can at least be friends again. I truly miss him in my life. You'll keep this to yourself and won't tell anyone? There's already enough gossip flying around here about me and Dutchy, and this would be fuel for the fire for sure."

Such a little island for so many secrets. "Mum's the word, I promise." Irma and I were the Mary-Kate and Ashley of dumb guy choices. If there were a class called Men 101, Irma and I should sign up and sit in the front row and take notes.

Irma shoved her now-nonexistent glasses

up her nose out of habit. "Huffy and Dwight weren't the only ones with an interest in our resident dead person." Irma reached for an issue of the *Crier* and ripped Speed Maslow's picture right off the front page and taped it to the suspect side of the cupboard. "Bunny and Speed used to be friends, then last week she made a comment over at the bank about how he couldn't be trusted. It was all over town in minutes, being as he's trying to raise money for the Speed Maslow Challenge. You'd think she'd be more considerate of someone she knew when he was a kid around here."

"Speed's from Mackinac?"

"Helped his uncle with a lawn maintenance business in the summers. We figured that's why he came back. He's got an apartment over his bike shop now, but I'm sure he has bigger plans. There's a lot of money here and people like him. Maybe Speed had enough of Bunny's badmouthing and decided to shut her up."

Irma held up the *Crier* with the big gaping hole where Speed's picture had been. "Says here that tonight's the kickoff up at the Grand for the Labor Day Jazz Weekend. It's one of those *asparagus and thin salty meat on water crackers* affairs and Speed's getting an award — Entrepreneur of the Year.

Everybody'll be talking about the Bunny Festival, and maybe somebody will let something slip." Irma parked her hand on her hip. "Bought myself a ditching-Dutchy dress, and it's time to take it out for a spin. I'd say you should go too, but it looks like you're coming down with a rash."

"Cat allergy — and try not to spin too fast, okay? We got to keep a low profile, or people will get nervous and clam up."

Irma dipped a spoon in the fudge brewing on the stove. She handed it to me, a glint of hope in her eyes. "Okay, here we go. Tell me — what do you really think of this batch? I'm getting better."

I really needed to enroll in lying school.

I headed off to Rita's trying to enjoy the relaxed, quaint, agonizingly slow little town coming to life. Wagons and drays plodded along, people who hadn't ridden a bike in years wobbled down the street, crashing into whatever got in their way, overnighters drifted into restaurants for breakfast. By some miracle of the island gods, and by using every ounce of patience I possessed, I didn't yell or shove anyone out of my way. I figured that made me an urban saint.

When I finally got to Rita's Fudge Shoppe, I waited for her and Dutchy to retreat back into the kitchen, then I slipped the bill and money for the fudge onto the counter. I went with the idea that they wouldn't care where the money came from for the five pounds of fudge and would have no reason to call Dwight about the order if they were paid in full. Now there was no reason for Dwight to call Rita's Fudge Shoppe and no reason for Rita's Fudge Shoppe to call Dwight. This was a lot of mess for two pieces of maple-nut fudge . . . but honestly, it was so worth it.

I snuck out the side door, blending into a milling crowd that was going absolutely nowhere. Turning onto Market Street, I avoided the bottleneck on Main as Sheldon beeped and vibrated my butt. It was a text from Mother. Leaving for Paris tomorrow AM. Check on Grandpa don't forget.

Right, the parents' trip to France for a month. Good for them, but the only thing Grandpa Frank needed from me was a lift back and forth to the airport when he headed off to Vegas for some R&B. He told Mother it was his love for rhythm and blues that took him to Vegas a few times a year, but I suspected it was more like roulette and bourbon. I sucked at lying, and Grandpa Frank had it down to an art form, except with me. We were buds. Maybe it was because I had his eyes or because he taught me how to drive a stick shift, but more than likely it was because neither of us fit the Bloomfield mold of society perfection and sublime snobbery. I like beer more than champagne, candy bars more than tiramisu and the Gap more than Saks. Grandpa Frank's favorite club is Canadian Club whiskey, and his idea of the perfect night out since Grandma died ten years ago is playing poker with his army buddies. Yeah, we were buds.

I passed the blacksmith shop, workplace of Smithy, another Bunny casualty. He had to resent the mother-in-law from hell, but how much? Did he just bitch and complain about her at the Stang over a few beers, or was it more *I'm getting rid of the old broad 'cause she's got it coming?*

The doors to the blacksmith barn were pulled together and locked tight, the shop and tour hours posted on the white plaque in front. Curls of smoke puffed from the stone chimney, the deep woody aroma wafting through the air suggesting the blacksmith was indeed *in.* Since I wasn't here to get shoed or branded or whatever else got done in such shops and I just wanted to talk with Smithy, I took the path around to the side to see if I could find him.

"Hello," I called out, knocking on the

screen door. "Anyone home?" I stepped inside to find coals glowing deep red in the hearth, the heat radiating all the way to where I stood. Tools I didn't recognize but that looked like something from the Old Testament hung on wood pegs, a buggy was parked in a stall and a black-and-white cat slept on a bench. Smithy couldn't have gone far — there was a fire blazing. "Hello?"

Steps that were split half logs trailed up the side of the barn and I took them into a big loft with arched doors wide open letting in warm sun and a cool breeze. Smithy wasn't here either, but he did have herbs and berries drying on big, flat screens held up on two-by-four sawhorses. The herbs smelled fresh and earthy and sweet, and there was a stack of little plastic baggies for storing them when the time came. I knew oregano from rosemary, and could pick out mint because I've had more than my share of mojitos over the years, but that was the extent of my herb awareness.

I gazed out of the loft, standing on top of the world, telling myself I didn't miss honking horns, the Chicago skyline and deep-dish pizza. I could see all the way to the bridge and beyond now, and it was very picturesque, if you liked picturesque, and —

I got shoved from behind. Hard! My neck

snapped back and I lost my footing on the old boards. Arms flailing, I grabbed for something, *anything,* till the bushes below rushed up to meet me.

9

I blinked my eyes open and saw Nate Sutter hovering above me. "Jail?"

"Not yet."

Another guy walked up. It was that hippie on *Scooby-Doo,* except bigger and with a silver stud earring and chewing gum. "What were you doing up in my loft?"

"Looking for you," I wheezed. I forced my eyeballs to work and gazed up. "Somebody pushed me."

"Why would somebody push you?" Sutter glanced at the loft. You got too close to the edge. Smithy said he watched you fall into the bushes and didn't see any badass characters standing around applauding the occasion. Can you move your arms and legs?"

I gave everything a test drive, then levered myself into a sitting position.

"Maybe you should visit Doc Evers," Sutter said. "If not for the fall, at least for the poison ivy. You're a mess."

"Cat allergy."

Smithy pointed to the red, blotchy back of my arm. "Leaves of three let them be? Sound familiar?"

"I live in Chicago. We count train stops."

Smithy shook his head. "Good luck with that allergy. I'm getting ready for the morning tourists, I've got to go." He stood and adjusted the strap on his worn overalls and tied his left boot, which had burn spots across the toe. Being a blacksmith wasn't for the puny. He grinned down at me. It was one of those nice-guy grins that made you want to buy the guy a beer, but when Sutter turned the other way, Smithy's smile died a quick death. "Stay out of high places, Chicago," Smithy added, steel in his eyes more than in his voice. "It's bad for your health."

Smithy sauntered off, my brain in a fog as much from the fall as the bad health crack. What happened to good old Smithy the brownie guy? I started to get up, except Sutter held me in place; this time it was his turn to give me the steely look. "What in the heck do you think you're doing?"

"Getting a double scoop of cherry chocolate chip to celebrate being alive?"

"You show up here and now my mother's suddenly blonde."

"She looks good blonde."

"She's wearing jeans."

"You're wearing jeans."

His brows knit together, and did he just growl? "What did you say to her?"

Don't light that match. "Your mom needed a little change, a makeover, updating — her idea, not mine. She's got a new spring in her step and really held her own in that fudge fight."

"What fudge fight?" Sutter ran his hand over his face, muttering a string of vivid Detroitisms, and ground his teeth, probably chipping a molar.

Okay, I got that Irma was embarrassed about Dutchy, and she had obviously kept it from sonny boy, for which Dutchy should be eternally grateful. If Nate Sutter had an aneurysm over jeans, contacts and hair, then stealing the cherished family recipes would land Dutchy in the bottom of Lake Huron. Of course, if sonny boy knew Mom and I were hunting a murderer, I'd be in the lake right beside Dutchy.

"You're not getting her involved in this Bunny thing, are you?" Sutter asked, as if reading my mind.

"What Bunny thing?"

"If you go upsetting everyone around here with your stupid ideas that Rudy's innocent,

I'm pulling the plug on Doud's freezer. I'll end this *hide the body* mess we got going, and I don't care how much business we lose. You understand what I'm saying?"

Screw you, is what I wanted to say back, but mouthing off to a city cop was never a good idea even if the cop wasn't in his big city. "Got it."

I wobbled to my feet, staggering, and Sutter grabbed me, his arm solid and strong and macho. Macho? Where'd that come from? My fall to Earth, or maybe a latent hormonal buildup due to being single and maybe not loving it as much as I thought?

"Are you okay?" Sutter asked, holding my shoulders in a firm grip. "You look weird."

"*You* look weird, like you're trying to catch your breath. Is that what happens at middle age?" He deserved that crack for calling my ideas stupid.

"Stay out of trouble, and get something for that poison ivy. You're scaring the fudgies."

He tromped across the street to the Lucky Bean, and I headed for Rudy's Rides at a much slower pace. Just when my knees had started to scab over, I'd bruised every bone in my body. Except I didn't do the bruising — somebody else did. Hey, I knew a push when I felt one. After years of mass transit rush hour Chicago commuting I knew all about pushes.

"What's cooking?" I yelled to Rudy. I limped past three more primed bikes in front of the shop that seemed to look more dingy by the day. I snagged Bambino from the pool table, petting his cute, fuzzy head and followed my nose to the kitchen. Rudy stood beside Ed stirring some concoction on a cookie sheet, the onion garlic smell making the shop more Chef Boyardee than Rudy's Rides. Neither guy said boo about my red, oozing skin, making me wonder what I looked like usually.

I put Bambino on the windowsill and got the cat treats from the cupboard as Rudy said, "We've been fooling around with this recipe since Ed talked me into retiring here when he did. We used to be poker buddies, and now it's euchre, and this is our secret lucky snack mix that we're passing off as trail mix to go along with biking." Rudy added handfuls of nuts. "I was thinking a bag of snacks with a bike rental is a gimmick just like you said. I'm going with BOGO Week to get our name out there like you see on TV all the time. Buy one get one."

"Rent a bike and get a bag of trail mix? Not bad," I said.

"More buy the trail mix and get a bike," Rudy laughed. "Twain says, *Many a small thing has been made large by the right kind of advertising.* Ed here had that hanging in his office in Chicago for years."

Personally I thought that was asking a lot of trail mix, but I just fell out of a barn, so what did I know? But why did I fall out, and why did Smithy go all Jekyll and Hyde on me? And how could he not have seen someone else up in that loft? Smithy didn't want me up there for some reason, but what was it? I pinched up a bit of the trail mix and set it in front of Bambino and Cleveland, then plucked up a cat treat and popped it in my mouth trying to make sense of what happened at the barn.

"Holy cow, this mix is terrible!" Drool pooled at the corners of my mouth, my tongue shriveling into the back of my mouth.

Rudy grabbed the bag out of my hand. "You just ate Friskies Seafood Sensations. The good news is you won't have urinary problems or hairballs."

"Herbs," I blurted. "A perfect addition."

"You didn't even taste it," Ed groused.

I tossed a handful of mix in my mouth. I needed to take another look at that loft and wanted an excuse to go now before any evidence got destroyed, and I didn't want to tell Rudy what was going on. "What about an upscale adult taste — throw in some rosemary or sage? Bet Smithy would sell us some. You know how everyone loves things homegrown."

I opened the back door. "I'll go see him right now." Not that I intended to chat it up with good old Smithy, who clearly didn't want to talk to me. It was Smithy's barn, but someone could have easily followed me. I had been admiring the scenery and not paying attention, so anyone could have pushed me.

"Stop at the medical center, get something for your poison ivy," Ed called, leaning out the door, knowing to avoid the broken step. "See if there's a psychiatrist hanging around. Think therapy. You're eating cat food."

I turned the corner onto Main thinking about my header into the lilacs and jumped back as Irish Donna whizzed right in front of me on the red primer bike she'd rented. Her hair streamed out behind her while horses reared and fudgies dove for the sidewalk, Donna screaming, "Whoa, Paddy, whoa."

The street leveled out, Donna dragging her feet, the bike slowing, then bouncing off a black-and-white porch post in front of Millie's Pub. Donna flopped over onto the street facedown, the bike toppling on top of her, fudgies gathering, staring, snapping pictures.

"Say something," I called out to Donna, people parting like the Red Sea when they caught a glimpse of my splotchy arms and face. I picked up the bike and helped Donna to stand. Squaring her shoulders, she sniffed in a lungful of air, shoved her red curls off her forehead and snatched her purse from the bike basket. She pushed a fudgie out of the way, then yanked open the pub door.

"Pour me a pint, Brad me boy," Donna bellowed to the barkeep. "I'm a woman in need." She sank into a booth, grabbed the hot sauce off the table and gave a big squirt directly into her mouth, smacking her lips in satisfaction. "Faith and begorra I'm restored!"

"What happened?" I asked Donna after I added an order of fried green beans — vegetables my way — to the beer request and took the seat across from her. Millie's was vintage island decor with a stamped tin ceiling, a mirrored bar reflecting liquor bottles stacked in front and those little black-and-white tiles like Grandpa Frank had in his downstairs bathroom right here on Millie's floor. A picture of Millie, the family hunting dog, hung on the wall. Around here everything was named after someone, and the pub was no exception.

"Ye know that saying *like riding a bike,* meaning folks don't be forgetting how it's done no matter how old ye get?" Irish Donna slapped her hand on the table. " 'Tis a big load of horse manure." She gulped down the Guinness and let out a burp that warranted a round of applause from the next table over. "So where ye be headed this fine day?" Donna asked. She tackled Guinness number two, the dark brew taking the edge off her bike encounter and putting color in her cheeks and reddening her nose.

"I got pushed out of Smithy's barn loft and I'm trying to figure out why and who did it," I said between bites of green bean.

Donna's eyes rounded, and she leaned across the table, hooking her finger for me to do the same. "It's the meddling about the Bunny Festival, it is. I've heard talk that ye not be thinking Rudy did the deed, meaning someone else around here did. Gets people jumpy as a pea on a drum. If ye ask me, ye got the black cloud to thank for things not going your way one bit."

She rolled her eyes upward and wagged her head in worry. "I can feel it this very minute, I can. It be growing around you getting bigger and bigger." Her hands made the outline of a cloud, and a chill snaked down my spine. She slid the gold chain with the shamrock from around her neck, kissed it and slipped it over my head. "For protection, me dear. Ye be needing more than me these days."

"Gee, that's really sweet."

"We can't be having any more occupants over there at Doud's with the place getting in a shipment of frozen juice and pies this very morning." Donna helped herself to the green beans. "Bunny's already squashed under the pizzas and tater tots, and another addition would be a true inconvenience to the store."

"God forbid we inconvenience the store."

"Amen, dearie."

We split the bill, and I followed her out to the porch. "Well, let's get on with it then," she said to me. "The afternoon tea fudgies will be arriving at the Blarney Scone, and Shamus never puts the doilies out right, and he flirts something fierce if I don't step in and put an end to it. The man has a roving eye and a weak brain."

"You want to go with me to the loft?"

"You're young and have your wits about you" — Donna studied my blotchy face —

"well, most of the time you do, and you're not the sort of lass who falls out of barns. I'd say someone was up there who followed you and is trying his best to scare you off from poking around the Bunny Festival. The question is, me dear, are you letting them get away with it and Rudy gets sent up the river for something he didn't do?"

My bones ached, I had massive poison ivy, probably from climbing up Dwight's trellis, I was on hit lists, the local cop wanted me behind bars but hey, my urinary tract was in good shape and I didn't have hairballs. What more could a girl ask for. "I work for Rudy's daughter back in Chicago. If I don't straighten this Bunny mess out, she'll fire me, and like you said, we can't let Rudy get sent up the river. He's a good guy getting a rotten deal."

Donna slapped me on the back, adding to the bone ache. "Then let's be getting on with it."

"What about your bike?"

"If luck be with us, it'll get pinched and we'll not be seeing it ever again."

Donna started off, and I fell in beside her. "There's a little problem you should know about. Smithy was not happy about me being up in his loft and told me to stay away."

"Well, he'd be drying his herbs up there

this time of year, and the man's fussy about his plants; says it's his healing therapy for Constance leaving him like she did."

"There's another possibility other than the herbs why Smithy wants me to stay away: Bunny killed Smithy's marriage and it could be that Smithy wanted to return the favor. Maybe he wouldn't like that I'm trying to get Rudy off because the guilty path might lead right to him."

Irish Donna stopped in the middle of the sidewalk, a crowd of fudgies nearly tripping over her. Eyes narrowing, she yanked me to the side. "What are ye thinking? Smithy's a dear boy, he is, not a mean bone in his body, everybody knows that. I cannot believe you're thinking he's the one who did the pushing. There are lots of others out there having it in for Bunny and not wanting to get found out."

Okay, this was going to be a real problem. Friends. Everybody around here knew everybody and couldn't believe the boy or girl next door was a killer.

"And why would Smithy be framing Rudy of all people? Tell me that, would you?" Donna added. "There not be a cross word between the two of them as far as I can tell. Ye gone daft in the head, girl, and I'll be no part of pinning a murder on a perfectly innocent boy like Smithy."

"I'm not pinning, but you have to admit that Smithy didn't like Bunny, and maybe he'd had enough of not seeing his daughter and blamed Bunny for the whole situation."

Donna snorted, wrinkled her nose and stormed off.

Being a nosy outsider would never compete with being a longtime friend, and I respected that, but Smithy was way up there on my *who knocked off Bunny* list. I strolled past the barn, the steady clang of hammer hitting metal vibrating into the fillings of my teeth. How did he stand the racket? Small wonder why he raised nice, quiet plants.

I turned for the side entrance I had gone in before and stopped at the screen door. Now I needed a distraction to get inside and up the steps to the loft without Smithy seeing me. Maybe I'd find a footprint or a gum wrapper or whatever up there to lead me to whoever wanted me out of the way. Heck, they found clues like that all the time on TV, right?

Red-faced, with sweat clinging to his forehead, Smithy swung the mallet, all his attention focused on the red-hot iron and the giant tongs holding it. Where I came from, we used tongs to snag the last olives out of the jar. I slipped off my shoes, waited for the hammer to hit the metal again then opened the door. The wood floor felt cool and smooth against my bare feet as I tiptoed up the well-worn steps as Smithy gave the iron rod another whack.

When I got to the top, the loft doors were still wide open, with the warm breeze drifting through them. The drying herbs and berries sat to one side, and I crept across the heavy floorboards to where I'd been pushed. The racket below suddenly stopped. I froze and waited a beat for the pounding to start up again, but instead felt someone come up behind me. Every hair on my body stood straight on end as I felt a hot breath against my neck.

10

Smithy was strong with a big hot forge to cook me to ashes; least I wouldn't itch anymore. I spun around, throwing my hands in the air with *Don't kill me; I have a cat to support* on the tip of my tongue, and Irish Donna slapped her hand over my mouth to squelch my scream.

I took a step back and gave her the *what the heck are you doing here* hands-up gesture. Donna pointed below to where Smithy was, did a swirly finger by the side of her head indicating Smithy was crazy. I didn't think Smithy was actually nuts, but something was clearly up with him. She pointed to me, then to the loft door.

She pointed to herself and the drying herbs and berries. From years of charades at Camp Wichicaca, I figured that meant I should look one place for clues and Donna would look in the other for some idea of who sent me airborne. I studied the floor by the open door for footprints other than mine as a woman's voice drifted up from below.

"These are my friends from Chicago," the woman said. "And we'd like a private tour of your blacksmith shop. We'd like to avoid the crowds."

"Tour's at three," Smithy said in his *polite historic guide to thick-headed tourist who didn't read signs* voice. "You and your friends are welcome then."

"You don't seem to understand." This time the woman had an edge — just short of rude, since she had guests. "I'm Helen, and my husband is Ed Levine, president of the Mackinac Yacht Club, and I'm on the board for the Lilac Festival, and my son's ad agency in Chicago does the publicity for free for the events on the island, so perhaps you can make an exception just this once for my friends."

A crash sounded behind me and I spun around to see Irish Donna standing over a toppled tray of dried blueberries, her cheeks chipmunk-full, sublime satisfaction in her eyes. She gave me an *uh-oh, look what I did* shoulder roll that didn't look all that sincere. She sucked in two more blueberries.

The woman below said, "Someone is already here right now; we can just join them and make it a small personal tour. That should work out."

"There's not supposed to be anyone up there," Smithy groused, a clatter of footsteps now heading our way.

Hide, I mouthed to Donna as Smithy, a woman in Bloomingdale's best and a man with hair on his chin and none on his head came into view at the top of the stairs. Irish Donna crouched down behind a drying table and I did a little friendly salute to Smithy and the gang, hoping to draw their attention my way.

Smithy and everyone else on the island knew I was snooping around to find Bunny's killer, but getting Donna involved would draw even more attention and drive the killer underground. Besides, the people on the island were Donna's friends. In a week I would be gone and forgotten, but she'd still have to live here.

"You?" Smithy growled, peering at me.

"I know, I know." I held up my hands in surrender. "You told me to stay away, but I couldn't. You see, I . . . I dropped my cell phone when I was up here earlier." I held up my constant companion, Sheldon. "I was admiring your lovely herbs, and —"

"Herbs," the woman shrieked, trotting over to the drying screens. "Oh my goodness, just look at these dried cranberries and blueberries; even the ones on the floor are perfection. These are amazing — so big and plump. And what's this?" She grabbed a handful of some grassy stuff. "I've never seen this herb before, and I'm a member of the CHS — that's the Chicago Herb Society — so I do know my herbs. It's something French, maybe? English? It smells like hay with a touch of oregano? And it's kind of sticky. Wonder what causes that?" She whipped out a wad of cash from her purse and shoved it at Smithy. "I simply must take some back with me to show the girls. How much?"

Smithy stuffed some rosemary in a baggie, thrust it at the woman then yanked away the grassy stuff and tossed it on the table. "Enjoy. No charge."

"I can get rosemary anywhere."

Smithy's brows furrowed and he pulled himself up to his big hulking blacksmith self and pointed a stiff finger at the steps. Without another word, we all followed Smithy, me bringing up the rear, giving Donna a wink and grabbing a fistful of dill — maybe it was dill. It was local and Ed wanted different, and this was different.

When we got to the bottom, the three o'clock blacksmith tour was already crowding the barn to overflowing. Smithy hurried over to the forge and pumped the bellows, igniting the fire. Everyone, including Helen and her entourage, gasped in surprise as sparks flew. The throng took a few steps back as heat blasted out into the room. With all the attention now on Smithy and the blazing forge, Donna snuck down the stairs. Together we faded out the door as Smithy started in on his *welcome to the Benjamin Blacksmith shop* speech.

"Did ye find anything before we got interrupted by her lord and ladyships?" Donna asked when we got to the sidewalk and headed down Market.

"Boot prints in the dust is about all, and Smithy wears boots, but it's his loft and —"

"And he could be the one giving you the old heave-ho earlier." Donna said, opening the white picket gate to the Blarney Scone.

"What happened to Saint Smithy?"

"Everyone's got a bit of devil in them, dear." Donna yanked me down onto one of the blue wood chairs; there was a small bouquet of yellow sunflowers in the middle of the small table for two under a tree. She leaned across and whispered, " 'Tis all about politics, the biggest devil of 'em all, if you ask me."

"Are we talking donkeys and elephants?"

"Votes on the town council. I got to thinking about that, and as much as I like Smithy, the dear boy, if Rudy's out of the picture with being in the poky, Smithy will be the one taking his place." Donna's eyes sparkled. "That's what I came back to tell ye."

"Smithy's a townie and Rudy's a townie, neither wanting the historical society looking over their shoulder. Their votes on the town council would be the same, so nothing changes. It's still a fifty-fifty split between the townies and the bluffies."

A sly grin creased Donna's lips. "The person taking Bunny's place on the council is on the side of the historic society, so nothing changes in the voting, but with Smithy it be different as peas and apples. The blacksmith shop and the other historic places on the island belong to the Park Commission. They aim to be keeping the island like it was back in the seventeen hundreds as much as possible and appeal to folks heading here for a bit of history and taste of nostalgia. Smithy's part of that, and it's job security for the dear boy. With him being on the council, the historical society gets his vote too, not the townies like you'd be thinking. The bluffies win."

Holy cow. This was a really good piece of information. "So Smithy gets even with

Bunny for the divorce *and* he keeps the island like he wants it. Why now? Why wouldn't Smithy do the Bunny Festival last year, or even six months ago?"

"Your talk about the herbs is what made me think of it. Smithy uses the barn to be drying his herbs, and Bunny made a fuss at the last council meeting, saying the barn wasn't Smithy's and he didn't have a right. Could be the dear boy had enough of the old biddy getting in his way with the herbs and his marriage and ended her once and for all. The thing is, I can't see Smithy as the murdering kind and hatching the idea."

"Could be bluffies helped Smithy come up with the idea."

" 'Tis a bluffy conspiracy," Donna gasped. "Blessed Saint Patrick." She snatched her shamrock, which was still around my neck, and kissed it. "Sneaks they are, the whole batch of 'em, and using the dear boy like that. Sinful, it is. So who would be doing such a thing?" Donna cut her gaze side to side, then whispered, "The island jazz festival is kicking off tonight up at the Grand, and Shamus got an invitation with being head of the volunteer fire department like he is. The townies will be there with the Better Business Bureau folks acknowledging Speed Maslow as Entrepreneur of the

Year. The bluffies will be showing off their baubles and designer duds and getting their pictures taken. Liquor will be flowing like a river and tongues wagging. Maybe I'll hear something."

"What's your take on Speed?"

Irish Donna fanned herself with a napkin. "He and his cronies are good for the cash registers around here to be sure, and it brings a bit of new blood to the place. But what I and every other female on this here island be liking most is the fine way he fills out a pair of black spandex biking shorts when pedaling around town. 'Tis a sight to behold, I tell you. One glance and I'm in need of two blood pressure pills to set me straight."

Irish Donna ushered a merry band of afternoon teetotalers into the Blarney Scone, and I headed for the medical center a few doors down and past Weber's Florist with the flying pig weather vane on top. The itching was driving me insane, and my left eye had swelled completely shut. I took the steps to the white clapboard with porch and rocking chairs that looked, from what I could see, more house than medical office. Right now I'd give a witchdoctor a try.

"I think I'm dying," I said to the nurse/receptionist behind the desk.

"We're all dying, just not today. Take a seat, roll up your sleeve and quit your whining."

11

"I didn't tell you what's wrong with me," I said to the nurse in a white jacket with rhinestones on the back pockets of her jeans.

I got the *duh* look along with a needle in my arm. She pulled out a book and pointed to a picture of leaves. "Count with me: One, two, three. Now say, 'No-no.' "

She handed over a tube of green goop. "Wash with this three times a day and try really hard not to croak in a public place; it gives the island a bad name. Image is everything around here, you know."

My one good eye shot wide open, and I sat up straight. "You mean I can die from poison ivy?"

"The *dying* part can be arranged if you keep poking your nose in where it doesn't belong, and so far you're off to a running start."

"But Rudy's innocent. What am I supposed to do? Just let the guy rot in jail?"

"Think about dialing it back a notch, okay? This island looks friendly enough, but there's a big dose of John Wayne rugged badass humming under the surface. It's the humming part you need to keep an eye on, and it's the part that's keeping an eye on you."

"I'm being too aggressive?"

"Bull moose comes to mind." Nurse/receptionist Jane Parker planted a hand on her twenty-something fudge-developed hip. "Rudy's a good guy, and no one's passing the crying towel for Bunny. More like buying a round of drinks down at the Stang. But Rudy's stuck in the middle."

"This big spender down at the Stang got a name?"

In answer I got the bill, a snarl and, "I was first in line buying drinks. My grandma had the corner table at the Christmas bazaar for her clam chowder every year till Bunny made a stink that the Historical Society should get that spot. Broke Grandma's heart. I got nothing good to say about Bunny Harrington and those snobby people up on the bluff, and that's pretty much how most of us townies feel."

I did the co-pay routine as another patient staggered into the office and dropped into a chair. Jane rushed over to what was either a heart attack or a sugar-fudge high — hard to tell the difference around here. I picked up my receipt, and right next to it on a sticky note were the words, *Alford's, Jason Bourne, propranolol.*

Alford's was the drugstore on Main Street. Beyond taking aspirin, I knew zip about pharmacology and I also knew zip about Jason Bourne. When I got to the porch, I stood on the rocking chair, tried not to break my neck, held up Sheldon and found three bars of the phone reception variety. I Googled *propranolol* — after trying a bunch of combinations of *O*s and *L*s to get the spelling right.

A beta-blocker? What was a beta and what was so bad about it that you had to block it? That part I didn't get, but the part about treating hypertension, anxiety and panic was pretty straightforward stuff. So, what kind of hit man who seemed to have a thriving business of doing people in had hypertension, anxiety and panic? You'd think they'd be cool as a cucumber; least they were in the movies.

I headed for the bike shop while reading three texts on Sheldon. One was from Lindsey saying Mother gave her a Chanel watch for making partner, and the next was from Mother saying she gave Lindsey a

Chanel watch for making partner. Both seemed harmless enough on the surface, but being from a family that turned being passive-aggressive into a science, the message was when was Evie ever going to warrant a Chanel watch. The way things were going the only watch I'd ever get was of the Mickey Mouse variety.

The third text was from Abigail asking how repairs and painting were going. I texted back that all was good and Rudy was glad to see me. I may suck at lying face-to-face, but I could lie like a pro in a text message.

"Hey, there you are. The great trail mix plan's working," Rudy said when I got back to the shop. "I rented ten bikes this afternoon alone. I think that red primer color is catching on around here — and where else can fudgies rent a bike and have darn good trail mix for five bucks? What a deal."

"I ran into Helen Levine over at the blacksmith shop. The woman puts the *hell* in Helen. Hard to believe she's Ed's wife. While I was there I got some of Smithy's herbs from his loft." I pulled the tangle of weeds from my pocket and gave a sniff. "Dill, I think. Smells pretty good."

Rudy stopped his primer brush mid-stroke. "How'd you manage to get that? He

145

guards those herbs with his life."

"Would you believe my ultra good looks and charming personality?"

"You look like you got the plague and half the town's volunteered to buy you a one-way ticket out of here, in or under the ferry. No one much cares which."

"Smithy was showing Helen around the blacksmith barn and I tagged along. He was giving away free herb samples." It wasn't a complete lie, and there was no need to worry Rudy about the *being pushed out of the loft* incident.

After adding the dill and a dash of chili powder to one of the trays brewing in the oven, I came back to the shop and took a stool beside Rudy's wicker rocker. I dumped primer into a paper cup and dipped my brush, ready to get to work. "You know," Rudy said as I tackled a bike, "we make a pretty good team. You're not afraid to get your hands dirty like a lot of city girls."

"Comes from art school. I was always covered in shades of magenta, indigo, cobalt or whatever. I think my parents were afraid I was going to cut off an ear and leave it on the dining room table; they never got me going to art school. I didn't go around spouting things like habeas corpus and due process and sue his pants off. It had to be

146

kind of scary for them, now that I think about it. So, how well do you know our resident scary person, Jason Bourne?"

Rudy added a swipe of dull red to the rusty back fender of a Schwinn bike. "No one really knows the man, and we all consider that a big step toward longevity. Bunny never had anything good to say to his face or behind his back."

"And look what happened to her longevity." My gaze locked with Rudy's. "If Bourne was fed up with Bunny, it would have been a snap for him to do her in. He could pick off the old girl with a scope and rifle from yards away, not cut her brakes."

"Except," Rudy said, adding more paint, "he's the only one around here who could pick off the old girl like that. He might as well hang an *I shot Bunny* sign around his neck." Rudy put down his brush. "Look, I know what you're thinking, Evie, and you can't go there. Jason Bourne is not a man to mess with, and there's too much gossip out there for some of it not to be true. Besides, why would he frame me for Bunny's festival?" Rudy leaned a little closer. "Your other eye's starting to swell shut."

"I thought the island was sinking. And why *wouldn't* Bourne frame you? I doubt that you're drinking buddies, and you're the logical candidate around here for a frame. Heck, if I were looking for a go-to frame guy, you'd be first on my list. You and Bunny were always at each other and everyone knew it. You have motive out the yin-yang."

Rudy took the paintbrush from my hand. "I'm not exactly sure where my yin-yang is, but you missed the bike and painted my knee. Least I won't rust."

"Jane Parker at the medical clinic jabbed me with some stuff. It should work, right?"

"We'll cross our fingers and light candles. Right now get a cold shower and take a nap. Maybe you'll unswell, though poison ivy is the least of your problems if you've been asking around about Bourne. People talk, and our sharpshooter's not going to be gone forever, you know."

"Maybe he's not as sharp as we think. When I was at the medical center, I saw a script for him for anxiety. What's with that? We got ourselves a nervous sniper?"

"It probably regulates the heart so he can pull the trigger between beats. It's crucial for making long-distance shots. It was in some De Niro movie, so it's gotta be true."

Far be it from me to argue with De Niro.

I rolled over in bed and stared into nothingness, everything in total black. Now both eyes had swelled shut? Least that's what I thought till I caught the lighthouses blinking in the night harbor and the silhouette of Little-bit perched on the windowsill. I winked one eye, then the other. Well dang, I could see, and I didn't scratch as much. Thank you, health insurance and Jane Parker.

I climbed out of bed, turned on the light, caught my reflection in the mirror and swallowed a scream. Okay, the swelling was down, and that was good, but my hair stood on end as if slathered with wallpaper paste. Needing some fresh air and food, I did the comb routine with marginal success and added the desperate tie-back with a scrunchie. I snagged Little-bit and took the steps down to the TV room.

Rudy was asleep in his blue Naugahyde La-Z-Boy, snoring like a hibernating bear, with his legs propped up, Bambino and Cleveland on his chest looking as if they belonged there. *Survivor* droned on from someplace in Africa with everyone doing a really bad job of riding elephants. Snagging a Chicago Cubs throw from the back of the green, worn couch, I covered Rudy up to where the cats took over, then added Little-bit to the mix. Two cats? Three cats? Maybe

Rudy would think he'd had three all along, and if he didn't he wouldn't care; he was that kind of guy. Heck, he took me in, didn't he?

Grabbing a trail mix baggie, I headed outside, where there was a horse-drawn carriage filled with the fashionably dressed trotting down Main and Fiona just ahead on the sidewalk.

"Nice dress," I said, falling into step, the carriage just ahead of us. "Hot date?"

"My mother says enough novenas that it should be. Instead I'm on my way to the Grand to cover the kickoff for the jazz festival and get some pics of Speed accepting his award."

"Always the hat?"

Fiona rolled her eyes up toward the purple sequins. "It's a warning so people know they need to smile when they see me coming and not be in the middle of a screaming match. The *Crier* is all about smiles. *Inside Scoop* was all about the smut." We followed the carriage onto Mahoney with clapboard houses and colorful window boxes.

"Do you miss L.A.? The excitement?" We turned onto Cadotte, which was congested with other equines heading up to the Grand perched up on the hill like a giant wedding cake.

"Like a toothache. I went there to do investigative reporting and ended up sneaking pics of stars and their sexual exploits. Bad job, worse boss. Peephole Perry had enough dirt on people to sink half the town; I'm surprised he's still alive. But L.A. doesn't have a monopoly on dirt." She gave me a sassy grin. "We've got a ton of our own. All the talk tonight's going to be about the Bunny Festival. You need to be there, girl. Maybe you'll hear something that will help Rudy. And the food's to die for."

I could so do with the food part. I pulled at my shirt and nodded to the drivers in top hats guiding carriages up to the staircase, the band playing "Mood Indigo" on the two-football-fields-long front porch. "The fashion police would have me in chains and leg irons."

"They've got to catch you first." Fiona stopped by the stone steps that led down into a wooded area. "Bat cave entrance. Follow the path and it takes you up the side of the hotel. Blend in like you're a gardener; gardeners always look splotchy and have poison ivy."

"You've done this."

"Not the poison ivy, but Julia Roberts and Ron Howard, to name a few, show up here once in a while. Smithy and I were celeb stalkers at an early age. I think that's how I got the L.A. bug."

"The L.A. bug's been squashed?"

"Flatter than a frog on a four-lane, if we had a four-lane around here. With a little luck I'll never lay eyes on Peephole again. There's sure no reason for him to come here. Find a shovel and you'll do great. Good luck."

I trotted down the steps. The wooded area came out at a greenhouse, tool shed and compost pile, a huge swimming pool and tennis and bocce ball courts just beyond. Thanks to Grandpa Frank and the gang at Sleepy Meadows Retirement, I kill at bocce ball.

"There you are." I was turned around to face a huge guy in jeans and a maroon polo with *Grand Hotel* embroidered on the sleeve. "HR said they were sending you over, and — Jeez, tuck in your shirt and do something with your hair, will ya? This is a classy place."

He draped an industrial-strength apron over my head, then jabbed a shovel, big bucket and thick gloves at me. "We got the uniformed guys cleaning up the front road; you take the rear where they make deliveries. We can't have the staff stepping in it and tracking it into the hotel, making the whole place reek. Get a move on."

"It?"

I got the *oh for the love of God* look. "Horses? The fragrant gifts they leave behind? The reason you were hired. Take the back steps, and you better do a good job or you're on the next ferry out of here."

This was all Fiona's doing with that *find a shovel* crack. She cursed me. Okay, I looked bad, I realized that. My hair truly was a disaster, and I'd slept in my clothes and I still had the *red plague* look and red primer splotches — but a human pooper-scooper? Really? How did I keep getting into these messes? Easily — oh, so easily that I scared myself.

"Well, what are you waiting for?"

For a beer, burger and fries, but since that wasn't happening anytime soon, I slid on the gloves that came up to my elbows and headed for the side steps lugging a big shovel and bucket. I could cut and run, but this joyful little experience might give me a chance to catch some conversations. At least I hoped so.

No one would pay attention to the local scooper, and they'd keep on talking, right? Plus, if I took off now, Mr. Crabby might alert Sutter that someone with poison ivy and painted clothes was MIA and roaming

153

around the hotel grounds where they didn't belong. Not too many individuals on this island fit that description, and I didn't need Sutter hunting me down and delivering another *mind your own business and stay out of trouble* sermon.

I cut around the side path of the hotel, avoiding the pretty people up on the porch. I took a sharp corner and came face-to-face with Smithy dressed in his work clothes right there on the path in front of me. We both stopped dead. "Why were you really in my loft?"

"Cell phone, just like I said. What are you doing here?"

Jaw set, Smithy took a step toward me and grabbed my shoulders in a tight grip. "Stay away from me and my business or you'll be sorry."

I swung my bucket, catching Smithy in the gut, which resulted in a solid *oomph,* then darted into the bushes, shovel and bucket banging into my legs. I tripped, landing on my hands and knees, and scrambled to my feet running like a scared little girl, because that's exactly what I was. What was that about *Smithy, the dear boy*? Ha! Strip off the overalls, plaid shirt and folksy leather apron and you got a lot of ugly white flab and one big scary dude. I wound my way up the side of the hotel to where the work drays and drivers were parked and I was never so glad to see people and animal excrement in my life.

"Jeez Louise, 'bout time you got here," a woman in a white uniform yelled from the doorway. "Start cleaning; this place is disgusting. If it tracks into the kitchen, the chefs will have a conniption and I'll get to hear about it and that means you'll hear about it, you get what I'm saying?"

I stared at the piles on the drive. Lindsey made partner today and was celebrating right this very moment with champagne and caviar. I'd just had the liver scared out of me by the local psychopath and was about to scoop the unmentionable. And to think my reason for coming here in the first place was to impress my parents. Yeah, this would impress the heck out of them.

I slid the shovel under the first *present* and gagged, the odor bringing tears to my eyes, my nose running onto my upper lip, my throat burning. Taking a deep breath — which was a really, really big mistake — I shoveled, choked and dumped.

"Ya better make sure you get it all up," Watchdog barked from the door as I moved on to the next pile. I must have aced scooping, because Watchdog went back inside as a waiter hurried out. He headed for the far delivery dray, a guy in a captain's hat and week's worth of scruff climbing down from the driver's seat.

Huffy's dad? He and the waiter seemed to know each other; they did the guy-ritual fist bump. Waiter guy said something about Huffy and Dwight and I stopped mid-shovel as the captain nodded in agreement. Agreement about what? What was this about Dwight and Huffy? Maybe that the two of them knocked off Bunny for her money?

I hoisted my bucket, kept the smelly shovel at arm's length and eyed a *present* over by the dray. Head down, I did the inconspicuous pooper-scooper shuffle, shoveling piles and picking up pieces of the conversation. Something about Huffy and Dwight being happy now and *my little girl finally getting what she deserves with Bunny out of the way.*

This kind of brought a tear to my eye, or maybe it was the surrounding fragrance bringing on the tear — hard to tell at this particular point in time. I scooped again, the shovel scraping across the blacktop. The captain may be a little rough around the edges, but he was a really good dad. Maybe he was too good? Just how much did he want to get Bunny out of the way so he could have a happy Huffy?

The server slid off his white jacket, the rite of passage to all things in and out of the hotel, and draped it over a bench. He heaved two boxes from the dray and headed inside. The captain grabbed three boxes and turned my way, our gazes colliding for a second through the darkness. Did he recognize me? Heck, I barely recognized me. He headed inside.

With only the horses for company — and they didn't look in a gossipy mood — I ditched the bucket, shovel, apron and big yucky gloves behind the bench and snatched the jacket. It covered me to my knees — thank you, big tall server dude — and I made my way to the runway-size front porch, the band now playing "Ain't Misbehaving." Wanna bet?

I snagged a discarded wood skewer from an abandoned plate, plucked off the uneaten shrimp and tossed it in my mouth since I never did get dinner, twisted my hair into a bun and speared the skewer through it, holding it in place. So I smelled a little fishy — better than the smell I had before. I didn't have a black tie like the rest of the staff, but in this hip-to-hip crowd no one would notice, especially if I had a tray of something delicious to pass — all eyes would be there, and not on me.

A waitress put down her silver tray laden with little dishes of ice cream covered in pecans drizzled with chocolate sauce to help a woman who'd spilled her drink. Another waitress parked her offerings of asparagus puffs to lend a hand. Asparagus versus chocolate, nuts and ice cream? No-brainer. I snapped up the ice cream tray, then scurried off, blending into the throng.

12

"Evie? Is that really you?"

So much for blending. I considered ignoring the greeting, but Irma wasn't the ignoring type, at least as long as I'd known her. These days she was more *I'm making a scene till I get what I want,* proven by the fact that she had on fake eyelashes, rhinestone earrings and a sapphire blue dress that plunged.

Well dang! "You look hot," I said as she tottered over to me on spiked heels. She giggled, blushed, then stopped in her tracks, eyes watering.

"What in the heck is that god-awful smell?" She fanned her red sequined chili pepper–shaped purse in front of her nose and took a step back.

Uh-oh. I took a whiff and got nothing; my smeller was on strike from the assault of the horse presents. I hitched my chin at the French doors, wide open on such a lovely, festive night to let people mingle about.

"Must be coming from inside. Some kind of accident?"

"Well, it sure can't be on purpose."

I shuffled over a few steps, getting to the railing and angling myself downwind. "Those are great shoes," I added for distraction.

Irma fluffed her hair, which was curled, set and shellacked. "I'm knocking them dead tonight. Good old Dutchy fell down the steps when he got a look at my girls here." Irma arched her plunge. "Guess I showed him what I got — or, in this case, *two things* I got — and he'd never get again."

Irma winked, then plucked a dish of ice cream from my tray. Three other guests eyed the desserts and approached from the upwind side. They got within sniffing range, paused, then hurried off in the other direction. Irma took a bite, total euphoria spreading across her face. "No one does pecan balls like the Grand," she said around a slurpy mouthful, a dribble escaping that she expertly caught with the tip of her tongue. "I hear they serve fifty thousand of these things every year."

She took another scoop. "I didn't know you got a waitress job up here."

"More of a volunteer position." I angled myself a little to the left. "Ed and Helen

Levine are over with Fiona getting their pictures taken, and I don't want them to see me. Ed will tell Rudy and then he'll worry that I'm snooping."

"Snooping? You?" Irma gave me a wink. "Ed and Helen are fat cats from Chicago; bluffies through and through, though Ed's not as bad as Helen. The Queen of England isn't as uppity as Helen Levine. Ed and Rudy are euchre buddies, and Ed talked Rudy into moving here. Enticed him with the fact that there weren't cars and he wouldn't be spending his days staring at carburetors and pistons. Rudy used to be Ed's mechanic." Irma nodded to Irish Donna and some handsome older guy at her side. "That's fast-hands Shamus," Irma offered. "And that pretty blonde he's got his arm around is not his daughter."

Irma licked chocolate sauce from the back of her spoon. "He had a fling with Bunny years ago that Donna doesn't think any of us know about but of course we all do, and just last week I caught him over at the post office making eyes at Winnie Bartholomew in her yellow polka-dot halter top."

Shamus's arm dropped to the pretty blonde's waist, giving a little squeeze followed by a seductive wink.

"I saw that," Donna yelled, loud enough

for us all to hear. She pushed the buxom blonde out of the way and decked Shamus right there in front of the crowd, his carcass flipping, ass over appetite, across one of the big white rocking chairs on the porch.

"Donna has some temper," I whispered to Irma.

"And she has a shotgun."

The band played a loud *ta-da*, drawing attention to an elevated podium instead of the marital drama at the Grand. Andrew Doud tapped the microphone to get everyone quiet. I recognized Andrew from the Bunny Ice Capades at his store. He welcomed guests and islanders and went on about Mackinac and business and the Jazz Festival. He introduced Speed Maslow as Entrepreneur of the Year and presented him with a framed picture of Speed in *Sports Illustrated*, on his bike, hands held high in triumph as he crossed the finish line, winning the Tour of Texas.

Speed looked surprised — or was that stunned? Guess he wasn't expecting the framed picture, and he didn't look too thrilled about it. Fiona snapped pictures, everyone applauded, women drooled and Irma put her empty plate back on my tray and grabbed another. "Brace yourself, Evie. We're in for one of Speed's *I am the greatest* speeches that he does for prospective investors, and there are a bunch of them here on this porch tonight with fat wallets." Speed smiled, but it was more forced than real as he accepted the framed picture and put it behind the podium. He said the race was a team effort and that he was honored and humbled to be here with so many friends, and he thanked everyone from the bottom of his heart. Speed had a heart? Who knew? He waved, then hurried off into the hotel without stopping for one single photo op.

The crowd stirred; it had been expecting more James Franco than Tom Hanks. "Who was that man?" Irma garbled around the spoon in her mouth. "And what have they done with big-mouth Maslow? Looked like he was having some kind of an attack up there."

"Maybe he's sick?"

"Being embalmed and six feet under wouldn't keep Speed from getting his picture taken and doing a sales pitch; he'd find a way."

To get things going again, the mini orchestra struck up Duke Ellington's "Take the A Train," which I recognized right off thanks to Grandpa Frank, a turntable and a stack of something he called his thirty-three and a thirds. A thirty-three and a third of what was a complete mystery, but I didn't care, 'cause the music rocked.

"Well, gee, look who's here," Irma said, a big smile on her face as she stared off into the crowd. "I had no idea Nate would be coming to something like this — a shindig at the Grand isn't exactly his cup of tea." She snagged another ice cream dish off my plate and held it up. "Yoo-hoo, Nate. Look what I got for you, dear."

What! My gaze followed Irma's to the main staircase leading up from the driveway below where the carriages left off passengers and saw sonny boy hustling right for us — for me.

"He's not smiling," Irma said, a *worried mother* edge to her voice. "Must be trouble on the island. I wonder what's going on now? Hope it's not something at the hotel."

"About that trouble." I put down the tray. "I have to go. My shift just ended. Give Nate some ice cream; lots of ice cream. It'll cheer him up." *And slow him down so I can get the heck out of here.*

"Why do you keep looking down the street, Chicago?" Rudy asked as I craned my neck around the corner of the shop for the ten-hundredth time. "Are you hoping for more customers? We already rented eight bikes

164

and we've only been open an hour. Business is picking up — but what in the heck is that smell hanging around here? It's like something died." Rudy sniffed the air. "Or worse?"

Crap! Literally. I did the *wash, rinse, repeat* cycle five times last night and was down to the *ep* of my epidermis and still . . . "Maybe something washed up on the shore?" I leaned out the door again, giving it a little push, as it kept sticking.

"You wouldn't be looking for Sutter, now would you?" Rudy asked behind me.

I spun around to Rudy, who was stirring primer. The Twain smile was in place, but his eyes didn't sparkle this morning like usual and there was a bank notice on the workbench. It didn't look like one of those *we love you as a customer* letters but more *you owe us money and we want it now* notices.

"Sutter? Why would I be looking for him?"

" 'Cause he's looking for you. Woke me out of a sound sleep right there in my very own TV room. Said you were posing as a server up at the Grand and they weren't happy about it. I told him it must have been another brunette with long hair, poison ivy and red paint on her jeans."

"Was he pissed?"

"He's a cop; they're always pissed. I gave him a cat."

Cat! I counted . . . Cleveland, Bambino, Little-bit. Ohmygod! Where was Little-bit?!

Rudy continued, "I don't know where the other cat came from, and Sutter looked like he needed to calm down before he popped something vital. Cats are good for calming. So tell me, what's the latest on Bunny?"

"That she's one cold, cold woman," Sutter said from behind us, obviously having come in from the back door. He pointed to me, dead serious in his eyes, jaw set. "We need to talk."

Two customers came into the shop looking for bikes and trail mix. As Rudy took care of business, Sutter snagged my sweatshirt hood and marched me toward the kitchen. "If you were this much of a pain in the butt in Chicago, they're never going to let you back in, and you are not staying here, and what in the heck is that smell?"

And you have my cat and I want him back was on the tip of my tongue, but I didn't say it. What was I going to do with a cat in a two-by-four apartment in Chicago? I was always at work, and that's not fair — he or she would get bored and pee on my clothes for sport. And maybe a cat would actually calm Sutter down. Though from the looks of things it wasn't working.

"You're about an inch away from jail," Sutter groused.

"There's a killer out there running around and you're going to lock me up? On what charges? Impersonating a waitress? Taking a white jacket that I'm sure was found later, borrowing a tray of ice cream or being a really bad pooper-scooper? And you better be good to that cat."

Sutter stilled, a smile playing at the corners of his lips, something I'd never seen before. He shoved his hands in his pockets and rocked back on his heels. "Wanna run that by me again?"

I grabbed him by the front of his shirt, surprising the heck out of both of us. "The cat — the furry thing that goes *meow-meow* and has whiskers and a tail. You'd better buy him toys and organic food and treats and the good litter, not the junk that sticks to his paws."

"I'm still back at pooper-scooper." Sutter's phone buzzed and I let go of his shirt, my cat-mommy adrenaline rush subsiding. I was suddenly aware of the scent of pine, sunshine and a hint of morning shower that wasn't me and smelled really good. Too good. Male good. Sutter? Why couldn't he be the one who smelled like pooper-scooper?

"I gotta take this," Sutter said, studying the phone screen and stepping out the back door. He caught the broken step and tripped, arms flailing, then landed flat-out on the deck with a solid thud, looking like a giant squashed spider. He scrambled to his feet and I retrieved the phone, which had skittered into the grass. I started to hand it back, then stopped, my steps slowing as I read the text aloud. *"SOS. Meatball and Partner headed to you."* I looked back to Sutter. "I don't think this means make a lot of spaghetti because company's coming."

Sutter snapped the phone from my fingers and shoved it in his jeans pocket. "How do you keep falling into everyone else's business? You got a built-in radar? Something goes sideways, and there you are right in the thick of it, making things worse. I gotta go."

I blocked Sutter's path. "No one sends SOS to a cop for kicks. What's this all about? I live here too, you know."

"Like I can forget." Sutter let out a resigned breath. "Sure, why not. Maybe you've heard something, and you can drive these guys nuts for a while and give me a break." Sutter raked back his too-long hair.

"Partner is the Partnership — the Detroit mob."

"In Chicago, it's the Outfit." That got me a Sutter double-take and a hint of respect for knowing more about Chicago than that it had good pizza and strong winds. "I come from a family of lawyers. You can't swing a dead cat around that city without the Outfit being in on it."

"Meatball is probably the capo, the boss. Street chatter is they're not coming to take in the sights. It's business, and it's personal."

"What are they going to do, shake down the fudge shops? Unionize the horses? Infiltrate the town council? Good luck with that one."

"I'm glad you're here," Irma said to me in a rush, hustling out the back door of the emporium, and across her backyard that connected to Rudy's. "We have to get . . ." The rest of her sentence died in her throat when she spotted Nate. Irma slapped a too-bright smile on her face. "Why are you here, dear?"

"Lately I've been asking myself that same question. And what do you have to get? I can get it for you. Just because I'm house-sitting over at HighSail with Bernie laid up in rehab, it doesn't mean I can't help you out." Nate kissed Irma on the cheek followed by a shake of the head at me. I wasn't up to speed on police mime, but my guess was Sutter wanted me to keep the info about the mob on the move to myself.

"Isn't there someplace you have to be?" Irma said to sonny boy, nudging him down the narrow walkway between the emporium and Rudy's Rides that led to Main Street. "Surely somebody's screwing up around here and needs a ticket to straighten them out," she went on. "Or maybe there's a nice robbery you can look into or a little old lady to help cross the street. You should go have a look around and keep us all safe; isn't that a great idea?"

Sutter tipped Irma's chin, his eyes peering into hers. "Have you been drinking?"

"Not yet, dear, but give it time." Irma nudged Nate with a little push out into the street. He stumbled as Irma waved him off. As soon as he was out of sight Irma rushed back to me, her eyes dancing. "He's come, he's come."

"The Lord?"

"Winslow! Dwight must have hit the panic button over his estate, and best of all, now it's my turn to make Dutchy and Rita sweat a little. This is gonna be fun."

13

"Winslow just got off Arnold's ferry and is probably walking up the dock right this minute," Irma said, grabbing my hand and heading for Main Street. She shoved two little kids and a Red Hat group to the side, weaving us in and out of tourists and past the Pink Pony and Huffy's Bike Hut. "Hurry it up; we don't want to miss him."

"Hold on," I said as we pulled up in front of the information center, where a crowd of disembarking fudgies was meandering up the wood pier. "How do you know what Winslow looks like, and how do you know he's here?"

"There's who you're looking for," said one of the luggage porters, rushing over to us. He pointed to a guy in a bad toupee and a red polo shirt carrying a leather briefcase and dragging a rolling weekender. The porter held out his hand. "Okay, so where's my ten bucks?"

"That's him," another porter said, holding his hand out to Irma. "You got your man, now I want my money."

"Screw you." Another porter elbowed the first and second porters out of the way. "I'm the one who called Irma; she pays me."

Another porter rushed our way, snagging Winslow by the arm and leading him over to Irma. "This the guy you want?" The porter yanked out his iPhone and held up Winslow's picture for all to see. He said to Irma, "You tweeted that you'd pay." He slapped Winslow on the back, nearly knocking him over.

"What is this all about?" Winslow asked as Irma frantically pulled bills from her pocket, the crowd swelling with porters and nosy tourists.

I whispered to Irma, "What happened to a low profile?"

Irma dropped another ten-dollar bill into a porter's palm. "It just blew up."

Except Winslow didn't know that. Drawing on the advertising theory that people like to feel important, I said, "Congratulations, Mr. Winslow, all this commotion is because you are our hundredth fudgie, I mean visitor, here to Mackinac Island this morning, and you get a free tour. Isn't that great?"

Before he could answer, I snagged the handle of his rolling weekender, hooked my arm through his and propelled him around a team of idling horses, through a maze of cyclists and across the street.

"But I don't want a tour," Winslow said, grabbing for the suitcase.

"But you won." I yanked the suitcase out of his grasp. "Nothing better than winning, right?" Any kind of winning was music to a lawyer's ears.

"Okay, okay," he panted, out of breath. "Just take me to Rita's Fudge Shoppe. I need to find out what's going on there and I have legal papers to deliver, and then you can get me to a house called SeeFar." Winslow smoothed back his fake hair and glared at me. "So?"

"So?"

"So tell me about the island. This is a free tour, right? I'm here, I won, I want a tour." Just like I thought — lawyers are all about the win no matter where or what.

"Uh, well this is Main Street, and . . . and there aren't any cars here — gee, can you imagine that?" I added, scrambling to think of enough stuff to talk about till we got to Rita's shop.

"We have a lot of fudge shops, a whole lot, and T-shirt shops and Rudy's Rides bicycle rental. It's just up the street, and they have some pretty kick-ass trail mix. Oh, and the tourists are called fudgies 'cause they buy a lot of fudge; isn't that clever?"

Winslow gave me a weird look. "You suck as a tour guide and you have some kind of rash; no wonder the tour's free. What's your name? I should report you to the visitor's bureau." He took a step back. "Are you contagious?"

"The English settled here in fifteen twenty-five," Irma rushed in, catching up to us on the sidewalk and pointing to the whitewashed Fort Something-or-other on the far hill. "And then the French paddled over from Canada, and you know how rambunctious those Canadians are — always in a snit about something," Irma prattled on. "And in fifteen ninety-seven there was the French and Indian War because nobody shared and they didn't have anything else to do but fight, and there were a lot of bows and arrows flying around, I can tell you that."

Winslow stopped in the middle of the sidewalk. "I thought the first settlement was Jamestown in sixteen oh seven and the French Indian War was seventeen fifty-four. What do you mean they had nothing to do? Bows and arrows flying?"

"There's Rita's," I said, nodding up ahead to the pink and chocolate awning. I grabbed Winslow's shirtsleeve and stepped up the pace, using the wheeled weekender as a battering ram out in front to clear away plodding tourists. This was not a time to plod.

"You go inside and take care of your business," I said to Winslow, who was huffing and puffing with a face red, heart attack imminent. "We'll watch your luggage and wait for you right out here so we don't get in your way."

Winslow swiped his hand across his forehead to mop up the line of sweat. "You're both bonkers, you know that?" He opened the door with the little bell tinkling; Dutchy was inside at the fudgie-congested counter.

"Okay, now we need to get out of here," I said to Irma while parking the weekender to the side. "If Dutchy and Rita see us with Winslow showing up in their shop, they might suspect something's up."

"No way." Irma parked her hands on her hips. "I want to see Dutchy and Rita Roundheels squirm when Winslow brings up the money issue. It's a little payback for stealing my fudge recipes. So far they've gotten away with it all scot-free. I just wish Winslow looked scarier — more Charles Bronson than Danny DeVito."

"He's a lawyer with papers. He's all Bronson, trust me."

"Think there might be some suing involved?" Irma pulled me to the edge of the window and crouched down with me hovering over her, both of us peering inside. "That always makes people sweat."

"Suing's always involved," I responded. "And what was all that talk about the French and Indian War and the Canadians?"

"Who listens to that tour stuff? It's just a bunch of pointing and blah-blah-blah and then someone in the crowd asks, *Where's the best place around here for lunch?* How'd I know we'd wind up with Mr. Encyclopedia of the history world?"

We watched Winslow hand over some papers with a blue backing, the official presentation package of lawyerese. Dutchy yelled something about never making a phone call. He raised his fist and did some pounding on the counter, Rita looking pale and shaking her head, customers fleeing for their lives.

"Hey, Evie girl, what's going on?" Fiona said, coming up behind me. "Are you thinking about getting some of Rita's peanut butter fudge to send to your folks like I get for my niece? It rocks; you won't be sorry. They'll love you for it."

Irma slowly stood from her crouched position below me and turned around, eyes beady, facing Fiona. "*You* shop here?" Irma yelped. "*You* eat this fudge from *my* recipes after you know what Dutchy did to me?"

"I mean . . . I mean . . ." Fiona bit her bottom lip. "It's just for variety, I swear, Irma, and I try to support all the shops on the island because I'm editor of the *Crier* now and need to be impartial, and personally I hate Rita's fudge. Yuck. It's too sweet and creamy. I like nice chewy fudge like yours, fudge you can sink your teeth into and that sticks to your gums and your gut and even beyond your gut and tastes like . . ."

Fiona looked from me to Irma, seeing that Irma wasn't buying any of it. "Oh what the heck," Fiona said. "I'm a big fat traitor, a Brutus and Benedict Arnold all rolled into one, and I'm sorry, Irma, I really am."

"Well you sure don't look sorry. You're grinning like a mindless baboon with a barrel of bananas." Irma folded her arms, her lips in a pout.

Fiona grabbed Irma's shoulders, the grin expanding to cover half her face. "To tell you the truth, I can't be sorry about anything right now. I just found out that Little Princess is coming to see her daddy for

Thanksgiving. Smithy is over the moon excited and I haven't seen him this way in a long time. Since Buttinski Bunny's doing Holiday on Ice over at Doud's and in no position to protest, Constance agreed to let Smithy have his daughter for a little vacation. This sudden change of attitude might have something to do with the fact that Constance and her new husband want to take a cruise and need a babysitter, but I don't care why she's letting her come. I'm just happy for Smithy." Fiona bit her lip. "But I do apologize about the fudge, Irma. How can I make it up to you?"

"For starters, you can tell everyone how great my fudge is." Irma jutted her chin.

"Uh, can you maybe think of something else I can do?"

Was that a growl coming from Irma? It must have been, because Fiona took a few steps away, turned and ran off just as Dutchy barreled through the double glass doors onto the porch. His face was red, eyes bulging. He pointed right at me, his lips curling in a snarl. "*You're* the one who used our phone two days ago. I remember seeing you in the kitchen with the phone right in your hand and making up some story about a fudge order from Dwight."

Uh-oh. I did the *dumb brunette* routine.

"Phone call? Hmm, I do remember now that you mention it. I was just trying to be helpful; that's what people do around here, right? No one was in the store and I was picking out fudge and the phone rang, so I took the call like a good citizen. Dwight said he'd stop by and pay the bill later on. So," I asked, all sweet and innocent, "did he pay the bill? Because if he did, that means he must have put in the order."

"I didn't order any fudge," Dwight said from behind me. A crowd was starting to gather to check out the drama. "I hate the stuff. But what I want to know is why did Rita call Winslow saying I owe her money, and how did she know Winslow was my attorney in the first place?"

Pale and shaking, Rita squealed, "I never made any calls about wanting money from the sale of SeeFar, I swear. I don't need any trouble with attorneys, or with you, Dwight."

"And you better remember that," Huffy said, stepping up onto the porch, which was getting a little crowded. "SeeFar belongs to Dwight, all of it, every last plank and window. His sister doesn't want any part of it, so it's ours, you got it? Ours, ours, ours." She jabbed her finger at Rita. "Now you just butt out if you know what's good for you."

"That's it," Winslow said in a commanding courtroom voice that didn't fit his Napoleon size. "Everybody just settle down. I have Bunny's will. I came to clear things up once and for all. I don't know what's going on here, but the bottom line is Dwight inherits the house and doesn't owe anybody anything, right, Dwight?"

Dwight did the guilty-man shuffle. "Right," he said in an unconvincing voice.

I might suck at lying, and the *leaves-of-three* thing was still a mystery — heck, everything I looked at had three leaves — but from years as the black sheep of the Bloomfields, I knew all about the guilty shuffle. The question here was what Dwight Harrington had to look guilty about, and it was something about SeeFar.

Dwight and Winslow flagged down an eight-legged taxi, and Dutchy draped his arm around Rita and said to Irma, "You're nothing but a troublemaker, you know that? You started the fudge fight to distract me so your Chicago sidekick here could make that call to Winslow." He dropped his voice. "You're going to be sorry you upset my little fudge muffin here. Look at her — she's all worked up. You're going to be real sorry."

180

Irma started to do her own version of the guilty shuffle, then stopped. She looked Dutchy right in the eyes, a bit of danger creeping into her own as she stepped close. "The only thing I'm sorry about is that I ever got mixed up with the likes of you."

"You're nothing but an old warhorse," Rita shot back. "You should be put out to pasture."

"Well, your darling boyfriend here sure had eyes on this old horse's heaving bosom last night up at the Grand Hotel. Fact is, he fell down the stairs right there in front of everyone, and it wasn't from too much hooch. He wasn't watching where he was going 'cause he was watching little ol' me."

"Heaving *what*?!" Rita yelped, fire in her eyes.

"Bosom," Irma answered, all smiles. "As in boobs, chest, melons, jugs, cans, gazongas."

Rita wiggled from under Dutchy's arm. "You no-good, two-timing jerk." She socked him right in the gut with a solid *whomp* and stormed back inside.

"But . . . but, fudge muffin?" Dutchy bellowed like a wounded calf. "I'm on your side. You can't believe Irma. She's a bitter old woman."

Irma tossed her blonde hair and puckered

her Pink Coquette lips. "Do I look like a bitter old woman? I look hot."

Dutchy shook his fist at Irma, then hobbled through the doors, fudge muffin pelting him with pieces of chocolate and my favorite maple-nut. Fudge muffin had a pretty mean right arm.

"Well, darn," Irma said. "I thought it would take longer for Rita and Dutchy to get onto us." We headed down Main Street, a slow grin tripping across Irma's face. "But it wasn't all snakes and roaches either. I got a bit of my own with those two for a change, and it sure beat sitting around with a case of the gloomies. And it's all thanks to you. I never wore jeans and Top-Siders or hunted a killer till you came to town. This is fantastic. I feel like a new woman."

"Maybe you should keep the killer part to yourself. And if Nate should ask, maybe tell him you're simply helping Rudy in his time of need. Think he'll buy it?"

"Not in this lifetime," Irma laughed, then glanced at the entrance to Rudy's Rides. She paused for a second, looking kind of sad, then turned for the emporium.

I hooked my arm through hers and turned her back to the bike shop. "Why don't you come on in and visit for a while?" I said in my *little miss matchmaker* voice — or, in this

182

case, *match maker-upper* voice. "Rudy has some new trail mix. You should give it a try; it's killer."

Irma fiddled with a strand of hair. "What if he throws me out?"

I gave her a little tug toward the shop. "What if he doesn't?"

14

Rudy lined up the six ball for the far pocket, took one look at Irma coming through the door and missed the cue ball, the momentum of the shot and his cast throwing him off balance as he fell headfirst across the pool table. "I don't think he wants to throw you out," I whispered to Irma.

"Hi," Rudy said to Irma, pushing himself off the table and smoothing out his Twain hair, which was never going to smooth.

"Hi," Irma said.

Not exactly *Romeo and Juliet,* but it was a start. "We got information on the Bunny Festival," I said to Rudy to keep things going.

"What Bunny?" Rudy asked, his eyes still on Irma. It was more *R and J* than I thought.

"Tell him what we found out, Irma," I said, trying for more conversation.

"There's a good chance Huffy and Dwight

orchestrated the Bunny Festival. Huffy even called SeeFar *our* house and you look good, Rudy, really good. How are you doing?"

Bambino made a flying leap from the pool table to Rudy's shoulder. Rudy didn't even blink; his eyes were fixed on Irma. "Dwight likes money and money's a big motivator and . . . and did you do something new with your hair? I like the color."

Irma blushed. "It's Adorable Apricot. Huffy and Dwight aren't the only ones who could have done in Bunny — there's Jason Bourne, and isn't that the shirt I gave you a few Christmases ago? It brings out the color of your blue eyes, Rudy."

This time Rudy blushed. "Speed could have done the Bunny Festival," he offered, a little smile on his face that had nothing to do with murder. "He wants my shop, and Smithy wants my place on the town council."

I'd heard my share of flirting at bars and restaurants, but flirting while talking murder suspects was a new one. I was about to tell them to maybe go get coffee when Fiona crept into the shop. She knocked into a row of bikes, and the racket of crashing metal on concrete snapped Rudy and Irma back to Earth — or as close as they'd get at the moment.

"Thought I heard your voice," Fiona said to Irma. "Look, before you start throwing rocks at me, I'm here to make amends for being a traitor. I feel really bad about the peanut butter fudge thing. Our families have been friends for years, and I want to keep it that way. So here's the deal: What if I help you come up with new fudge ideas? We can work on it together. I searched online for some recipes, and I'll feature the emporium on the front page of the *Crier* to bring in business. What do you think? Am I forgiven?"

Irma dragged her gaze away from Rudy. "What fudge?"

Fiona held her hands out, palms up. "You look sort of funny — and what's wrong with Rudy? I think he's having some kind of attack. I think you both got something."

There may be snow on the roof, even some dyed-apricot snow, but there was still fire in the furnace. Rudy hobbled over to help a customer studying the baskets of trail mix, and Fiona pulled a bottle of peach brandy from her purse and held it out to Irma. "Look what I got," she said. "Dad left it behind in the bottom drawer of his editor's desk. I brought it for inspiration. Dad said he always got the best ideas when he'd had a swig or two. Let's go on over to

186

your place and start cooking, we'll do some small test batches."

"I know what's going on," Irma said to Fiona, a twinkle in her eyes. "You're worried that if your mother finds out about you buying Dutchy's fudge she'll come back here and beat you with a stick," Irma said.

"It crossed my mind." Fiona flashed a grin, kissed Irma on the cheek and they left out the back door, stepping over the cracked step.

I straightened the fallen bikes back into a neat row. Rudy put down the phone and turned to me. "Can you do a bike delivery to ShadyNook up on Huron Road? It's for a friend's nine-year-old grandson, but it's not Huron Road on the bluff side or Huron that leads to Arch Rock, but Huron Road that winds up behind the fort. The founding fathers weren't a creative lot with naming streets. Irish Donna is tied up at the Blarney Scone, and taxi delivery costs an arm and a leg and I'm already down one of those."

Rudy took my hand. "Ya know, at first I didn't want you here 'cause I was a stubborn old man. Well, the age hasn't changed, but now I don't know what I'd do without you to hold the place together like you are. Sure hope that promotion you want is worth all this grief of poison ivy, painting bikes and trying to keep me out of the slammer." Rudy did the guilty shuffle. "But can you give me a few minutes before you take off? I need a haircut."

It was the eternal question of whether or not to stick my nose into a situation that was none of my blankety-blank business. Considering all I'd done since I got there was stick my nose in other people's business, I went with it. "You have great friends," I said trying to ease into advice I had no right to give. "Irma's really nice, and she's got spunk and not afraid to try new things, and you two would have a lot of fun together if you give her a chance and —"

"Irma's the one that got away." Humming, Rudy took off, a little spring in his crutch.

Wow, I'd never been *the one who got away.* Fact is my last experience of the male variety was with *the one who ran away.* Rudy headed off and I studied the stash of sad bikes in the shop, found a smaller one and tried to picture a kid happy to ride it. Like that was going to happen. I whipped out cans of black paint and found some yellow and a little bit of white. I painted Darth Vader on the front bumper and light sabers on the back, added the Death Star spaceship and R2-D2 and made the bike helmet more *Stormtrooper* than *my grandmother made me wear this stupid thing.*

"You look terrific," I said to Rudy when he bounded back into the shop.

"The terrific ship sailed about twenty years ago. Right now I'll settle for decent."

"Rudy, not only are you a terrific guy, you're a total dude." I kissed him on the cheek, then *Star Wars* on wheels and I headed for Fort Street. The neat thing about the island was that during the day the weather was warm to hot and at night you needed a jacket or fleece. That was the summertime, of course. From what I heard, in the winter, the place was Doud's freezer times a million and everyone dressed like the Michelin Man.

No wonder they built a fort on top of this hill, I thought as I headed up Fort Street. The enemy would take one look at the effort needed to get there and go find someplace level to attack. Sweating, with legs cramping, I pushed the bike, the island breeze the only thing keeping me from keeling over. I passed the governor's summer home, took the next fork to the right and found Shady-Nook, a blue clapboard in a cul-de-sac behind a privacy screen of tall yews. Privacy from what? This was a freaking island.

I parked the bike on the front part of the wraparound porch, then started back for town, noticing a line forming by the white picket fence at the governor's abode. The plaque out front of the house said it was open for business. I guessed that when the governor of Michigan was here vacationing he didn't appreciate people wandering through his domicile seeing him wearing PJs and sipping a Bloody Mary.

A tall, lanky guy in pleated khakis and a plaid bowtie stood guard at the door with one of those counting clickers in hand. He allowed a certain number of visitors in the house at a time, with no exceptions till Helen Levine pranced up the sidewalk, cutting in front of everyone. She said something to the guy with the clicker, flashed a smile, and her party of three passed straight on through.

Okay, so what were the rest of the people waiting in line? Chopped liver? This smelled a lot like *we bluffies stick together.* I hated line-jumpers and I hated people who thought they were better than the rest of mankind. And there was the distinct possibility that maybe the bluffies were in cahoots with Smithy in framing Rudy

"Hi," I said to the guy at the door as he finally clicked me into the lovely stone and wood home with views of the harbor and the Grand Hotel off to the right. "I'm a friend of Rudy's, and if Smithy, the guy from the blacksmith shop, takes Rudy's place on the town council, that'll be just what the people living up here on the bluff want, right? Care to comment on that or the Bunny Festival?"

The guy dropped his counter. Okay, I could have handled that better but I was tired and running out of time to save Rudy. The tourists behind me stared, and the guy with the counter snagged my arm and tried to usher me down the steps, but I wasn't in a budging mood.

"What do you think you're doing, saying things like that?" he hissed. He caught the eye of one of his staff. "Call the police right now."

"What's this about a bunny festival?" one of the tourists waiting in line asked, with others smiling and nodding. "Somebody was talking about it over at Doud's Market. Seems to be a pretty big deal. Is it going to be like the Lilac Festival? What's the date? The kids will love it; we'll have to come back. I gotta make reservations."

"Will Bugs Bunny be here?" one of the kids in line asked. "He talks funny."

I got up in the guy's face. "Smithy taking

Rudy's place on the town council shifts the vote to the historic society. Maybe they got together with Smithy. Heck, maybe they planned the whole Bunny Festival?"

"Chicago!" It was Sutter, and how'd he get here so fast? I turned around to Detroit cop on horseback, just like some Wild West movie, except in this case the damsel was *causing* the distress.

Sutter slid from the saddle like a man who knew one end of a horse from the other, flipped the reins over the fence, jumped the pickets and tromped my way.

"She's a menace," the counter guy bellowed, jabbing his finger at me. "She's upsetting everyone."

"She's not upsetting us," a man in a ball cap with three happy kids in tow said to Sutter. "She's telling us about the Bunny Festival. We've heard talk in town but we don't know when it is."

"Will Rabbit from *Winnie the Pooh* be there?" asked one of the kids. "He's my favorite rabbit ever."

"What about the Velveteen Rabbit?" asked a mother with a toddler in her arms. "The kids will have a good time with this. They can dress up and be in the parade."

"The Energizer Bunny with his drum is so cute," a teenager said.

"I wouldn't mind seeing a Playboy bunny," a twenty-something guy quipped.

"Get her out of here!" The guy with the counter stomped his foot and pointed his bony finger at me.

Sutter had on his *Detroit cop* face. There was no standing my ground this time, so I followed him. He climbed on the horse and held out his hand. "Put your foot in the stirrup and get on. You're wasting my time; I've got to get back."

"Ya know, I'm not that crazy about horses. No turn signal, no brakes."

"Think of it as a convertible."

I swallowed the rest of my lament, gave him my hand, and instantly found myself perched on the back end of a horse. Of all the places I wanted to be, this was not one of 'em.

15

"Hold on," Sutter ordered.

"Where's the seat belt?"

In answer, Sutter took off, and I grabbed for the only thing available . . . him! I flung my arms around his middle, my boobs rubbing up and down against his back, my butt smacking against horse butt, jarring every bone in my body. "I just bit my darn tongue back here. Slow down."

"I'm not going fast. Feel the rhythm of the horse," Sutter yelled.

"What rhythm? Ya' think this is Arthur Murray, and watch that tree, there's a kid up ahead and you're too close to the edge of the road and you took that corner too fast and I'm sliding off this thing." And how did Sutter get to be so blasted ripped for a guy over forty! Didn't guys go to pot after forty? Where was the beer gut?

Sutter pulled to a stop, pried my arms

from around his chest and looked back at me.

"Dear God, are we there yet?" I asked.

"Where's *there*?"

"How the heck should I know? You're the one driving this thing."

"We stopped 'cause I couldn't breathe from your death grip. Did you have to sit so close? And you're a freaking back-saddle driver."

I socked his arm. "A horse's rump isn't all that roomy and I didn't want to be back here and you were the one galloping like a madman down that hill. Was it to scare me? 'Cause it worked."

"It was a trot."

I socked his arm again for good measure, then grabbed the waistband of his jeans, not paying one bit of attention to his trim waist, and slid down one side of the horse's rounded rump, dropping to my knees. While I was down there, I kissed the grass, glad to be on it again.

"Very funny," Sutter said, peering my way. "I got a call coming in from Detroit. I wasn't expecting a nine-one-one from the governor's house saying that a woman with a ponytail and rash was causing trouble. Gee, who could that be?"

"Get a nine-one-one from anyone else?

There may have been a slight misunderstanding over at Rita's Fudge Shoppe earlier with Dwight and Huffy. Doesn't it seem a little off that they didn't call the police to complain about it?"

"You mean to complain about you?" Sutter's mouth tightened. "My mother wasn't in on this, was she?"

"Of course not." I looked down to check if my pants were on fire. "But maybe they didn't call because they didn't want to get the police involved in what they got going on."

I got closer to the horse than I wanted to be. "I think Dwight and Huffy could have planned and carried out the Bunny Festival. With the furry one in hibernation, Huffy and Dwight are free to do the *happy ever after* thing and they get the house and the money and Winslow makes it work. Huffy was adamant about that house. They are up to something."

"Who's Winslow?"

I buried my face in my hands, muttering, "You're missing the point. There are other suspects out there." Except Sutter had Rudy as his prime suspect, and unless I had something more than theory to show him, he wasn't flipping his opinion. "How's my cat?"

"What cat?"

"You're impossible."

"I try." Sutter put the horse in gear, leaving me once again staring at the business end of a large, undiapered animal.

I went into Doud's and got cereal, milk, eggs, Doritos and other essentials of life, then headed for the checkout desk. "Did you hear about the Bunny Festival?" the gal in the green apron at the cash register asked.

"I did," I said in a loud voice so everyone around me could hear. "I was up at the governor's house this afternoon and the tour guide up there, the one in khakis and a bowtie is in charge of the festival all by himself. He volunteered right there on the spot to head it up. Said he wants as much input as possible with suggestions and plans so he can make this the biggest and best event this summer. Just let him know what you have in mind. Call him anytime day or night to talk as often as needed."

In light of my latest experience with Mr. Bowtie, I felt I had a right to add some excitement to his life like he added to mine. If there were a conspiracy between Smithy and the historic society, my encounter at the governor's house would light a fire under someone's behind, and chances were good someone would let something slip.

I lugged my grocery bags out the door and ran into Irish Donna coming down Fort Street with not one huff or puff on her lips. She took one of my bags. "Let me help ye with that. I was just dropping off scones and would be glad to lend you a hand. After the day you've had over at Rita's Fudge Shoppe and up there at the governor's house ye must be a pooped pup. 'Tis good to see you're sharing that dark cloud you got going on with people who truly deserve it around here."

"Guess I'm not making many friends these days."

"Odds are running two to one over at the Stang you be winding up in jail before Rudy gets himself there, but I got twenty bucks that says Rudy'll beat you." She winked. "I know about the cloud, ya see, and figure you got one foot on a banana peel. I'll be the one winning the betting pot at the Stang and me and lovely Shamus can afford that trip to Florida when the weather goes right to the dogs up here."

"So glad I can add to your vacation enjoyment, but didn't you just push the lovely Shamus over a rocking chair up at the Grand for flirting with that cute little blonde?"

"He looked right handsome sprawled out

on the floor if I do say so. Didn't even mash the rose in his lapel."

"And that's okay with you?"

" 'Twas my favorite color rose off my prize bush."

When we got to the bike shop, Ed was holding the door, and Rudy was balanced on one crutch tightening the hinge, a straw hat on his head to keep off the sun. "You look more like Tom Sawyer than Mark Twain," I said as I ferried the groceries back to the kitchen.

"The place is falling apart around my ears." Rudy picked up another screwdriver. "This is paying the price for putting off those spring repairs. Ed here's been trying to fix a few things, sawed off the bottom of the door here so it wouldn't stick. He's a handy guy to have around."

"The way I see it, ye be shut down any time now," Donna chimed in. "The shop is looking sad, it is, and it doesn't matter to the town council if ye be Mark Twain or that Tom Sawyer person." Donna paused, a new glint in her green eyes. "Unless we can be making it matter. What if we do a little Tom Sawyering of our own?"

"Build a raft and sail the Mississippi?" I said, taking over hinge duty from Rudy. With a house full of lawyers, someone had to know how to put more than an appeal together. "The way things are going around here, it's not a bad idea."

"I was thinking more like we can be painting the place up and having it look like fun and get the tourist kiddies in on the act, just like Tom Sawyer did when painting the fence," Donna offered.

"And if the town council gives us grief," Rudy added, sounding a lot happier than he did a minute ago, "we can say that over there at the Museum House they're having Native American basket making for the kids and at the Biddle House it's weaving and sewing classes. All the fudge stores do a class now and then. We can paint this place by making it look like history coming to life. Make it into a tourist attraction, since Twain did indeed stay here and give lectures about his books."

Ed snorted. "Never going to work. Unless it's some kind of phone, pad or screen, kids'll never go for it, and Tom Sawyer painted a fence, not a shop. I'm telling you, the only way out of this mess is to get Abigail here and find a good attorney." Ed held up his hands defensively. "Not that I'm calling her. Rudy here put the kibosh on that idea. But she needs to know what's going on with her own father."

"I'll sketch a picket fence on the front of the shop to make it all look like part of the book," I said, adding another screw to the hinge and trying really hard not to think of Abigail showing up. "And it doesn't matter if the kids buy into the painting idea or not. Fact is, it's better if they don't; we're just using them and the Sawyer idea for a cover. We can get more done around here without them in the way. As long as it looks like we're doing Twain, we're good to go."

"Never going to work, I tell you." Ed checked his watch. "I have to meet Helen and the most boring house guests on the planet Earth for a sunset cruise. They're Ed Junior's potential clients. They do some big ads on TV and Lord knows he needs the business. And this is one way we can keep writing off that boat as a business expense."

Ed patted Rudy on the back. "It's going to be okay, pal. I didn't get you out to this rock to wind up visiting you in the slammer. We'll figure this out together."

Ed headed for the docks, Donna went off to make an apple-walnut scone delivery up on the West Bluff and Rudy did his *worry, thump step* pace with Bambino perched on his shoulder. "I should have stayed in Chicago," he said. "I never had all these problems in Chicago."

I packed up the toolbox. "You had wind, dirt, noise, crowds. And if you'd stayed there, you wouldn't have met Irma."

"Or broken my dang leg, though I like your take on the situation a whole lot better than mine." Rudy absently petted Bambino and nervously bit at his bottom lip. "So what do you think I should be doing about Irma? I'm not too good at this courting thing."

"Uh, you're talking to someone whose fiancé chose a baseball game over the altar. Now, if you want ideas on how to totally tick people off, I got that one covered."

A few more customers frequented the bike shop to pick up trail mix and not rent bikes. With no business, Rudy closed early to watch *Big Brother* and see if Alex finally got kicked off. I volunteered to make a cat food run, since we were running low — and I wanted to take a bag to Sutter's house as a reminder that yes, he did have a cat!

A big harvest moon hovered at the horizon, casting a wavy ribbon of gold across the lake, and Fiona wobbled out of the emporium glassy-eyed, blouse untucked, sequin hat in hand. "How's the great fudge challenge going?" I asked.

"After two glasses of peach brandy anything tastes good. That stuff is gross. Hope it tastes better in the fudge we made up and I can redeem myself with Irma."

Fiona leaned against the lamppost, gulping in fresh air, and Sheldon beeped from my back pocket, heralding a text message. My gut clenched, my jaw tightened and the little hairs on the back of my neck stood straight up. "It's my boss," I said to Fiona. "I can feel her vibes all the way out here. I think the woman sleeps at the office and eats from the vending machines."

I pulled out my phone and read, Ev, need Clawson files.

"She calls you Ev?" Fiona asked, reading over my shoulder. "Least Peephole knew my name."

"That she remembered the first two letters of who I am is a huge improvement. Usually I was *hey, you.* Think I should tell her that Rudy's doing great and not to worry?" I weighed the options of my being struck by lightning for lying my ass off versus Abigail coming here to check on her dad. "I'll chance it."

Fudgies and locals were sitting on blankets at Marquette Park to enjoy the view while a jazz quartet at the gazebo did a decent version of "Moon River."

"It's a perfect night," Fiona sighed, a breeze drifting off the lake. "Except for the little fact that there's a killer on the loose and the wrong guy's set up to take the fall. Got any ideas what to do about that problem?"

"I can't imagine that Sutter is absolutely positive Rudy did the deed when I have so many doubts. Sutter has to know more than he's letting on, don't you think?"

"I could poke around at the police station and see what's going on," Fiona offered. "Molly the desk clerk's got a weakness for strawberry smoothies."

"Maybe I should poke around his house."

Fiona's eyes widened to cover half her face. "Now that's a really great idea. I'm in."

"What happened to talking to Molly?"

"Are you kidding?" Fiona straightened her hat. "This is investigative reporting right here in front of me. Who would have thought? Sweet. So what are we looking for?"

"For openers, a cat Sutter doesn't know he has. If Sutter's around, we'll try reasoning with him about Rudy. If Sutter isn't there, we'll snoop and see if he has any suspects he's not telling us about. He's hiding something, and with his office at the police station not really being his, I think he'd keep notes or whatever at his house till he was sure."

"There's something I don't get," Fiona added. "What's a Detroit cop — a detective, no less — doing here for months on end? Usually we get retired cops wanting a free vacation to fill in when we need it."

"Maybe Sutter just wanted to visit his mom for a while?"

"You really think that's it?"

"Heck no."

Fiona and I stopped at Doud's and bought two bags of cat food, two slices of pepperoni-and-mushroom pizza, two flashlights, and two bottles of OPI nail polish — that's Berry Daring and Flashbulb Fuschia. We paid at the cash register, ogled some hottie's cute behind, then headed out into the night.

16

We dropped one bag of cat food and the nail polish off at the bike shop, then started for Sutter's house, which was really Bernie's house.

"Best I can remember," Fiona said as we started up Church Street, the dim streetlights casting our shadows onto the uneven sidewalk, "is that HighSail is that big faded blue house with the overgrown bushes and dirty windows over there." She pointed.

"It's got a nice mansard roof and widow's walk."

"If the gutters and railing weren't falling off." Fiona shook her head. "No wonder Sutter doesn't know he has a cat; it probably got lost in rotting floorboards. Either Bernie was one crappy housekeeper, or he was in the middle of fixing up the place."

I knocked on the front door. There were no lights on inside and no Detroit cop telling me to get lost. I put the cat food on the front porch by the door, handed Fiona a flashlight and followed her around back to a version of *wild safari invades Mackinac.*

"Can anyone say 'lawn mower'?" Fiona stepped around a low branch with thick cobwebs catching the moonlight.

"If anything fuzzy or crawly with beady eyes slithers across our path, I'm out of here," I said with a little shiver. "I don't do bugs."

"Girl, if Sutter catches us, bugs will be the least of our problems." Fiona tried the back door. "Locked."

"Island boy left the window open." I slid out the screen and we stepped into a tidy but tired fifties kitchen with scuffed tan linoleum, matching Formica, a wood table and two chairs and dishes drying in the rack and a packet of Baby Ruth candy bars in the fridge. I just had to look. I tossed Fiona a Baby Ruth. "Dessert."

"Here kitty, kitty, kitty," Fiona sang out around a mouthful of chocolate, caramel and peanuts.

"I'll look down here," Fiona said. "You take the upstairs." She put the flashlight on the counter and pulled open kitchen drawers.

I took the steps to the second floor, the old wood creaking with each footfall. Four rooms were in various stages of repair and repaint, with a toppled ladder in one, plus a splash of green paint across the floor. Looked like playing *This Old House* is how Bernie messed up his back.

I tore open the Baby Ruth and went in the next room to a hand-carved dresser and a humpbacked trunk with rusted locks, weathered straps and probably doubloons inside. Bernie had some interesting furniture. The floors were bare wood, and moonlight fell across a massive four-poster bed with its sheets and blankets tossed, an indent in one pillow and a robe at the bottom that was obviously all Sutter.

I stopped dead, swallowing a whole bite of candy in one gulp. My ex's bedroom smelled of dirty socks and gym shorts. This room smelled warm and woodsy with a touch of spicy aftershave and a hint of danger. Not *gun* kind of danger, but more *who was this guy and what would I do if I ever found out?* I couldn't breathe, and my heart was doing a slow, heavy thud, perspiration slithering between my boobs and other private areas I forgot I had.

This was the personal side of Sutter, the sexy side, the all-male side and more about the man than I wanted to know. Yeah, right. I backed out of the door and into the hall, then felt something brushing my ankles. I screamed, jumped, lost my balance and bounced down the steps like a hundred-and-thirty-pound bowling ball, landing at the bottom in a big, round heap. "Crap."

"Don't pass out! Don't pass out!" Fiona pleaded as she smacked my cheeks. "We can't have Sutter finding us in his house. He'll kill us dead."

My side hurt, my head hurt and I tasted blood. "Do I have all my teeth?" I asked Fiona, giving her a toothy grin.

"Split lip but no gaping holes. What the heck happened?"

"That's what happened." I aimed Fiona's flashlight up the steps to Little-bit sitting in a pool of moonlight at the top.

"I think he's laughing at you."

"One day with Sutter and the furry little cretin's turned into mini-Sutter." I slowly unfolded myself, Fiona helping me up.

"We've got to get out of here," she said. "You made a heck of a lot of noise."

We headed for the door and Fiona handed me a napkin from the kitchen table so my split lip wouldn't dribble telltale blood. We stumbled out the back door into the night, through the cobweb branch that had us swiping at our faces and whining like little girls. We rounded the corner to Church Street.

"Why, there ye be," Irish Donna yelped, drawing Paddy to a stop. She scooted to one side of the cart and patted the empty space beside her. "You best be getting in, my dears, there's a commotion at Rita's Fudge Shoppe and Sutter be asking around for Chicago here. He's wonderin' where she be."

"Why doth Thutter think I dith anything?"

"When things be going haywire these days, ye always seem to be in the thick of it. And what happened to your mouth?" Donna held up her hand, looking from me back to the house. "Never ye mind, there are some things I don't need to be knowing about, but if you and Fiona here show up together, Sutter might get suspicious you two were into something you shouldn't be."

Fiona helped me into the cart. "Evie has a split lip, talks with a lisp and looks like she was shot out of a cannon — the *suspicious* ship has sailed."

Donna hit the horsey accelerator by flicking the reins. I waved to Fiona while every bone in my body tried to fit back in place where it belonged to make an upright person.

"Hoth you know I wath here?"

210

"Mira Brindle be living next door for fifty years now and watching with her telescope. Her Herman used to be staring at boats out there in the bay. 'Tis my guess he did a lot more staring at Jeannette Holloway's bedroom, but that's another story. Since Herman sailed off to that great harbor in the sky, Mira's seen fit to be taking over telescope duties. CNN and Joan Rivers all in one, she is, and at times she sees things we all wish she didn't. She said you and Fiona were in Sutter's bedroom looking around. She heard a thump over there and then she gave me a jingle on the phone being as that you and I've been spending time together."

"I wath trying to see what Thutter knoths about the killer."

Donna patted my hand. "No need to explain; we all be looking around a man's bedroom one time or another, dearie. It's when you stop looking and start doing that gets ye in trouble, mark my words." Donna pointed down Main Street. "All the commotion must be in back, and I think there be a hint of burning in the air."

She parked Paddy at the curb, and we headed for the alley behind Rita's Fudge Shoppe, where the back doors were propped open wide. Rita and Dutchy and a gathering crowd stared wide-eyed into the smoke-filled kitchen as the stink of burned sugar filled the air. Sutter, Shamus, Smithy and nurse Jane Porter coughed and choked and sprayed the kitchen area with giant fire extinguishers, killing all the flames in sight with clouds of white foam.

"You did this," Dutchy yelled at me, his face red, hair standing on end, finger pointing. "You called that attorney guy and you tried to burn us out 'cause you don't like me and you don't like Rita. You should be in jail," Dutchy went on. "You're a public nuisance. You should be off the streets. You're ruining this island. Nothing's been the same since you got here."

"Thath's crazy," I said, my mouth still a mess. As I looked around, I could see that no one believed me and everyone believed Dutchy . . . except for Huffy? She stood in the front of the gathering, balanced on her bicycle, arms folded, glaring daggers at Rita and Dutchy and not me? I was not public nuisance number one in everyone's eyes?

"That's it. Everyone go home," Sutter bellowed as he came out of the kitchen smudged with soot. "Fire's out. Looks like papers were set too close to the stove and ignited some towels and aprons is all."

"It's arson, I tell you." Dutchy pointed to me again. "And that Chicago girl did it.

We're not cooking fudge this time of night; the stove's not in use. She came in and set the fire while Rita and I were out front closing up for the day. And you really think I'd leave papers by my stove?" Dutchy kicked at the dirt. "I'm not that stupid."

"Accidents happen," Sutter said, holding up the charred papers. "Get some help to clean up the place, and you'll be up and running by noon."

Dutchy started another rant, then stopped dead, his eyes now focused on Huffy. He looked back to the scorched papers in Sutter's hand, then back to Huffy and swallowed.

"Fine." Dutchy's voice dropped several decibels and sounded a lot more reasonable than it had seconds ago. He held on to Rita, never taking his eyes off Huffy. "We can fix this," he said. "It's all going to work out just as it should. We got the message."

"Glad to hear it." Sutter cupped my elbow in a tight grip. "And you and I need to talk. Now."

"You're arrethting me?"

"What happened to you?"

"I'm innothent."

"You should put that on business cards and hand them out." Sutter's mouth pinched together tight, drawing the soot on his face into hard lines. He fast-trotted me out of the alley, every cell of my body screaming to slow down, just like when we were on the dang horse. With no crowds to slow us down and not bothering with chit-chat, we headed for the white clapboard building with the courtroom on the second floor and the police station below. Sutter barreled through the *Police Only* door and past the night clerk Molly, who was sipping a smoothie, and took me down the hall into a small office that was probably his.

"Sit." He nodded at a plain wood, really uncomfortable-looking chair. "Do not go anywhere. Do not touch anything."

He slammed the door, leaving me alone for the moment feeling cranky 'cause my mouth hurt and there were no folders on his desk to rifle through. On TV there were always files on the desk that had great info and they were lying out in plain sight for the hero . . . somebody like me . . . to find. Clearly Sutter needed to watch more TV.

At least my lip had stopped bleeding; but the front of my shirt was dotted in stained-forever red. I wadded up the napkin Fiona swiped off Sutter's table and tossed it in the trashcan by the desk. A list of scribbled let-ters on the napkin stared back at me: first *t-t-a,* then *e-l-o* and *a-l-l.* The rest of the letters were folded underneath where I couldn't see them. I'd gotten this napkin off Sutter's table at his house. Maybe it was a phone message and he didn't have paper so he used a napkin? Been there, done that. It meant something if he wrote it down, and the biggest somethings right now were the Meatball mob and the Bunny business. That, or Sutter was into Words with Friends.

"Here," Sutter said, barging in as I snapped my hand out of the trashcan minus the napkin. Sutter wiped sooty smudges from his face as he handed me one of those red, white and blue popsicles — would you expect anything but red, white and blue popsicles on Mackinac Island?

"Thanths," I said, the ice instantly numbing my throbbing lip, which must be the size of a softball by now.

"You don't like Rita and Dutchy, I get that. So, did you set the blasted fire or what?" Sutter grumped.

Okay, here we go. Breaking and entering in the police chief's house versus arson. Which to confess to? What happened to the days when my choices were deciding whether I want fries with that? I reached in my pocket and pulled out the half-eaten, totally gross and smashed-up Baby Ruth and slapped it on the desk. "I left cat food on the porch."

Sutter looked from me to the candy bar and back, his eyes widening in recognition. "You were in my house!"

"It's Bernie's house, so don't get all snippy, and I was checking on my cat, who is now most definitely *your* cat, so I couldn't set fire to Rita's shop 'cause I was busy falling down the stairs because Little-bit scared the heck out of me." There was no reason to drag Fiona into this.

"What kind of name is Little-bit? I call him Winchester."

"You're naming him after a rifle?"

"It's dignified; sophisticated; a place in England."

I gave him a *you really expect me to believe that line of baloney* look.

"Okay, it's a rifle. I should throw you in jail for breaking and entering."

"I didn't break a thing, and not a court in the land will convict me for looking after the welfare of a cat named after weapons, and in case you missed it, Huffy had more fire in her eyes than there was in the fudge shop, and she sure wasn't looking at me."

"She was staring at Dutchy and Rita."

"You didn't miss it."

"Got any idea what Huffy and Dutchy and Rita got going on?"

"How about a little quid pro quo?"

"How about a little find your quid in jail?"

I took a bite of popsicle. "All I know is that with Bunny out of the way, Huffy gets Dwight, and the girl's really obsessed with his house. For some reason" — *that shall remain a mystery to protect the guilty, like Irma and me* — "Huffy sort of thinks Rita and Dutchy might have a claim on SeeFar, and she's not thrilled about it."

"What's that got to do with the fire and Huffy?" Sutter pulled the charred papers from his jean pocket and tossed them on his desk, ashes scattering across the top. "Looks like an accident to me."

"The back page is blue. This pack of papers is what's left of the legal documents an attorney gave to Dutchy and Rita stating the house was all Dwight's, down to the last board and step. I'd say Huffy wanted to make sure Dutchy and Rita got the message and started a little fire to underline her sincerity." I plucked up a corner of the blue page. "Here's what I think's going on."

"I can hardly wait."

"I think Huffy knocked off Bunny to get what she wants, and it's a good bet Dwight was in on it."

"Murder his own mother?"

"Depends on the mother, and on how

much can a guy put up with, and for how long, with no end in sight. How old is Dwight — forty or so? And you saw the look in Huffy's eyes tonight. It wasn't *let's all be friends and toast marshmallows.* And think about this: Rudy's not the most stealthy of individuals with a full-leg cast and a crutch. If he's guilty of doing in Bunny, why don't you have an eyewitness by now?" I snagged the napkin out of the trash and tossed it beside the smashed candy. "And who are these people?"

Sutter tossed the napkin back in the trash and leaned over me, hands on the arms of my chair, face inches from mine, smelling like smoke with a hint of fudge. "You're . . ." He stilled, eyes suddenly black as the ashes on the desk. He swallowed hard, gently ran his thumb across my lip, then bolted upright and walked across the floor — actually, it was more of a Rudy hobble. My stomach flipped, my mouth went dry and my lungs quit working. All this because of Sutter?

"I'm what?" I finally managed.

"You should think about going home to Mommy and Daddy."

"I think I'm getting close to the real killer," I said, my brain starting to function after my body read a lot more into Sutter's one little touch than it should have. "Right

218

now Huffy and Dwight get my vote as prime suspects, or maybe Smithy or Speed could have planned the big Bunny surprise. They all have motive, something to gain if she was out of the picture, and even I could figure out how to cut a brake cable."

Sutter turned back, shut his eyes for a second and ran his hand around the back of his neck. He puffed out a breath of air. "What am I going to do with you?" he said in almost a whisper, more to himself than to me.

For a split second I remembered the bedroom and the tossed sheets and moonlight and the hint of danger and imagined just what Sutter could do with me. I had some imagination. Except that was never ever going to happen. My ex was not only a jock, but a cop; another blasted know-it-all cop, hard-headed cop. And I wasn't going back down that road. No, thank you.

"What you can do is let me out of here." I got up and tromped to the door.

17

"Okay," I said to Rudy as the first morning taxis trotted down Main Street with loads of fudgies, all passing by Rudy's Rides. "I got three cans of beach-baby blue pried open. I painted the outline of a picket fence across the front of the shop here so we look like we're following the book. I bought paintbrushes from Doud's. And this old sheet spread out should be good enough to catch drips and spills so we don't make a mess of the porch."

"You really think this will work?" Rudy smoothed out his Mark Twain jacket and sat in the wicker rocker that I'd pulled out onto the sidewalk.

"I'll have this place painted and looking good before the town council realizes what we're up to. That plus sprucing up the bikes should keep them from shutting you down. It won't make money, but it keeps the doors to the place open till we figure something out."

I handed him a copy of *Tom Sawyer.* "Here you go. Now all you gotta do is rock away and spout things to passersby like *Just because you put syrup on the top doesn't make it pancakes.*"

"Twain said that?"

"It's from the back of a cereal box, but you get the idea. I'm going over to Irma's for cover-up clothes for the kids to paint in so we look like we want them to participate. We'll scatter 'em around, along with the brushes dipped in blue."

"You sure you're up to all this after that fall you took last night and busted your lip? What in the world happened to you?"

"Too much catting around." I headed for the emporium and let myself in the back door to dead quiet.

"Anybody home?" I called out. The aroma of chocolate and something else sweet and a little fruity was scenting the air. I strolled into the front of the shop to find Irma stretched out on one of the marble tables, apron over her eyes, bottle of peach brandy wedged between her enhanced Victoria's Secret breasts.

"Are you okay?" I asked.

"No need to yell," Irma mumbled from

under her apron. Her finger pointed to the slab of fudge on the second marble table. "Peach brandy fudge." She hiccupped. "Taste it. Pretty darn good, if I do say so myself."

"It makes you drunk?"

"If you put more of the booze in you than in the fudge it does." Irma laughed, hiccupped then moaned. "Least if I die now I'm already on a marble slab."

I took the booze then helped Irma to sit. She wobbled, slid off the table onto the floor, legs wide apart and hair wild. She blinked and gazed up at me. "I think my legs fell off."

I hoisted her up, and together, the three of us — Irma, me and the brandy — stumbled into the kitchen. I deposited Irma in a chair, located some aspirin, dumped out two multivitamins, got a pitcher of water, made toast and charged up the coffeepot. Hangover Therapy 101 — one of the better things I learned in college.

Irma stared, bleary-eyed, at the remedy I had spread out on the table and made a face. "I'd rather have that bite of the dog cure."

"I think it's hair of the dog, and this is better. Do you have a few old shirts you don't want? We're doing some painting over at Rudy's."

Irma held up a vitamin, studying it in the sunlight. "Do you think Rudy takes Viagra?"

Yikes! I dumped the rest of the peach brandy down the drain, put all the pills in Irma's palm and looked her right in the eyes. "Take these right now and keep drinking the water till it's gone and you have to pee like a racehorse and we will forget this conversation ever took place. Where are the clothes?"

"Upstairs hall closet on right. Saving 'em for the island swap we do 'cause it's hard to get rid of stuff. I got on one of Bunny's sweaters right now. She got one of my scarves — not that she's got any use for it now."

The floor plan was like Rudy's, except the kitchen was much bigger. Taking the back steps, I found the closet at the top with the boxes stacked inside. I pulled open the top one and saw neatly folded T-shirts that would be great as cover-ups for the little Rembrandts who I hoped would never show up — and a copy of *The Highwayman's Revenge* by Sophia Lovelace. Right there on the cover were a half-naked chickie and a bare-chested dude tangled in sheets and each other, getting it on in the moonlight and sprawled across a big four-poster bed way too much like Sutter's.

My blood boiled. My latent hormones kicked into overdrive. I slammed the box closed, kicked it back in the closet and locked the door behind me, then leaned against it. This was God getting even with me for sneaking into Sutter's house and stealing his Baby Ruth.

"Are you okay up there?"

I took the shirts and galloped down the steps. "Thanks," I said to Irma when I got to the bottom.

"You're all red and sweaty. What happened up there?"

"Hot flashes."

"You're too young for hot flashes."

"Wanna bet." I ran out the door and turned toward the front of the bike shop, where three little kids were merrily slapping blue paint on the front of Rudy's Rides as parents snapped pictures like it was a day at Disney World.

No, no, no, this was supposed to be the bad idea, the one that flopped. Breaking into Sutter's abode was supposed to be the good idea that succeeded, getting me lots of info to help find Bunny's killer. Rudy smiled for a family doing selfies with him, then he helped a little girl of about six into a cover-up T-shirt and handed her a brush. I found the little artist a section of fence to decorate, then backed up, letting parents get that perfect-moment shot of their offspring as a white bulldog, more a basketball with legs than a canine, charged up Main Street barking, *Free at last, free at last, holy cow, I'm free at last.*

Okay maybe the little dog wasn't really barking that, but he looked like he would if he could, and the problem was that a four-horse dray was fast-trotting right for him. The driver couldn't see the little dog, and even if he could see him, the one thing I knew about horses was that they did not brake to a stop like a Ford pickup.

18

Kiddies screamed, parents looked horrified and I ran for the dog. Puppies getting smooshed by big horses with fudgies looking on did not happen on Mackinac Island. Me getting mangled rated a human-interest story that would be good for business if I lived to tell about it.

I ran, scooped up the dog in one hand then tripped face-first, bracing my fall with my free hand as sixteen iron hooves thundered my way. I one-arm, two-knee scooted as fast as I could with a wiggling basketball in my grasp, and by luck and expert driving, the dray went the other way. *Thank you, Jesus.*

A woman in a red hat helped me up, dusted me off then hit me with her purse. "You need to keep your pet on a leash. What's wrong with you?"

"It's not my dog."

"He's licking your face like he's your dog.

You should be ashamed for not owning up to your responsibility."

Others nodded in agreement, and the dog added more licks, confirming their suspicions. I looked down Main Street, hoping to see a distraught owner rushing my way with a hefty reward in his hand, or at least an apology. When that didn't happen, I got a few more evil looks from the dispersing crowd and checked Basketball's collar. No cute doggie name like *Mr. Wiggles,* but there was a phone number. I managed to hold on to Basketball with one hand and slide Sheldon out of my back pocket with the other, then punch the digits.

"Who is this?" a woman on the other end snarled.

"I have your dog."

Voices sounded in the background, with a bunch of yelling and cussing. "What do you want?"

"Uh, to give him back?"

"How much?"

"All of him? Where are you? I'll bring him to you."

"SeeFar, come alone, no heat."

"It's already eighty degrees out here and there's nothing much I can do abo—"

The line went dead. What was going on up at SeeFar now? The place was like a

227

three-ring circus. The whole island was a circus. I thought about the brochures advertising Mackinac as a place of peace and tranquility. Wasn't there some law about truth in advertising?

Rudy seemed to be holding down the fort okay. Fudgies were snapping his picture with their kids on his good knee, and Rudy passed out bags of trail mix for free. He was the island summer Santa. Basketball was heavy, but the six-buck taxi fare to SeeFar was more then I wanted to shell out, and there'd probably be an extra charge for the dog. If I knew how to ride a bike, I could do the *pup in the basket* routine. I really should learn how to ride. I looked at my again-bloody knees and scraped elbows — and my lip still hurt. Or maybe not.

Cradling Basketball like a basketball, because no way could his short stubby legs take the east bluff steps, I headed up as Winslow galloped down, pushing other stair-climbers out of his way. A sleeve of a white dress shirt and toe of a sock stuck out of his suitcase, and his face was ghost white, not overheated red like it should be. "Are you okay?" I asked as he raced by me at marathon speed.

"I will be," he called back. "As soon as I get on a ferry and get the heck out of here.

I came to straighten out Bunny's estate and get Dwight's signature on some papers so he can take over the house, and now he doesn't even own the blasted house. Dwight's gotten himself into a big mess this time, and I can't help him. He's on his own."

Winslow tore across Marquette Park and I lost sight of him as he turned onto Main. What was wrong with Winslow, mild-mannered attorney and history buff? Shifting Basketball to my other arm, I trudged my way up the third flight, plumpy puppo perfectly content to be carried rather than do the walking himself. Smart dog.

I got to the top, took a left past the petunia flowerpot for SeeFar and walked up to the wrought iron gate that marked the entrance. A dray was parked at the curb, with two men unloading boxes and a lady at the door. Basketball scrambled up the porch stacked with boxes and into the arms of the lady dressed in a gray cotton skirt, pink cardigan and Dr. Scholl's. She had hair like Rudy's. "How much for the dog?" she asked me.

"He's yours. He's free."

"What are you, some kind of wise guy?"

"I get called *troublemaker* a lot — does that count? Good luck with the dog." Under the *SeeFar* plaque there was now another plaque that hadn't been there before — *The*

Seniority. Just like on the envelope marked *Urgent* that I'd seen in Dwight's room when I cased his place.

"Is Dwight around?" I asked. "His mother just passed away." Not that I was all tea and sympathy for Dwight, but the crazies had landed, and this was his house . . . maybe.

"He's cooking us dinner. Go away. Don't come back." The door slammed shut, leaving me on the porch. Us? Who was us? Bunny mourners? How long were they staying? With all these boxes, it looked like they'd be here awhile — and Dwight could cook? Who knew. A rear window flew up, clouds of smoke puffing out along with the stench of burned meat. From the sounds of the yelling and screaming and barking inside, it was a good guess Dwight was not the Julia Child of Mackinac Island.

I got back to town, where Rudy was in his element as Twain, with both kids and adults eating it up. Considering all the action out in front of the shop, I could get away with painting the back of the shop, and by evening three sides of it had a first coat of beach-baby blue. Guess all those painting classes I took in college at five hundred dollars a credit hour counted for something after all.

"You need a break," I said to Rudy after

we closed up Twain and the Tourists. "Go play euchre and bring me back a burger and some fried green beans."

Laughing, Rudy balanced on his crutch and studied the front of Rudy's Rides, which looked like an impressionist painting caught in a rainstorm. "The kids had fun. I had fun. Guess what? They call me Uncle Rudy. Never thought of myself as uncle before. I like it."

He pointed to the corner of the shop. "And whatever you do, don't paint over those marks there that you see. It's how tall Mark, James, Lilly and Kaitlyn are. We put their names and the date. They come to the island every year, and we're gonna keep track of how much they grow."

"You need grandkids, Rudy."

"Tell your boss — but my guess is she's not the sort you tell much to these days. Kids aren't high on her priority list; making money is. Right now I'd be happy if she had a date once in a while. All she does is work, drive her fancy car and act important. I'll bring you back a pasty from Millie's." He looked me in the eyes and put his hand on my shoulder. "We did good today, Chicago. I didn't think we could really pull this off but we did. You got gumption, lots of it and you're a good painter."

"I think I like being here," I said, a little surprised by just how much I meant it.

"I can tell." Whistling, Rudy thumped off to the Stang, the soft glow of lamplights in the foggy night and the absence of cars giving the place a quiet, eighteen hundreds seaside town feel. If one of those big square-riggers sailed into port and Captain Somebody disembarked with a parrot on his shoulder and yelled, *Arr, matey,* I wouldn't have batted an eye. I knew I should stop painting for the night or risk blowing our cover, except I already had more paint on me than what was left in the can. The sooner I got this done, the sooner I could toss out these clothes for good and never paint anything blue again.

I went inside the shop for a fresh paint roller, figuring if I stayed in the back no one would see me and I could paint by moonlight. People did lots of things by moonlight . . . like paint, just paint, and I was not going to think about HighSail and that big four-poster and moonlight ever again. I cut through the kitchen and stepped outside onto the deck, coming face-to-face with . . . the Godfather? The age was about right, except this godfather had a diamond stud in his ear and a thin scar across his right cheek. The bulge in his jacket suggested he

232

was not making a social call. So much for the seaside town and square-riggers.

"Want a bike?" I squeaked, using two shaky hands to steady the paint tray.

"Came by to say thanks for saving the dog. I'm Angelo." His eyes were cold, calculating but nonthreatening, at least for the moment, and if they changed, I didn't want to be within a city block of the guy.

"Rosetta would be lost without Meatball around. Rosetta's my sister, and you know how cranky sisters can get."

"Actually, I do."

"If we can assist you in some way, just say the word." Angelo took a step closer. "We pay our debts. Always." And I didn't doubt him for one nanosecond. He rounded the corner of the shop and I finally remembered to breathe. Angelo did not fit the profile of your average Mackinac fudgie. And there was the bulge in the jacket to consider, and . . . and . . . "Meatball!"

I dropped the roller on the deck. It landed with a solid *thunk,* splattering paint everywhere. *E-l-o* were the last three letters in *Angelo* and *e-t-t-a* were the final letters in *Rosetta* and then there was *a-l-l* for *Meatball.* The words on the napkin! Meatball wasn't a mob boss but a mob pet. The bucket-list chapter of the Detroit Partnership was alive and well . . . depending how dinner went . . . and bunking in with Dwight up at SeeFar! A senior contingent had taken over SeeFar as their retirement home? Everyone had to retire sooner or later, but why here?

Sutter needed to know what was going on. It wasn't so much that I felt obliged to share information, because Sutter sure didn't share anything with me, but the Partnership was way out of my league no matter what their age. If something happened to Dwight, it would be my fault, and there was no more room behind the ice cream and tater tots, or so people kept telling me.

I sealed the painting paraphernalia in a plastic bag so I could pick up tomorrow for more painting escapades with Twain and the fudgies. I pulled out Sheldon and blessed AT&T that I got reception and called the Stang. Sutter wasn't there so I headed for HighSail. Strollers on the boardwalk stared at my blue camo outfit, little kids were pointing and laughing and two teens said I was *rad* and asked where I got it done.

Sutter's kitchen had the light on. I went around back and banged on the door. Apple in mouth, Sutter peeked out the side window, muttered something unflattering and opened the door with, "What now?"

"You're not going to believe this."

"I wish that were true."

19

I pushed past Sutter, went to the fridge, got a Baby Ruth, tore off the wrapper and chomped. "Dinner," I mumbled around a mouthful. "The Partnership is here, right on the island. I rescued their dog." I took another bite. "They're up at SeeFar holding Dwight hostage, although he was cooking for them, so who knows what that's all about."

"Can't you just watch TV and go to bed like everyone else?"

"Angelo met me in the alley and thanked me for saving Meatball. Meatball is Rosetta's rotund dog with a really bad overbite, and Angelo and Rosetta are names on that napkin I got here at your house. It all ties together." I pushed Sutter toward the door. "So do your thing. Go arrest them."

"For what? Making Dwight cook? Probably the only real work he's done in years. Should give them a medal. How old are these guys?"

"Seventyish. They're kind of scary."

Sutter swiped blue from my face. "Lot of that happening around here lately."

"This is serious. What are they doing up at SeeFar? The front porch was stacked with boxes and a freight dray outside unloading more, like they're moving in."

"I bet Dwight learns to cook really fast."

"That's it?" I waved my hands in the air. "We're discussing culinary skills while the Detroit mafia is camping out on the east bluff days after Bunny bites the big one and . . . and . . ."

I finished the Baby Ruth and studied Sutter, who was standing all relaxed on one foot, that darn moonlight in his hair as he calmly munched an apple. Forget the moonlight! "You knew about this?"

"We got the geriatric mafia plus dog, and as long as they don't break the law here I can't do anything. Seems Dwight pulled a fast-shuffle real-estate scam on the wrong people and they've come to collect what's owed — like his house."

I sucked in a quick breath, nearly choking on a peanut. "They're going to kill him?"

"Dead people don't pay up, and the paying up part is the important thing. Dwight's got himself a house, and now his visitors have got it."

"That's it! That's it! The mob knocked off Bunny so Dwight would inherit and they'd get what they had coming to them. It's a perfect motive."

"It's a stretch. And they just got here on the island today. Bunny bit the dust days ago."

"So they paid someone to do it like . . . like . . . like Jason Bourne! This just keeps getting better and better."

Sutter dropped the apple core in the trash and put his hands on my shoulders, his big brown eyes serious and dark and really nice. "Listen to me, Chicago. You can't go around accusing people without proof; especially the mob and a hit man. The Seniority may look a little wrinkled on the outside, but it doesn't take much effort to pull a trigger and ditch the body, and they're pros at both. The only thing Jason Bourne's guilty of is a really stupid name, but I guess it beats Lady Gaga. Cutting an old lady's brakes isn't the mob's style."

"And you think it's Rudy's style?"

Sutter went to the wall and banged his head against it. "I know what you're going to do. I should lock you up for your own protection."

"I'll be discreet."

"You're covered in blue paint, half the town is ready to throw you in the lake and now you're adding the mob to the list. You wouldn't know *discreet* if you tripped over it on a sunny day and it bit you in the butt.

Sutter threw me out of his house with an apple instead of another Baby Ruth and a blah-blah-blah lecture on some decisions not being good for my health. Guess the *health* part is why I wound up with fruit, instead of another candy bar, like I really wanted.

In all fairness, I got where Sutter was coming from about the mob being risky business, but how could I walk away from Uncle Rudy? He marked the kids' heights on his shop for Pete's sake. He bounced them on his knee and brought me pasties, and he was innocent. I had to figure out some way to follow up on this mob–hit man connection and try not to wind up in the freezer or the lake myself.

The crazy Labor Day weekend was three days off, but tonight, downtown was quiet, the family fudgies enjoying their last days of vacation before school started. The only action was in bars like the Pink Pony, the Gatehouse and Goodfellows, and the Stang for the locals. Mission Point, the Grand, Chippewa and the other big hotels on the

239

island had their own, more upscale, evening entertainment for guests.

Sheldon buzzed my butt. It was a *Call me now* text from Abigail, who was probably still at work fine-tuning the pitch for Mr. Big Client. I figured that Rudy had been putting her off these last few days, just like I'd been doing all along. If one of us didn't give Abigail something to chew on, she'd suspect a cover-up and get herself here ASAP no matter what. I did not need ASAP Abigail — the mob arrival would pale in comparison.

I took a selfie of me in my paint clothes to reassure her I was working hard and helping out, then texted, Shop looks great, Rudy playing euchre, all's well. I hit *send* and crossed my fingers boss lady bought it.

A breeze ruffled through the treetops, the temperature dropping, with the promise of autumn on its way. The last ferry of the night revved its engines and motored off from the pier rounding the harbor lighthouse that blinked green every ten seconds. A few tired tourists ambled up the dock, and right there in the middle of the ambling was Jason Bourne, a smile on his face and a spring in his step. That was pretty much my reaction to beer and pizza.

He climbed on the taxi, handing his

overnight bag to a porter and keeping the silver attaché case cuffed to his wrist by his side. Looks like Mr. Bourne had a good trip; least for him it was good. Did he send a *welcome to the island* basket to Angelo, Rosetta and Meatball? The Seniority hiring Bourne to do the deed was a perfect fit because they'd get SeeFar. It that was the case, maybe Bourne would pay the new kids on the block a visit tonight to see how things were going. Spying on the mob and the local hit man didn't smack of the brightest idea I'd ever had, but if I could take pictures of the meeting and send them to Sutter, he'd see the connection with his own two eyes. He'd have to believe my hit man–mob theory held water and look into it . . . right?

Considering the stops along the way to let off other passengers, Bourne's taxi would take about twenty minutes to wind its way to his house. I could run the steps — right now I was so tired it would be more of a crawl — but Irish Donna and Paddy trotting down the street toward me offered another option. I held my thumb out in a hitchhiker stance to get Donna to stop. Like my blue-splattered ensemble wasn't enough to make her curious.

"If ye looking to get a pint, my dear, hop on board and let's get to it. The night's not getting any younger, and with that outfit of yours we might get a round free of charge just for entertaining the customers."

"Can you give me a lift up to the East Bluff?" I climbed in beside her, and Paddy took off in a slow horsey clop. "I need to . . ."

Yikes. I needed to what? I was walking into Don Corleone does fudge island, and I couldn't let Donna be part of that. Her being in on the barn loft exploits and risking getting yelled at by Smithy was one thing, but this was a whole different ball game.

"To take pictures of the island," I said, holding up Sheldon as we trotted along with a few others out enjoying a nighttime buggy ride. "My parents want to see the view of the Mackinac Bridge all lit up at night. They're thinking about coming here for vacation next year."

"Ye be the worst liar I ever encountered, Chicago. I know what you're up to, and it's checking out those new folks moving in with Dwight. Everybody's talking; they be kind of a scary lot with taking over SeeFar like they have. I think we should pay a visit and see what's what."

"There is no *we* this time, okay?" I said as we started up Mission Hill. "Just drop me off at the top and you go back to the Stang."

"The town's dead as a bedpost tonight — nothing going on. So what we be looking for now that we're here?"

I took one of Donna's hands in mine and looked her dead in the eyes so she'd know I was serious. "Bunny's out of the picture, and three days later SeeFar has new occupants from Detroit? It's too much of a coincidence, and I don't want you caught in the middle. From what I've heard, Dwight kept company with some pretty rough characters, and this could be the cream of the crop."

Donna folded her arms and pouted. "You think you're smarter than me 'cause you're from the big city and I'm just an old island hick."

Good grief, where'd that come from? "I don't want you in the line of fire — if there is fire, not that there will be fire. Forget fire." Did I have to mention fire? Like waving red in front of a bull.

Donna grinned, eyes sparkling. "Now you're talking. There be some serious action going on, and I can be putting it on my Facebook page. Bet I get myself a bunch of *likes* over this one."

The mob going viral was not what I needed. "Stay out of this and I'll buy you breakfast tomorrow at the Pancake House and tell you everything, I swear."

Donna had one foot out of the carriage.

"I'll give Paddy a bath."

"And ye make the scone deliveries for me tomorrow afternoon?"

"Sure, whatever, just go home." I thought about what I was saying. Tomorrow afternoon sounded really specific — *planned* specific. "You're playing me?"

"Our delivery boy's off to camp and we need to be making the delivery. Shamus and I have a big group of our own coming in for high tea."

"I think I've just been had."

"Maybe a wee bit, but you're catching on." I climbed down from the buggy. Donna climbed back in, waved, then flicked the reins. Paddy started down the road toward town, passing the taxi coming up. Bourne sat all alone in the back, still looking really happy about something. Maybe this time he'd knocked off a bad guy who had it coming.

I ducked behind the big petunia pots, thinking I should start paying rent on the space. Peeking around the edge, I spied Bourne disembarking and heard the *clack, clack, clack* of his weekender rolling up his sidewalk to his front door. He pulled out keys, unlocked the door and went inside, and I saw the living room light come on.

Shivering as much from the cold as from what I was doing up here all by myself, I waited till the coast was clear, then slunk to the back of SeeFar, doing a clam-crawl again to keep below the window line. I knew this house way better than I wanted to. Lights were on in the kitchen and the window was open, probably from another Dwight-created gastronomic fiasco.

I slipped down between a white concrete statue of the Blessed Virgin that hadn't been there before and a big bush. I made sure none of those *leaves of three* were hanging around. If Bourne came calling, I'd see him. Or maybe this was a wild goose chase and they'd all just go to bed; they had to be tired. Heck, I was tired to the bone. I'd painted a house and rescued a Meatball.

I settled back against the side of the house, trying to get warm. I gave Mary a pat on the back for being such a great mom. My eyes closed for a little rest and at the moment I was too beat to think about any creepy crawlies occupying my hiding space. Right now I was in an exhausted, *live and let live* frame of mind.

"What are you doing here?" said a rough voice hovering over me.

"Rudy?"

"Guess again."

The flashlight clicked off and I blinked my eyes open to angry black ones and Angelo pointing a gun right at my forehead.

20

"How'd you know I was here?" I asked Angelo as he lowered the gun.

"My turn to unload the dishwasher and I heard snoring outside the window."

I jutted my chin and sat up straight, squaring my shoulders. "I do not snore."

"We're talking buzz saw. Why are you here keeping Mary company, and why are you blue?"

Think, Evie, think. Praying? Drunk as a skunk? Blue is the new black? I held up my hands. "I got nothing." I crawled out and stood. "If you were going to shoot me, you would have done it by now, right?"

"Be a big sin to shoot you with Mary here looking on."

Otherwise it would be a little sin? Probably best not to press the point.

Angelo held out the gun. "Besides, the thing doesn't even have bullets. Rosetta tossed 'em out last year when I shot up her best drapes thinking we had an intruder. She ragged on me for a month about the dang drapes. You'd think they were made of gold. I still carry my piece here 'cause I feel naked without it. So spill it, what gives?"

"It's an island, people are curious and it's my turn to get the dirt."

"Ya gotta be the worst liar ever." Angelo nodded toward the back steps. "I was making cocoa, extra marshmallows when I can get away with it. Rosetta's always on me about my blood sugar levels. Want some cocoa? It's cold out here and you're shivering."

More like shaking from sheer terror.

"Rosetta and Meatball are watching reruns of *The Untouchables*," Angelo added as I followed him up the back wood steps and into the kitchen. "I think Dwight's hiding under his bed. He made oatmeal cookies. Half of 'em burned. We can scrape off the black part and they might not be too bad."

"Why do you have Dwight cooking for you?"

Angelo nodded to a ladder-back chair by a maple kitchen table complete with a green fringe tablecloth and a bowl of wax apples in the middle. I sat down, and Angelo spooned cocoa into a saucepan and whisked the milk. "Dwight sold a bunch of us some real estate in the Keys for a winter place. The problem was, he didn't own it. We thought a long walk off a short pier might even the score, but then he inherited this house and we figured a summer place might be nice. Rosetta and I are here to get things organized for the others coming in a few weeks. We like the house, but it's too bad about Dwight's mom."

Time for the loaded questions. I eyed the back door, figuring it would take me maybe two seconds to get there and run screaming into the night. "So." I swallowed, scooting to the edge of the chair for a fast getaway. "How did you know she died? It's pretty much hush-hush."

"We had someone keeping an eye on Dwight, 'cause he was in to us for a bundle. We got the word about Bunny and hiding the body in a freezer so as not to upset the business community till after the holiday. Now we got ourselves a cook and a summer house."

"You didn't facilitate Dwight's inheritance?"

Angelo stopped whisking the cocoa, giving me a slow look. "You mean like did we snuff out Dwight's mom to get this house? We'd never do that to an old lady. What kind of people do you think we are? You were friends with Bunny?"

"I'm friends with the guy accused of knocking her off, and if it wasn't you doing the knocking, then it's got to be somebody else on my list."

"You got a list?" Angelo looked wistful. "I remember the days when I had a list." He dropped a handful of little marshmallows in the bottom of two *I ♡ Detroit* mugs and poured out the cocoa, the scent of chocolate permeating the air and steam curling over the top of the little pillow-puffs of white.

"So who do you think snuffed Bunny?" Angelo asked, taking the seat across from me.

"She wasn't loved by one and all around here, including her own son and his girl-friend. She was kind of a pain in the neck," I said, plucking a chocolate-infused marsh-mallow off the top and dropping it in my mouth. "There're two other bike shops on the island," I added. "Both would like to take over my friend's shop and cut the competition, so framing him fits. Then there's a blacksmith and the neighborhood hit man, Jason Bourne. Neither of them got along with Bunny either."

Angelo stopped the mug halfway to his mouth. "Jason Bourne? See, that's what gives this profession a bad rap. Cheesy nicknames make us all look bad. Maybe you should have a look around this Bourne guy's place, since he's a professional. Could be someone wanted Bunny out of the way and hired local talent; makes better sense than a DIY job. You know what you're getting when you hire local. Think global, buy local." Angelo laughed. "A little hit man humor. So when are we busting in?"

"We?" I splashed my cocoa across the table.

"You helped us, now I can help you."

"I appreciate the thought, but I can't be busting anything. That cop here has me on a short leash, and if he catches me doing one more thing —"

"Catching's not gonna happen. Where's this hit man live?"

"Two doors up."

Angelo took a sip from his mug, and a white line clung to his upper lip. Guns, breaking and entering with the mob and a marshmallow mustache . . . It was one of those nights.

"Let's see now," Angelo said. "I signed up for Pilates at noon at the Lilac Tree Spa 'cause the arthritis in my shoulder's acting up from packing heat all these years. There's a butterfly talk up at the Grand I want to catch, and Dwight's having a yard sale here to pick up some cash. We'll do the bust tomorrow night. Eight's good? Meet you at the back door here. Have somebody get this Bourne guy out of his house for an hour. And you need to ditch the blue; you stand out like a neon sign."

The next morning I added another layer of lotion to my abused skin after scrubbing paint off my body for an hour the night before and thinking about my new BFF from Detroit.

"Rudy?" I called out, tromping downstairs. Except there was no Rudy in the kitchen with fresh coffee waiting for me, just two cats hovering over a half-empty food bowl as if Armageddon and starvation were imminent. I filled the bowl, made coffee then knocked on Rudy's bedroom door. Getting no answer, I headed outside, figuring he was probably getting a head start on the great Tom Sawyer project, except he wasn't — he wasn't there either, and with all that was going on around here I didn't like Rudy being MIA. Somebody framed Rudy for taking out Bunny; the next step might be to take out *him.* Last night I was in bed before Rudy came in; that is, *if* he came in.

I pulled out Sheldon and dialed 911. "Yes, it's an emergency," I barked to Sutter when he picked up. "Rudy's missing. I don't think he came home last night. Do something — and don't give me that forty-eight-hour missing person speech like they do on TV for a person to be officially gone. Here everyone knows where everyone is twenty-four/seven. Do something!"

I could hear some papers rustling in the background.

"Are you listening to me?"

"I dropped my doughnut." The phone went dead, and little red dots danced in front of my eyes. I was going to kill Sutter with my bare hands! It was one thing to ignore my killer theories, but Rudy was not here, and that mattered. We got along, we were friends and painting buds and he fixed me breakfast every morning.

I grabbed a jacket, slammed the door and headed for the police station, but then I saw Sutter on a bike pedaling my way. " 'Bout time you got here. No horsey?"

"He's eating breakfast, like everyone else on this island." Sutter parked the bike and nodded at the emporium. "Lights on in the back. Did you think that maybe Rudy's having coffee with Mom? They're friends. She's up, he's up, it's early."

"Coffee?"

"Black stuff, cream, sugar, maybe a doughnut, unless it ends up on the floor when you're answering a phone call from some crazed female."

"Look," I rushed on, trying to explain. "I'm just a little jumpy with all that's going on around here."

"You're jumpy?" Sutter took a step back and laughed. Oh, that's rich. Got any idea the impact you're having on the rest of us around here? We passed jumpy two days ago. The whole island's destined for Prozac." Sutter put his hand on my back and none too gently shoved me up the walk to the back door of the emporium. Irma was busting about inside, copper pots simmering on the stove, ribbons of steam curling out over the top.

"Well, hello, dears," Irma said, all smiles, eyes bright and cheery as we walked in. She nodded to me and kissed sonny boy on the cheek.

"See, no Rudy," I said with a *so there* edge to my voice. "He's missing, and I bet he's in trouble, I can feel in my bones that something isn't right, and —"

"Irma, do you have an extra towel? This one's . . ." Rudy stopped in the doorway between the kitchen and the hall. Sutter's eyes rounded to the size of golf balls, and you could have knocked me over with a wet noodle. Not exactly the kind of trouble I had in mind, but with a gun on Sutter's hip it was headed that way.

"Rudy," Irma giggled. "You look better in that blue robe than I ever did."

"I gave you that robe." Sutter stared, not moving a muscle. "What . . . Who . . . Why . . . Mom!"

"Well now," Irma said, handing a fluffy, just-out-of-the-dryer towel to Rudy and giving the pot another stir with a spoon the Jolly Green Giant would have found useful. "You know the *who* well enough, and as for the *what* and *why,* I don't think that's any of your business — no offense, dear."

"You're sixty-seven."

"Sixty-eight, dear."

Sutter looked from his mother to Rudy, who was slowly backing into the hallway. "How can you do this?"

"How?" Irma patted her son's hand. "There's a book upstairs in your old room. Thought we went over this when you were ten or maybe eleven. Been a while for you, has it? Don't worry, you're young; you have time to figure it out."

"But . . . but . . ." Sutter muttered, then headed for the door in a near-run, slamming it behind him.

"Is he gone?" Rudy asked, peeking around the corner, this time in his pants and shirt. "I'm sorry, Irma, I didn't mean for this to happen."

Irma put her hands on Rudy's shoulders and gave him a sassy smile. "I thought it happened pretty well, if I do say so myself."

Yikes! "I'm out of here. See you back at the ranch," I blurted to Rudy. I exited through the front of the emporium in case Sutter had passed out right there on Main. Sutter was nowhere in sight, but Fiona pulled her cart to the curb and climbed down, a big brown basket in her arms.

"Did you happen to see our local police officer?" I asked her.

"Strangest thing, he was pounding on the front door of the Stang, yelling something about being desperate and they had to let him in or he'd shoot the lock off the place. Wonder what that's all about? Did you do something new and not include me?"

"For once I'm innocent. What's in the basket?" I asked as a diversion from questions I didn't want to answer.

"Here, let me show you. You're gonna love this." Fiona flipped open the lid. "The brandy fudge was a big hit — Irma sold out in half a day, so she's decided to aim for the more adult palate."

Fiona pulled out a jar and held it up. "This is ancho chilies and smoked paprika sea salt, and Smithy makes this special herb butter from his garden that he keeps in the back of his fridge, so I grabbed a tub. Irma's leaving the maple-nut and chocolate chips to the rest of the shops on the island, and changing the name from *Irma's Fudge Emporium* to *The Good Stuff.* We're appealing to a niche market, giving senior discounts. This is going to put Irma on the map, and maybe get me out of the doghouse."

By afternoon, most of the bike shop had a second coat of beach-baby blue as Rudy/Twain told stories to the kids about the big fish in the lake and explained that the best way to toast marshmallows was on a stick you found in the woods and that there were more stars in the sky than grains of sand on all the beaches on Earth. When I came around to the front to paint, I saw that Rudy had added *how tall I am* marks along the entire front of the shop, along with dates and names.

"What are we going to do about the kids?" Rudy asked me. "We can't paint over their marks. Look right there: Allison Bell is thirty-two and three-quarters inches tall and Dominic Carter is forty-three-and-a-half inches tall. They'll come back next year and be looking to see how much they've grown, along with all the other kids I've got up here. We can't paint over it and we can't leave the shop looking run down."

"I'll think of something," I said with a lot more conviction than I felt. "I have to help Donna deliver some scones, and I'll be back soon. Hold down the fort." *And if you see Nate Sutter, run.* I didn't add the last part, but probably should have.

I did a quick change then headed for the white picket fence of the Blarney Scone. "You're looking more and more like one of the Smurf people," Donna said as she opened the back door. She gave me three long, white boxes and a threatening look. "Don't drop these; they be some of my best work ever. Got a fine assortment made up and been baking like a banshee all night."

"This is perfect."

"You're not the one up all night trying to bake with a broken oven. Good thing I've got another on order."

"Sorry about the oven, but you need to have Jason Bourne come here to the Blarney Scone for a scone tasting. Say around eight o'clock tonight. There's a good chance he had something to do with Bunny biting the big one and I want to look around his place.

You can tell Bourne you're trying a new recipe and want his input, with him being one of your best customers."

Donna took a step back. "Blessed be Saint Patrick, you know that obituary piece we were working on the night you got here, now I'm thinking I'll get a chance to use it. And how do you intend to get yourself inside Bourne's house? The man's got the place locked up like Fort Knox."

"I'm working on that part. You'll call Bourne?"

"He's not one to be chatting on the phone, but he will pick up for me. Since we're talking Rudy here, I'll make the effort, since he took our part on the town council like he has." Donna patted my cheek. "Ye best be real careful, Evie girl. Mr. Bourne's a mighty private person, and if the man catches ye . . ." She bit her bottom lip. "Does Rudy know your next of kin to be contacting?"

21

The scone delivery was at the top of Crow's Nest Trail, better known to me as the steps from hell. Drenched in blue-tinged sweat by the time I got there, I went around the side porch of the huge Victorian to the gardens in the back. Tables with white linens dotted the grass, the whole place decked out in late-summer red and pink geraniums, purple asters, dahlias, yarrow, coneflowers and the like. My mother's garden was not as elaborate as this, but close. I wondered how the parents were doing in Paris? Stupid question — everyone did great in Paris.

"There you are," a maid in a white apron grumped as I came inside the kitchen. She snagged the boxes out of my hand. "I need to get things set up, we're running late. Grab that silver tray with the pink doilies and get the napkins and for God's sake don't get blue on them."

I followed Grumpy outside, put down the

tray, then headed back to town. Instead of taking the steps, I turned toward SeeFar, hoping to catch Angelo between the butterfly lecture and Pilates. I needed to see if Angelo and I were still on for tonight and to let him know that Donna had a plan to get Bourne out for a few hours.

I opened the squeaky gate and cut across the grass. I didn't see Angelo, but Dwight was surrounded by a small crowd of shoppers and a collection of boxes, furniture, a few rugs, tables with books, framed pictures and a set of old china. Nurse Jane Porter had two ugly lamps picked out, Doc Evers hauled off a brass coat rack, Speed pawed through a box of photos and Smithy test-pedaled a stationary bicycle. Jason Bourne had a box of paperbacks tucked under his arm and was haggling with Dwight over the price of a nice-looking tie — the perfect accessory for the well-dressed hit man — as Huffy stormed her way up the sidewalk.

Everyone pretended to be consumed with the sale, but no one really wanted to miss a word of "You got me into this, you creep, and it's all gone wrong and you're going to make it right if it's the last thing you do, Dwight Harrington."

"But sweetheart, we can work this out, I swear it's going to be okay." Dwight put his

arm around Huffy and took cash from Jane
Porter for the ugly lamps.

Huffy wiggled away, eyes on fire, lower lip
in a pout. "You said we could be together
and have things our way, and now you've
gone and ruined it all. No house, no money.
How could you let this happen? My father
knows what's going on and he won't let you
get away with this."

Huffy got on her bike and pedaled off
down the road, leaving Dwight looking pale
and sick as Smithy paid him for the stationary bike.

"Huffy's been after Dwight since Helen
and I bought the Merry Widow six years
ago," Ed said, coming up behind me, a
bunch of pictures tucked under his arm.
"And now when those two could finally be
getting together, Dwight goes and loses it
all. He's one of those guys always after the
fast buck, and this time it bit him in the
butt. I keep trying to tell Ed Junior that hard
work gets the job done. He needs to be
more like Abigail. She's got her head
screwed on right, a real go-getter."

"Abigail has no life."

"Ed Junior could do with a little less of a
life. A Ferrari? Where's that money coming
from? What's he thinking? Not about business, I can tell you that. He's driving me

crazy. But then I'm the one who spoiled him, so I can't complain. I just need to help him out once in a while to make things right, or so Helen keeps telling me." Ed glanced around at SeeFar. "Maybe the new owners will make this place right and put some more money into it. Bunny had the roof done last year, but the outside could do with a paint job."

Speed walked up and slapped Ed on the back old-buddy style. He had a smile on his face that was more teeth than *I'm so happy to see you.*

"I'd like to buy those pictures from you," Speed said, pointing to Ed's eight-by-ten glossies. "They're of me when I used to cut Bunny's grass a long time ago. We were great pals, and she gave me a lot of encouragement when I was just getting into cycling."

Ed pulled out an article from the *Crier.* "Bunny kept this with the pictures. It says right here that she gave you the name *Speed* from the way you sped around the island so fast it was like you had a motor on your bike. You were destined for greatness even then." Ed held out a pen. "I'd love to have you autograph the pictures. I'm hanging them in my den. Great local interest."

"I'll give you five hundred bucks for 'em."

Speed reached for the pictures and Ed pulled them back. "A thousand," Speed added. His smile got tighter, his eyes darker, all pretense at friendliness gone. "I want to put them in my shop. Bunny promised me those pictures and never got around to giving them to me. They are some really fond memories." Except Speed sure didn't sound fond; he sounded pissed and mean and maybe a little desperate.

Ed held the photos a little tighter. "I'm sure you have other pictures you can put in your shop — like the framed one of you in *Sports Illustrated* that you got up at the Grand the other night, and . . ." Ed let the rest of the sentence hang; Speed was already halfway across the yard.

"Helen would kill me if I gave these up." Ed glanced at one of the pictures of Speed in his early teens, all lean with sun-bleached curly hair, alongside a young and pleasant Bunny. It was hard to imagine Bunny pleasant.

"While I'm here I'll get Helen some of those books I saw earlier in an L.L.Bean box by the folding table," Ed added. "I think Helen has a thing for steamy reads. I found *The Highwayman's Revenge* hidden in a copy of *War and Peace* on our bookshelf and *The Duke's Decadent Proposal* in *The*

Comedies of William Shakespeare. I know I sure didn't put them there." Ed laughed. "I read a few pages, and *wow.* The back cover says the author's a Vegas mystery woman who tells all. Surprised the books don't set the house on fire and . . . and they're gone."

Ed nodded to the folding table. "They were right there in a box. I didn't see anyone check them out with Dwight."

"Must be another closet reader." My brain fogged over with images of the four-poster and the moon, and was that Sutter coming up the walk?

"I've got to go," I said to Ed. "Don't let Speed fast-talk you out of your pictures. They'll look great on your wall."

When I got back to the shop, it was after five and Rudy had himself balanced on a bike right at the front door. He had his one crutch lying across the handlebars, and there was a wild look in his eyes.

"I'm gonna ride down to the VI and have a walleye fish sandwich for dinner and onion soup, and chips, I'm dying for some chips, Those fat ones that make a big crunch when you bite into them."

I put myself smack in front of the bike to block Rudy's way. "You're hungry, I'll make you dinner. You can't ride to the Village Inn.

You've got a broken leg, remember?" I rapped the cast with my knuckles to emphasize my point. "See, no bend, stiff as a board. You can't pedal. Big problem."

"I got one good leg left . . . Actually, it's my right." Rudy laughed, his eyes not focusing. "A little crutch humor. All I need is one leg." Rudy waved his hand. "Out of the way, Chicago, I'm on a mission here. Irma, that hot little number, brought over some fudge that she cooked up all by herself today. Best fudge I ever had."

"Must have been the brandy fudge. You're drunk as a skunk."

"I could really do with a KitKat. I love KitKats — and did I mention chips?"

"Listen to me, if you take off on this bike, you're going to kill yourself, and then Abigail will kill *me.*" I grabbed the crutch then hoisted Rudy up, the bike toppling over with a crash. Rudy wobbled and leaned on me, all one hundred and whatever pounds, plus cast, and together we did the hop-shuffle back to the kitchen. I couldn't imagine the alcohol content in fudge being enough to make someone this blammed. I wasn't cook of the year by any stretch, but I'd made enough Christmas fudge with Mother to know that too much liquid — too much of any liquid — made for really soupy fudge.

I plopped Rudy in a kitchen chair and he banged his fist on the table. "Chips."

"What if I make pork chops?"

"Lots of chips."

It was like dealing with an inebriated two-year-old. I got out turkey bacon and eggs and repeated the Hangover Therapy 101 lesson that I had laid out for Irma. I cooked up breakfast for dinner so there'd be something in Rudy's stomach to sop up the alcohol.

"Here," I said, putting the food in front of Rudy. "Eat this, all of it, and don't move from this chair, and no bikes. I'm going to check on Irma."

"Give my little cutie-pootie a big old smooch for me, okay?"

"I'll let you handle that one." I headed out the back door and across the deck, which was still splattered with blue paint from when I dropped the roller when Angelo showed up. I cut over to Irma's, where I could hear some Bob Marley blaring inside the shop.

Who knew alcohol in fudge could be so potent? I gripped the doorknob, prayed for strength and cut through the kitchen to the main room, where the bass was vibrating so hard on "Three Little Birds," my teeth hurt. An old turntable with big speakers was set up on the display case. People sat on tables, legs dangling, eyes not focusing, arms in the air, swaying back and forth and singing along — or slurring along, depending on how zonked they happened to be.

Irma shuffled about passing out Doritos and Fritos. The majority of the people in the shop were on retirement road, and they were all three sheets to the wind, thanks to that senior discount Fiona had mentioned earlier.

"Come on in, the water's fine, dearie," Irma yelled over the din of off-key warbling. She gave me a big wave and a lopsided smile. Dishes of fudge were making the rounds, everyone helping themselves and sending their cholesterol and sugar levels through the roof.

"No Woman, No Cry" filled the room to cheers and more swaying. I wasn't exactly a wallflower, and never in a million years had I seen myself as someone who got in the way of a good time, but this was it. If I didn't break up the party, people would start passing out on the floor. I pulled the plug on the music and climbed on top of a table to wolf whistles, catcalls and shouts of "Show us what you got, baby!"

"The party's over," I yelled.

That got me boos and hisses and a pummeling with junk food.

"You are all wasted. What would your kids say if they saw you all like this?" Did those words really come out of my mouth?

"We don't give a flying fig what our kids say," a guy in a red and blue plaid shirt called out. "We'll just cut the little bastards out of the will."

Giggling filled the room, and two women fell off the tables. Everyone thought it was the funniest thing ever, so it was followed by more giggling. It was like being back in junior high.

"We need more chips," someone called. "More chips, more chips, more chips" was chanted through the room at brain-numbing decibels. But the good news was that I could do chips — and that would get everyone out of here!

"Follow me to the best chips in town!" I found Bob Marley's "Kaya" on my phone, cranked it, jumped off the table and started a swaying line out the front door. I headed for Horn's bar, holding Sheldon over my head, with the band of mellow oldsters pied-pipering behind. I figured Horn's knew how to handle drunks better than I did, and maybe they could sober them up. Right now it would take all the coffee on the island to sober them up. How could this happen from fudge?

When I got back to the bike shop, the cannon up at the fort boomed the six o'clock warning, Taps floated out over the island, marking the end to another day in paradise, and I found Rudy facedown in his bacon and eggs, snoring. Some days in paradise were better than others.

I half dragged Rudy to the La-Z-Boy to sleep it off, then headed for the shower to get fancied up for my eight o'clock date with Angelo. I dressed in breaking-and-entering black, twisted my hair up and pinned it in place. I added black eyeliner 'cause I hadn't been on a date in months and needed to keep my makeup skills honed. I left Rudy a note saying there was a sandwich in the fridge and that I'd be back around ten, then locked the shop up behind me.

22

I wanted to think I was getting better at climbing the death steps, but in truth they kicked my butt every time. All the locals around here must have the constitutions of rhinoceroses. Moonlight lit the bluff, a few carriages were out and about, one pulling up beside me. Fiona leaned down and gave me a closer look. "Evie? If you had pointy ears, you'd look like Catwoman. Holy cow, dressed like that, you're up to something." She jumped from the cart, then glanced at SeeFar. "You're sneaking around there? Why? Not that I'm complaining." Fiona's eyes danced with excitement.

Great! Fiona's investigative reporter radar was on full alert. There was no getting rid of her now. "I saved Angelo's Meatball and he's helping me sneak into Bourne's house. I think maybe someone paid Bourne to knock off Bunny,"

"Bourne? Angelo? Meatball? This gets better and better."

"Let's hope Angelo thinks so." Fiona tied her horse and cart to a bench and we tiptoed around to the back of SeeFar. Angelo was waiting by the door in a black suit, white shirt, yellow silk tie and matching handkerchief in his breast pocket. Uh-oh. Breaking and entering goes *GQ*?

"I can't make it tonight," Angelo said to me. "Rosetta wants to go dancing at the Grand. I told her I had business, but she's not buying it. Said we were retired and she didn't take all those Author Murray classes for nothin', and who the heck is this?"

"Fiona. She runs the *Town Crier.*"

"You brought along a reporter?"

"It's Mackinac, she only reports on things that smile, and what do we do now that you're going dancing? I got Bourne out of the house and everything. Can't you go dancing another night?"

"When my sister sets her mind to something, it happens. I'll show you and the reporter here how to get in on your own. I did a little walk around that Bourne guy's place and got some ideas. The front door has a motion-detector light, so that's not gonna work. The back door has another one, and a keypad lock, making it a little tricky for a beginner, but there's a porch on the second floor. You can go in there, piece of cake."

"What if our piece of cake is equipped with an alarm system?" Fiona asked, and I added, "I can't get arrested; I'm already the black sheep of my family."

"Hey, every family needs a black sheep," Angelo said. "But this place won't have an alarm that's hotwired to the cops or some agency. If Bourne's who you think, the last thing he wants is the law showing up. He's probably living off his reputation. Ya know, like what kind of idiot would break into a hit man's house?"

"Can't imagine," Fiona said, grinning ear to ear.

"The porch lock is one of those fancy bio-matic fingerprint locks that get so much press," Angelo said. "They look techy, but lucky for us it's a piece of junk and opens with a pass code and a hidden place for a key. The key's your in. I'll give you a crash course in lock-picking."

"A course in lock picking!" Fiona hugged Angelo and I asked him, "How can you tell all this lock stuff by just looking at it from down on the ground?"

"A decent pair of binoculars. It's the family business." Angelo looked to Fiona. "Don't print that." He handed her a pen flashlight, then slid a thin leather wallet from his breast pocket and flipped it open to —

"Dental tools?" I asked.

"That would work too." He took a long, thin, pointy thing from the pouch and then something shaped like an L. He stuck the L into the lock on his door. "We'll practice. This is a tension wrench; it holds the cylinder in place. Turn it just a little bit."

He put long pointy into the lock. "They call this a hook pick. There're pins holding the lock in place so you can't open the door. This pushes the pins up and out of the way. When they spring back down, they land on the cylinder 'cause you turned it. Turn the cylinder the rest of the way like you would a key, and bingo."

"We are so going to hell," I whispered.

"And it's so worth it," Fiona gushed.

Angelo handed me the tools. "Bobby pins, nail file or a paperclip work too if you were in a pinch, but these do a better job. Feel for pins," he said to me as I stuck in the wrench then the pick.

I fished around and there was a snap. Angelo ruffled my hair. "You got it. You're a natural. I'll give you two a boost up to the porch, then I gotta go rumba."

We crept across the neighbor's yard,

hopped a little iron fence and wound up in the back of JB's place. No lights were on there, leaving the yard black as a tomb — bad choice of words. Angelo made a cup with his hands. "Try not to get my suit dirty. You can drop back down into the shrubbery when you want out. Make sure to lock the place up and put everything back the way you found it."

More landing in the bushes; my life was not improving. Up I went, grabbing the wood railing, then pulling myself over, falling headfirst with a hard thump.

"Shh," Angelo hissed from below as he boosted Fiona.

I peered over the edge and gave a thumbs-up.

"There could be cameras," he stage-whispered as he started back to his house. "You never know about these hit man types; they're a whacko bunch. Keep your head down low so they don't see your face, and slouch — that hides how tall you are. Oh, and hunt around for a hidden room. Hit men keep their ammo out of sight. Otherwise it freaks the pizza delivery guys when they come. One look at an assault rifle and you can kiss your pepperoni with extra cheese good-bye."

Angelo faded into the night, and Fiona

turned to me, eyes huge. "Cameras? Ammo? Hidden room? How'd I get so lucky?"

"I came to town and Bunny croaked." It took me twice as long to do the *piece of cake* lock as it had taken to do Angelo's, but I finally turned the cylinder and clicked the door open. Fiona gave me a high-five. "You know," I said, "we really are going to hell for this."

"Yeah, but right now life is sweet. We're in Jason Bourne's hallway."

We crawled to an open door that was obviously JB's room. The bed wasn't made and clothes were flung across a chair. No desk; a dresser with the usual array of clothes; and a nightstand with Tylenol PM, Tums and a smiley-face stress-relief ball.

"Looks like being a hit man isn't all flowers and sunshine," Fiona whispered.

We scooted to the next door. "It's locked," Fiona said, turning the knob. "It's one of those old door locks like in the Disney version of Cinderella."

"Except there aren't any cute little mice headed my way with a key to save the day." I stuck the wrench tool in the lock and fished around till it caught on something, then I gave a hard turn, but it slipped. I tried again then again with no luck.

"We're wasting time." Fiona said and

started downstairs. I kept the flashlight aimed at the floor and away from the big windows that offered a killer view of the night harbor and Mackinaw Bridge.

The dining room held a table, a hutch, six chairs and a layer of dust. Across the hall in the living room, the red coals of a smoldering fire offered the only light, with a box of logs sitting right in front. My flashlight reflected off a silver briefcase by the couch, handcuffs dangling off the side. "It's *the* briefcase," Fiona gasped. "Open it."

"*You* open it."

"Looks like it has a combination lock, and Angelo didn't cover that in Lock-Picking, the Beginner Class. What are we looking for again?"

"Bourne's client list, something that says somebody paid him a bundle to knock off Bunny, and my guess is it's in that locked room." Shaking with fear, disappointment and the sinking feeling I was getting nowhere fast in finding the real killer, I slunk over to the hearth to get warm and to try and come up with at least one good idea, since I hadn't had any in a really long time. I reached for a log from the box to add to the fire and kick up the heat, then stopped dead. That *four-poster bed with moonlight and the chickie and delish dude* book was right there in front of me.

"What?" Fiona asked coming up beside me.

"It's Lovelace books from Dwight's yard sale. I recognize the L.L.Bean box they were packed in."

"A half-burned copy of *The Duke's Decadent Proposal*'s smoldering here in the fireplace. I've read this one. My guess is it caught fire all by itself." Fiona fanned herself with her hand. "There's a bedroom scene on page —"

"Why would a hit man burn books? Why *these* books? I get that romance is not everyone's cup of tea, but setting them on fire seems a little extreme, don't you think?" I picked up *The Secret Diary of Miss Collette* and photos of a man in a brown leather jacket, bad mustache and fedora who had a silver briefcase cuffed to his wrist fell to the floor.

"It's Bourne in disguise coming out of an office building, or maybe going in — hard to tell," Fiona picked up the pictures. "It's some contemporary building with big glass doors and windows all across the front." She passed me the photo with the 375 address in silver numbers over the entrance. "375 where?" I asked. "The building has a big-city feel, but why is this photo of Jason

278

Bourne and this particular building important? Why would someone take it?"

"Why put it in a box headed for the fire," Fiona added. "Bourne wanted it destroyed, not just tossed in the trash.

I pulled out Sheldon and snapped pictures of the pictures, then emailed them to myself as a key turned in the front door. Fiona's eyes covered half her face and my heart dropped to my toes.

23

The front door opened, and Fiona hunkered down beside the couch, pulling me with her. Humming, Bourne walked into the living room and stood by the hearth. Humming was good, right? People didn't kill people if they were happy — unless killing was their job, and they really liked their job.

He put a pink Blarney Scone bag on a little table by an overstuffed chair, and instead of turning Fiona and me into worm food, he picked a book out of the box. He heaved a sigh, tore out some pages and tossed them onto the hot embers, which burst into a soft yellow glow. He added more books, crumbled the photos and added the pieces to the blaze.

He headed for the bookshelf and fiddled with something there, then opera filled the room. He started for the kitchen and I followed Fiona to the steps, swiping a blueberry scone from the little pink bag along the way. Four scones or three — JB would never know the difference, and we needed to get something positive out of this evening.

Following Fiona, we tiptoed up the steps, timing footfalls with the loudest opera shrieks. I split the sugary scone in two, handed half to Fiona then reset the lock and closed the door behind me. We climbed over the railing and landed in the bushes, staying put for a few minutes to finish off the pastry and to see if bodies falling from the second floor happened to have caught Bourne's attention. When nothing happened, I thanked Puccini or Verdi or whoever had penned the opera bellowing inside, and we made a dash for the street. We climbed in Fiona's cart, neither of us saying a word for a full minute. "Gee, that was fun," I finally managed.

"You bet it was," Fiona agreed, and meant every word. "We need to get in that locked room. The question is how?"

Fiona dropped me at the shop, retrieved her bottle of That's Berry Daring nail polish and took off to finish up an editorial piece for the *Crier.* I checked in on Rudy, who was still zonked in the La-Z-Boy. I'd seen my share of hangovers, but fudge hangovers were something else. I got my laptop from my room, hoped it had some juice left and headed for the Pink Pony for free Wi-Fi and some fried green beans. The bar was packed, and a guitar player was warbling on about Alabama being his sweet home.

I found a stool at the end of the bar behind the cash register and away from the turmoil. I ordered a beer and beans and pulled up Google Images. Dropping in the picture of Bourne and the glass office building, I did a search by image. This works great for well-known stuff, like pinpointing the location of Machu Picchu or the Washington Monument, but this office building was pretty obscure, and — holy cow, it worked! Smooches to Google. Bless the guys who rode around with those cameras strapped to the hoods of their cars. I wondered if the island had cameras strapped to the backs of some horses. They should!

Bourne's 375 office building was on Hudson Street in New York City, and that it was designed by some famous architect gave it notoriety. My beans came and I munched, staring at the picture trying to think what it meant, and it meant something or Bunny wouldn't have had pictures of it.

"Moving up in the world?" came Sutter's voice from behind me. He pointed to the computer, getting my attention there, then snagging a fried bean. I quickly closed my computer. Sutter flipped it back open, bought the guy on the next stool a beer, making sure he saw the police patch on his Windbreaker, then politely asking him to move.

"Surprised you don't have some fancy iPad." He took another green bean.

"Not enough kick for the software I use in my job," I said, trying to get his attention onto something else. I sure didn't want to tell Sutter how I got this photo. "So, what do you do back in Detroit?" I asked Sutter.

I got the *duh* look.

"Right, you're a cop with a three-month vacation. I think I want your job." The Pink Pony was bar-loud, and Sutter leaned closer, his woodsy scent of soap and aftershave washing over me. Little shower droplets still clung to his hair, there was a light scruff across his jaw and his brown eyes were intense — always intense — and my heart skipped two beats, then kicked into overdrive.

"You need to laugh more," I said, wanting to somehow get my mind off scruff, eyes and overdrive.

"I was working on it, then you showed up. Why are you collecting pictures of Jason Bourne in New York?"

"Why are you hiding out on Mackinac Island?"

"Who says I'm hiding out?"

"Only Congress gets three months off with pay."

"Where'd you get this picture?" He nodded to the screen and snatched another bean.

The thing with spilling my guts to Sutter is he could shut me down before I could put this all together. On the other hand, he thought like a cop and knew how bad guys operated. I thought like a designer and knew how to sell soap, cars and soft drinks. "Bunny had it mixed in with some books that Bourne bought at Dwight's yard sale. What I don't get is why Bunny would care that Bourne was at this particular New York location — and how did she get the picture in the first place?"

"Who's in the building?" Sutter snagged another bean. "Unless you think JB was there to admire the architecture, he was there because of someone inside."

I did a search on the tenants. "This one's a high-end advertising firm; I recognize the name. And there's a publishing house. The books!" I Googled *The Highwayman's Revenge.* "This publisher puts out the Lovelace romance books. They're hot, steamy sexy books about delicious guys with . . . with black hair who need a shave and smell like . . ." I looked at Sutter, my insides on fire.

"Okay, so you got a picture of Bourne outside a building where there's a publisher."

"What building?"

Sutter took my beer. "How many of these did you have?"

I grabbed my beer back. *Get a grip, Bloomfield.* "Bourne was burning a box of Lovelace books, and he burned the pictures too. Why would he do that?"

"How do you know about the burning?"

"A little bird told me."

Sutter leaned closer still, his breath hot on my face. "How did you get into his house?" His eyes shot wide open. "Angelo?"

"I saved his dog, and Angelo pays his debts. He makes great hot chocolate."

"You're breaking into a hit man's house and consorting with the mob."

"Define *consorting.*" Sutter closed his eyes and muttered some creative expletives. I closed my computer and slid off the stool. Then I ran for the door to get away form Sutter — and for more reasons than one.

Rudy slept in, least that was my guess,

because he wasn't outside the next morning being Twain, and I sure wasn't checking out his whereabouts after the little surprise party at Irma's. Without Rudy/Twain to pull off our tourist attraction, I had to improvise. I shrugged into jeans, got the straw hat Rudy used when fixing the door hinge and went for the Tom Sawyer effect on my own.

I rented out a handful of bikes and sold off the rest of the trail mix. A few kids gave painting the fence a try, but I was no match for Rudy's stories. By noon the trim on the shop was bright white, setting off the beach-baby blue, and I added a curly frame around the kids' heights so it looked like a picture and did a sketch of Rudy on his rocker next to it. The shop wasn't exactly the Taj Mahal, but it didn't look bad.

"Is that supposed to be me?" Rudy said as he stumbled out of the shop, coffee cup in hand, eyes squinting against the sun, ice pack strapped to his head with a belt.

"It's a caricature of you as Twain. I even put in Bambino and Cleveland. Are you okay?"

Donna and Paddy plodded up to the curb. "Saints above," Donna said to Rudy. "You be looking like death warmed over and served on a platter. You're in no condition to be riding with Paddy and me out to the freight docks to check on me new oven and pick up those bikes for Ed that finally made it here."

Rudy leaned heavy on his crutch. "Don't know how I got this way. Yesterday I started off feeling really good after eating a few pieces of Irma's herbal fudge, then switched to the fudge with booze, and *bam,* it hit me like a ton of bricks. Bad combination. Worst headache ever."

"I'll just be bringing Chicago with me, paint and all," Donna said. "It's getting to be we wouldn't recognize her any other way, though the blue was a bit more becoming than the white. Makes you look sickly, dear."

"I'll keep that in mind." I climbed in the buggy, Rudy handed me a screwdriver to attach the seat and the pedals to Ed's bikes so I could drop them at Ed's boat on the way back then Irish Donna, Paddy and I plodded out of town. Main Street was congested this time of day. Well, it was as congested as it ever got in this part of the world, moving at horsey and bicycle pace. We rounded Mission Point, where fudgies played croquet and tennis and sat in white Adirondack chairs looking out at the sparkling, sun-splashed water. The road circled around the whole island for eight miles, no GPS needed — you wound up where you started. Hiking or biking the interior paths got more complicated, not many signs and you never knew where you'd wind up.

"Now we can get to talking," Donna said as we left the crowds behind. Main Street turned into Lake Shore Boulevard with sandy beaches on one side and straight-up cliffs on the other. "How did it go at Bourne's place? There be any skeletons in the closet for real? I kept stuffing scones and tea down the man's throat best I could to buy you some time I did."

"He got back to his house while Fiona and I were still there."

"Fiona?"

"We get around."

"Holy Saint Patrick!" Hand to heart, Donna flopped back against the carriage seat. "And ye lived to tell about it? 'Tis the luck of me shamrock that's keeping you alive these days, it is."

I pulled out Sheldon and showed Donna the photo of Bourne by the glass building. "It's in New York City, and Bunny had this photo in with some Lovelace books that Bourne stole from Dwight's yard sale. He was burning them. Can you think of any connection between Bunny, a New York publisher and a hit man?"

"Sounds like a title of a mighty bad book,

it does. Bunny worked on her snooty family history for years and went to New York more than once to try and sell the piece of malarkey. She made a big deal out of it, not that it ever amounted to much. Maybe she came across Bourne when she was there and snapped his picture?"

"New York isn't Mackinac Island. Bunny and Bourne showing up at the same place at the same time is too much of a co-incidence. Whatever got them there, it was a planned event." I sucked in a quick breath. "Good grief. Are you thinking what I'm thinking?"

"That Bourne's mustache looks like a dead caterpillar these days? The man's in need of an overhaul, he is. Think there's a hit man magazine he can take a look at?"

"That Bunny was Bourne's target. He knew she was going to New York to try and sell her book, and he followed her to this publisher."

"Faith and begorra!"

24

My brain snapped back to what Angelo had said about *think global, buy local.* "What if someone here on the island paid Bourne to off Bunny?" I said to Irish Donna as we clip-clopped our way out to British Landing. "A hit in New York doesn't stand out like it does here — except Bunny got to Bourne before he got to her. Miss Congeniality probably suspected someone might be after her. She'd messed up Smithy's marriage and kept Huffy and Dwight apart, and who knows what's going on with Speed. She took the picture, and maybe she threatened to tweet it and ruin Bourne's reputation. Something like *the worst hit man ever* would be really bad for Bourne's business."

"So ye think Bourne did the old biddy in here by cutting her brake cable when things fell apart in the city?"

"I think she blackmailed him with the pictures; that's why he wanted them back.

She was suddenly getting money from somewhere to start fixing up SeeFar. Either Bourne had enough of paying her off and decided to take his chances, or the person who hired him to do the deed in the first place took matters into his or her own hands."

"So why was Bourne burning books?"

"He used the box of books to get the pictures out of the sale without looking suspicious. Bourne's bookshelves are more Hemingway than *The Highwayman's Revenge,* so he got rid of them. I need to get back into Bourne's house," I said, thinking about the locked room. "He's a businessman. He keeps records. If I can find something that links him to Bunny . . ."

"We can't talk about that now, dear," Donna said as British Landing came into view. "Sometimes even the rocks have ears, and things have a way of getting back."

Soft waves lapped against the freight docks as workers offloaded crates and boxes from a working ferry that was nothing like the sleek white ferries that whizzed fudgies to and from the mainland. Containers of trash from the island lined the dock to make the return trip. Living on an island was like living in a too-small house — there was only so much room and then something had to go, namely the garbage.

"There ye be, Captain," Irish Donna called out to the guy I'd met that foggy morning in front of SeeFar. He had on the same stained sweatshirt and beat-up captain's hat. "I'm checking on me stove that's finally come in," Donna said to the captain as she climbed down from the carriage. "Chicago here's picking up two bikes."

The captain tipped his hat to Donna, then sent her and a dockworker off to a storage building to find the stove. He checked his clipboard. "Only one bike made the trip this time," he said to me. "The other one will be along in a day or so, and we'll deliver it free, since the order got split. The boys here will load you up, but you need to sign the delivery papers in the office." He gave me a once-over. "Don't I know you from somewhere? Hard to tell with all that paint. You're kind of splotchy."

"Just here to help Rudy." I gave him the *innocent* look and followed the captain to the front part of the storage building. Two desks, shelves, computers, printers, a bulletin board, a Keurig coffeemaker and a water cooler cluttered the little green room. The captain picked up a stack of papers and flipped through them, a photo of what looked like a cone of black-and-white waves slid out onto the desk. For a second I thought it was the lake or sky at night, except *Mackinac Straights Hospital and Health Center* was stamped at the bottom along with a date.

The captain caught me staring at the picture and scooped it into the top drawer of the desk and slammed it shut. "Sign here." He thrust the papers at me, his brow furrowing. "I remember where I saw you. You were standing outside SeeFar that morning I was taking a walk."

He leaned across the desk, eyes cold, voice low and menacing. "I told you to mind your own business then, and I'm telling you again. If you think you know something, you don't know nothin'. It's a deep lake we got out there, missy. I'd remember that if I were you."

I dropped the clipboard on the desk and tried not to run as I went back to the safety of the buggy. Donna was ready to go, the box with the bike wedged in the back. "Is it the right stove?" I asked her as we started off.

"That it is, and I can't wait to start baking. The boys will be bringing it on out tomorrow first thing. That old stove I have now is a time bomb waiting to go off."

"Yeah, I know what you mean about waiting for time bombs."

"Are ye feeling poorly, dear? You're white as can be under all that . . . white."

I could feel the captain watching us as we headed down Lake Shore. "Where is Mackinaw Straits Hospital?" I asked when we got out of sight of the captain.

"Over there in Mackinaw City. It's where we go for the big health issues Doc Evers can't handle. Pretty much where you're born and where you die if you're a local — and you're looking like ye could be headed there right now."

Born? The black-and-white picture was an ultrasound. I'd seen my share of them from the girls in the office back in Chicago. "You know how Huffy's been a little intense lately, even for Huffy? She's got a reason — she's pregnant."

Donna sniffed, her mouth in a deep frown. "I'm gone five minutes now, just five, been on this island for twenty-five years I have, and the captain takes you into his confidence as soon as I turn my back and tells you something like that? You sure know how to be sweet-talking a man."

Oh for the love of . . . "There was an ultrasound picture on his desk, and unless the captain's personally headed for a medical miracle of that persuasion, I think it's

Huffy's. The captain shoved the thing in his desk as soon as he saw me looking at it, then proceeded to inform me about the depth of the lake and told me that I should keep it in mind."

Donna grinned. "Well, now I'm feeling better. Thought I was getting out-gossiped by a fudgie."

"Saints preserve us."

"Amen. The thing is, I'd be watching my step if I were you, me dear. The captain's not one for saying something he doesn't mean, and the man is sure protective of his Huffy. He always has been since Mrs. Captain ran off with the saxophone player from up at the Grand years ago. But you're right in why Huffy's acting like a nincompoop, and it explains plenty. She's wanting a father for her baby before he comes into this here world, and she wants to be living at SeeFar."

"And now the father is broke, he's the cook for the mob and they're the ones who own the house. Poor Huffy."

"She's never been a *poor Huffy.* The girl's not a *sit back* kind of person, she's more of a *this is mine and I'm taking it* kind of gal."

"To the point where she'd knock off Bunny to make it happen?"

"Without blinking an eye, she would."

Donna leaned a little closer, even though no one else was around. "Just between us, I wouldn't be putting it past her to have planned the whole thing — the being pregnant, I mean. She's not getting any younger, and Dwight and that house of his are what she's wanted her whole life. And the other part to be thinking about is that the Captain himself must be in a state that things aren't going well for his little girl. Somebody needs to be paying for the situation. Dwight got her with child, lost the money and the house and has no way to take care of his Huffy the way she deserves."

Donna heaved a long sigh. "Wouldn't ya know it, we had this Bunny business figured out, we did, with Bourne being our man, and now I'm thinking Huffy or the captain himself coulda done the deed."

Or Speed or Smithy. Lake Shore turned back into Main Street, and Paddy stopped at the curb in front of the yacht club. "I'll drop off Ed's bike," I said to Donna as I wrestled the box out of the back of the carriage. "I can walk back to the shop from here."

Donna and Paddy faded down the street, and after convincing the dock master that even though I was a little rough-looking at the moment I was indeed here to make a delivery and not to abscond with a pricey boat, I dragged the box across the wood planks till I got to *Helen's Heaven,* a really fine sailboat if you liked sailboats. It was moored near the end and bobbing lazily with the lake swells.

I hated bobbing, swells or any up and down movement on the water. I was a *feet firmly on the ground* sort of girl who fervently believed that if God wanted us in or on the water we'd have gills.

I tore open the box and attached the pedals and seat to the really cool new folding bike that was perfect to store on a boat. My stomach rolled in time with the waves as I carried the bike onboard, then headed for home, the sun setting over Mission Point.

I checked in the few bikes we had rented, letting Rudy nurse his throbbing head, then closed up shop for the night. Miles Davis tunes drifted in from Marquette Park, but I was too beat to appreciate anything but a bath and sleep.

The next morning I added the final touches to the white trim as Fiona, complete with purple sequin hat, stopped her horse cart at the curb beside the bike shop. "Girl," she said as she climbed down, "every time I see you, you're a different color." She stepped closer. "Any fallout on our JB adventure?"

"That glass building we saw is in New York City. Maybe JB was hired to knock off you-know-who, and she figured it out and got a picture of him in the act and was blackmailing him."

"And I thought my putting out a special edition on the great Mackinaw Bridge walk was exciting."

"But I don't have any proof . . . yet. So, tell me about the walk."

"Every year they shut down the bridge and people walk across, unless it's too windy and walkers might get blown into the lake. It's been a tradition for as long as I can remember. The walk part, not the being blown into the lake part."

Fiona sighed, a smile tripping across her face. "Ya know, I'm glad I'm back here, I really am. I was bummed I was fired from the *Inside Scoop* — kind of embarrassing to get the ax from a second-rate rag. But now you're here and we've got suspects and bodies and talking motives."

"Huffy's dad threatened to throw me in the lake."

"Well, there you go. This place is great. Think I'll buy a new snowmobile for when the lake freezes over. Then we can buzz back and forth to the mainland."

"Snowmobiles?"

"NASCAR, Mackinac style." Fiona nodded at the Good Stuff. "That fudge Irma and I cooked up must be something. It's not even ten o'clock and there's a group of oldsters sitting on the rock wall, barefooted, scarfing chocolate fudge from there and giggling like preschoolers. There's even fudgies coming out of Doud's Market eating chips by the handful, bags from the Good Stuff swinging from their arms. And there's a line of customers waiting outside Irma's shop."

"With a guy strumming a guitar," I added as I closed the paint can and studied the scene. "Usually the only thing the senior set waits for around here is the early bird special over at the Yankee Rebel or the ferry. And why Irma's fudge? There's a bunch of them on the island. How much alcohol do you think Irma uses?"

Fiona gave me an *oh boy* look and we headed over to the Good Stuff. "Is the fudge here really that good that you're willing to queue up for it?" I asked a blue-haired woman with a straw purse waiting in line.

A woman in a tangerine orange jacket and white slacks looked me dead in the eyes. "Honey, I'm here to tell you that my arthritis has never been better than when I eat the Good Stuff. That there Bourbon Bombshell fudge is mighty tasty, I'll give you that, but it's the Herbal Euphoria fudge that's the best, and I'm keeping it all for myself and not sharing it with anyone, I don't care who they are."

Everyone nodded in agreement and a woman in a sun hat adorned with pink and purple straw flowers added, "Why, I haven't felt this good since a jar of white lightning got accidentally-on-purpose dumped in the church punch five Christmases ago. It's like I'm back in college again."

"It's better than Prozac for chasing the blues," a bald-headed man added, the guitar player now strumming "Like a Rolling Stone," with everyone swaying to the tune. Another guy took off his tie and fastened it across his forehead. The woman with the hat yanked off a big pink flower and stuck it in his headband.

Fiona and I looked from the happy guitarist to the people giggling on the rock wall to another group coming out of Doud's. Fiona sucked in a breath. "We got bags of Doritos, Cheetos and Fritos and a guy with a flower in his bandana playing the guitar."

"Herbal Euphoria?" I asked the bald-headed man.

"Gives you a terrible case of the munchies, but you sure do feel good."

Fiona grabbed my hand and held it tight. "Smithy's herbal butter, the munchies, giggling like kids and feeling really good?"

"Holy Chicago!"

25

"I'm going to strangle Smithy with my own two hands," Fiona growled as we pushed our way into Irma's shop, Fiona elbowing customers to the side, something she probably learned in getting the *Inside Scoop.* "Do you know what you're doing here?" Fiona asked Irma when we got to the marble-top table.

"Hello, dears. I'm selling fudge, lots and lots and lots of delicious fudge. Don't you just love the rainbow icing peace signs I drizzled across the top of this batch, and the little flowers in the middle? Isn't life won-der-ful, completely won-der-ful?" Irma was dressed in a flowered skirt with a pink geranium stuck in her hair and no shoes.

"Do you have any idea why everything is so wonderful?" I asked her.

"The fudge I'm making is won-der-ful; just ask anyone here." She touched Fiona's cheek and smiled. "I have so many wonder-ful customers buying my fudge and having fun. We're having lots and lots and lots of fun. Don't you love my skirt? I had it packed away in that box with my Lovelace books. No one even knows who she is. I think I'll get the books out and read them again. They are won-der-ful, just like my fudge."

"Look," Fiona said, a hint of sternness to her voice to try and get Irma's attention. "You can't do what you're doing, it's against the law — at least in this state it's against the law."

"What's against the law?" Rudy asked, shuffling out of the kitchen area. He had on shorts, sandals and a flowered shirt, with his hair pulled back into a . . . ponytail? Really? More peace signs decorated his cast, along with inscriptions like *We love you, man* and *Hang loose.*

Rudy gave Irma a peck on the cheek and put his arm around her. "We're over twenty-one; we're legal."

Irma tickled Rudy. "And some of the stuff you do should be against the law, you silver fox."

"What are *you* doing here?" I asked Rudy. "You're already in enough trouble."

"I'm making trail mix and helping Irma."

"Let me guess," Fiona said. "You're both

using the herb butter I got from my dear brother Smithy, whom I intend to beat to a pulp."

"Best stuff ever," Irma said, a silly grin tripping across her face. "Makes us even for you buying the peanut butter fudge over at Rita's." Irma kissed Fiona on the cheek. "You always were such a sweet girl. Maybe you can get more of that butter; business is booming. I bet Smithy's cooking up another batch right this minute."

Fiona gave me an *Oh dear God in heaven* look, and I said to Irma and Rudy, "You got to get rid of this . . . stuff — every bit of the Herbal Euphoria fudge. And the trail mix has got to go. If Fiona and I can figure this out, so can Nate, and he's going to come barging in here and have to arrest his own mother and you'll all be in jail braiding each other's hair and singing 'Kumbaya.' Do you get what I'm saying?"

"Throw it out, both the fudge and the mix?" Rudy wagged his head. "Everything? Why?"

"Into the lake it goes," Fiona said. "And you've got to do it immediately. Think of it this way: You'll make a lot of fish really, really happy."

"I don't get it," Irma said, her eyes dreamy.

"You lived the sixties," I said, trying to reason with them. "Bob Dylan, flowers, lava lamps . . . you're playing 'In-A-Gadda-Da-Vida' on a turntable, for God's sake! Doesn't this seem a little familiar? My guess is you both ordered beads and Birkenstocks online this morning, and Doud's is no doubt completely out of every kind of chip imaginable by now."

Rudy looked from me to the fudge, a hint of sanity returning. "Oh."

"Yeah, *oh*. Fiona and I have to get to Smithy before this goes any further. Promise me you'll shut down and clean this place out right now. And do not eat or sell any more fudge!"

Fiona and I ran for the door and climbed in her horse cart as Rudy started telling everyone the Good Stuff was shutting down for the day due to a family emergency . . . like the possibility of Irma winding up in the pokey stoned out of her gourd, with her son standing guard.

"If Smithy's brewing another batch, we got to stop him before Nate shows up," Fiona said. "If Smithy winds up in jail, the parents will totally blame me."

We did a fast trot past Trayser's Trading Post and Thunderbird Gifts. Fiona was the Tom Petty of the horse cart world. We passed Speed's bike shop with a banner saying the Speedsters were having carb night at Goodfellows. Well dang, I should learn to ride a bike just for the pasta. We cut up Astor to Market Street, and the blacksmith shop was just ahead.

"The double doors are open," Fiona said. "The blacksmith is in, probably lecturing a group of tourists. Just wait till he hears the lecture I'm going to give him."

Fiona pulled the cart to a stop and hopped out, with me following, trying to think of some way to keep Fiona from flattening her brother. She made her way to the front of the crowd and growled to Smithy, "We got to talk."

"I'm in the middle of a presentation."

"We need to talk *now,* brother dearest." She looked Smithy right in the eyes; his face was red and sweaty from the hot coals. "Butter."

Smithy dropped his hammer, his eyes now the size of goose eggs. "You know what happened to my butter?"

"It ain't pretty."

"That's all for today, folks," Smithy said to the crowd. "Everybody out. Come back tomorrow." He spread his arms wide, backing everyone through the doors and onto the front lawn. "We got a horseshoe emergency here. I gotta make a barn call."

Smithy came back into the barn and slammed the doors together, locked them then faced Fiona. "Where is it?"

"It wound up in fudge that is selling like all get-out over at Irma's."

"You took my herb butter?"

"How was I supposed to know it was that kind of herb! Now we have a bunch of toasted seniors wandering the streets and passing out flowers and flashing the peace sign. Chances are good they might start flashing something else."

"You really need to give it back."

"That's the whole point — it's gone, consumed, digested. I helped Irma with a new fudge recipe, and that butter was the new part and it's a really big hit. You got a nice side business going on here, way beyond growing oregano and sage. Bet you're making a killing with selling it off. How could you —"

"He's not selling off anything," Nurse Jane Porter said, coming down the steps from the loft, a bag of herbs in her hand. She sidled up close to Smithy and slid her arm through his. "This terrific guy is my hero; he's a hero to a lot of people around here."

"Let me guess," I said, stepping in since Fiona looked close to a stroke. "You two are the president and vice president of the island feel-good society?"

Jane Porter smiled up at Smithy. "You could say that. The butter is for two ladies on chemo, a man suffering from depression and another from MS. They got prescriptions for the stuff, but do you have any idea how expensive those prescriptions are? And it's not very good quality. I see these folks week in and week out struggling, and it just broke my heart. I knew Smithy had a garden and I asked him to help me to help them and we came up with a plan." Jane batted her eyes and sighed. "He's terrific."

"P . . . Prescription?" Fiona muttered.

"Sorry about pushing you out of the loft," Smithy said to me. "I couldn't have you blowing the whistle on us."

"I make *special* brownies once a week," Jane went on. "Evie saw Smithy that night at the Grand. He was making a delivery to a bartender with MS. With the busy jazz weekend, he couldn't get to the clinic."

Fiona sank down onto a little wood bench by the forge and looked from Jane to Smithy. "So you two are an item?"

"For almost a year; ever since we started this." Smithy winked at Jane. "We both had bad breakups, so we kept our relationship to ourselves. And I have a daughter to consider. We wanted to make sure this was the real thing before we let the cat out of the bag."

"But I'm your sister."

"And you're a reporter."

"And you didn't kill Bunny?" I added.

Smithy looked confused. "I thought Rudy did her in — not that I blame the man." Smithy hugged Jane. "Constance and I probably would have muddled through our marriage and been unhappy for years. Thanks to Bunny being Bunny, we didn't. She did me a favor; probably the only favor she's ever done in years, even if she didn't mean to."

"Listen to me," Fiona said, wagging her finger big-sister-style. "You guys really need to lock up the butter and get it to a better hiding place."

"Better hiding place for what?" Sutter asked, coming in through the side door, the screen slamming shut behind him and Jane standing right there with a bag of *prescription* in her hand.

Fiona and I exchanged *uh-oh* looks, and I stepped between Sutter and Jane, saying, "Smithy's dried blueberries are so amazing that everyone on the island's going to be wanting some, and they might even steal them, so he better hide them."

Once again proving beyond all doubt that I sucked at lying.

"I think you're all crazy." Sutter sighed, then turned his attention to me. "But right now I don't care. I've been looking all over for you."

"Me?" I sighed. "Why?" There was getting to be a long list of *whys,* and at this particular moment I had Angelo's lock-picking set in my back pocket so I could return it to him.

"There's a woman over at the station," Sutter said. "She won't talk to anyone, won't even give me her name, but she insists on talking to you, and she's . . ."

"What?"

"Rich, demanding, obnoxious, a pain in the ass even worse than you — hard to imagine." Sutter rocked back on his heels. "So which bluffie did you tick off now, Chicago, to get someone like this in your life?"

Lately that covered a lot of territory. "Let's go," I said, grateful for a reason to get Sutter out of the barn. I followed him to the side door and glanced back at Fiona giving me the *okay* sign.

The police station was close, so Sutter wouldn't encounter many seniors off in la-la land. I figured if I could keep him occupied for a few more hours with this woman, the whole island would slowly shift back to reality. No matter who this bluffie was or how obnoxious or snotty, she was a blessing. I followed Sutter into the station, past Molly the desk clerk, her eyes round and terrified, then to his office door, which he opened to reveal . . .

"Mother?"

26

"What are you doing here?" I asked Mother from the doorway of Sutter's office. "You're in Paris . . . Eiffel Tower, Notre Dame, crepes."

"Well obviously I'm not in Paris, Evie." Mother straightened her pink scarf and smoothed her white linen skirt, which would be a pile of wrinkles on anyone else but would not dare do such a thing on Ann Louise Bloomfield. "And I am sure there's a very logical explanation as to why you're painted white?"

"I was helping a friend with some repairs, and where's Father?"

"Last I saw of the man he'd taken up with a twenty-something topless dancer from the Lido and was drinking wine, eating cheese and sketching nudes in a studio apartment on the Left Bank."

"You . . . are so funny?" I said hopefully.

"Evie, as you know, I am never funny, and

I have flown for twelve hours to get here. I couldn't face your siblings at the moment. They don't understand things that are not perfect, and for you, it's simply a way of life. And I need to have the right spin on this situation before I get back to Chicago. People will talk."

Mother stood. "Now where should I have my luggage sent? The hotels and bed and breakfasts are full due to some holiday they seem to be having. I'll stay with you. I trust you're up at the Grand Hotel? I do hope you insisted on a decent room with a view."

"I'm staying with a friend in a room over his bicycle shop."

Mother let out *the* Mother sigh. "Of course you are. I'd forgotten I wasn't traveling with Lindsey and Trevor. I suppose *Over His Bicycle Shop* is a quaint boutique B and B. We'll just have to make do."

She held out her hand to Sutter. "Since my daughter has lost all sense of decorum, I am Ann Louise Bloomfield. I take it you are Bernie Fletcher, since that is the name on this little plastic plaque on the desk. You need a cleaning lady; the place is filthy."

Sutter took Mother's hand. "Actually, my name is —"

"It doesn't matter," Mother said, making her way toward the door. I followed her,

313

mouthing *I'm sorry* to Sutter, who was enjoying this a lot more than I was. I mouthed *I'm sorry* to Molly, who looked close to tears, and to the taxi driver Mother paid to retrieve her luggage, along with a dissertation on how to not steal anything.

"You must be hungry," I said to Mother as we headed for Main Street, trying to think of something to keep her busy. "The Yankee Rebel is just around the corner and has great fish."

"I'd rather nap. I can have luncheon sent up to the room."

"How long do you plan on being here?" I tried not to whimper. "You have a law practice and clients and —"

"A few weeks. I should have some things sent over from Chicago."

"There you are," Angelo said to me as he hurried out of Little Luxuries, two bottles of wine nestled in a bag. "I need my —"

"Later would be better," I said to Angelo in a rush. "This is my mother — my Chicago attorney mother." I hitched my head toward Mother, hoping Angelo would get the message that I couldn't exactly whip out the locksmith tools right in front of her and hand them back.

"Is that right?" Angelo stilled, a slow smile sliding across his face and brightening his eyes. "*This* is your mother? I would have expected someone covered in paint."

Mother laughed, and Angelo's smiled widened. What the —

"I have a bunch of lawyer friends back in Detroit," Angelo continued. "In fact, our family business couldn't survive without them — there's always trouble — but none of 'em are as pretty as you." Angelo gave Mother an appreciative once-over. "Va-va-voom. Enchanté, mademoiselle."

Va-va-voom followed by really bad French? I waited for Mother to take out her American Express platinum card and stab him through the heart with it.

But she didn't. Instead, she extended her hand and blushed; at least, I thought it was a blush. Mother never blushed, so it was hard to tell for sure.

"I am delighted to meet you," she said in a pleasant voice that I'd never heard.

"Can I take you to dinner tomorrow evening?" Angelo offered. "I know this is sudden, but I've just moved here to the island. You and I can explore this place together. Could be fun."

"Fun." Mother's eyes softened. "Yes, I think *fun* would be perfect."

Okay, in my whole entire life I never remembered Mother using the F-word. The mob boss and the lawyer? Stabbing Angelo with the card would have been better. "I'll take you to dinner, Mother," I blurted.

"I already have plans with . . ."

"Angelo."

"Angelo," Mother repeated kind of breathily. "An enchanting gentleman from Detroit. My friends call me Carmen."

"Who the heck's —" A swift kick to my ankle shut me up. *Ouch!*

"Seven o'clock at the Woods, Carmen? One of the taxis will take you there. I look forward to our evening together." Angelo kissed the back of Mother's hand and strolled off, Mother glowing, Angelo humming, and my brain in meltdown.

"About Angelo," I started. "He's —"

"Just what I need."

"Oh, trust me, I really don't think so. You have no idea what you're getting into."

"Evie." Mother grabbed my shoulders and peered at me through lowered eyelids. "Your father's taken up with a French harlot and is painting nudes. I am now Carmen; not a word of this gets back to Lindsey, Trevor or your grandfather or you're out of the will; and I need to go shopping for something with black lace."

Before I could get my brain to function after the black lace comment, Mother was

316

halfway down the next block. I should let her know that the best shopping for evening wear might be up at the Grand Hotel or Mission Point, but telling Ann Louise Bloomfield, aka Carmen, where to shop was like telling Martha Stewart how to bake cookies.

"I've got a problem," I said to Rudy when I walked into Rudy's Rides. He still had on his flowered shirt, but his hair was no longer ponytailed and he had on a shoe. Yes, island life was shifting back into normalcy. He was fixing a bike at the workbench. "It's been a day of problems."

He winked at me. "The fish are now happy, so that particular dilemma is taken care of, and Irma made up your bed for your mother and you can sleep on the pull-out couch in the TV room down here."

"How did you know about Mother?"

"The fudge vine. It's the island grapevine dipped in chocolate. Heard she has a date tomorrow with that mobster guy up on the bluff who took over Bunny's house."

Rudy stopped working on the bike. "You should know that I might be spending some time with Irma. I'm just telling you so you don't wonder where I am. We figure the way things are going with the Bunny Festival, we may not have much time left." Rudy's smile slipped a notch. "To think we lived next door all these years, and when we finally get together . . ."

"Hey, you can't give up on me," I said, a lump in my throat. "Thanks for helping with Mother."

"Thanks for trying to save my behind. You've outdone yourself, and somehow I don't think it was all for a promotion. We're good friends, Evie Bloomfield."

I bit my bottom lip, that lump in my throat getting bigger.

"Maybe you can paint up a few bikes so the place looks a little more *country vintage* instead of *old and depressed* for your mom. Think I'll go see what Irma's up to while I still can."

Rudy hobbled off, his gait a little slower, his back not quite so straight, sadness sitting in my gut like a rock. I rooted around under the workbench and found the paints Rudy used for bike touch-ups but instead of making the whole bike one color, I painted swirls of blue hydrangeas with yellow centers, long stems, big green leaves and white butterflies. Hey, I could vintage with the best of 'em, and I needed some cheer at the moment.

I added a clear coat of polycrylic to set the paint so it wouldn't run or wear off.

Not exactly Rembrandt, but better than primer red, and it gave a shabby-chic feel to the shop. I got pink potted geraniums from Doud's, put them in the basket attached to the front and parked the bike on the sidewalk.

"Looks good," Ed said, pulling up beside me as evening settled over the island.

"Yeah, but what if it's too late to make a difference and it's all for nothing? Rudy's over at Irma's place if you want to see him."

Ed stepped closer. "I came to see you. I've got a lead. Remember those pictures I bought at Dwight's yard sale of Bunny and our local celebrity? Well, they're gone. I had them on the dining room table at my place and they disappeared. There's something going on with Bunny and Speed, and it's not just cutting grass and nostalgia. I'm going to talk to him. I know he took those pictures and I want to know why."

"He won't admit anything, but I think it has something to do with when he was young — maybe something that Bunny had on him, and that if it got out it could hurt his fund-raising?"

Face pinched with worry, Ed raked back his graying hair. "We need to take it to Sutter. We're running out of time, and I'm going to lose my best friend. If we just plant a seed of doubt, maybe Sutter will let Rudy off the hook. I hate this more than you know. How could this happen?"

"Unless we have proof, Sutter's not going to listen. He knows we're both on Rudy's side. Let me poke around; I'm getting pretty good at it."

"Is that bike for rent?" a woman in khaki shorts asked as she came up the sidewalk. "I have a garden party luncheon tomorrow, and if I pedaled up on this and a hat I have that matches, it would make a big splash. Bet I could even make the front page of the *Crier.* Always wanted to do that."

Big splash, Ed mouthed, giving me a thumbs-up. He might be retired, but he sure knew his advertising stuff. Best promotion is word of mouth.

"You can rent the bike for free," I said. "Just tell everyone you got it here at Rudy's Rides."

The woman toed up the kickstand. "I can do that. Got any bikes in roses or lilacs? A lilac bike would be a great hit at the Lilac Festival. I'm not looking to win races; I want something fun to ride while I'm here, something I don't have at home. And my sister's into cooking, so she'd love a bike with that theme."

"I can do that," I gushed. "Just give me a day."

The woman pedaled off, and Ed patted me on the back. "How good are you at painting roses and pots and pans?"

By six I had three rose bikes, a chef bike with mixing bowls, aprons and the like, a jazz bike with notes and instruments and song titles, and a smaller bike done up as Batman. Mother sauntered into the shop all smiles. I had no idea what to do with all smiles, since it had never happened before.

"What do you think about this little number?" Mother said, holding up a black dress with red lace that looked way more Carmen than Ann Louise ever did.

"Mother, how many Manhattans had you had when you picked that out?"

"If you must know, three, and I got these shoes." She opened the box. "I've never had red satin shoes with rhinestones."

And there's a reason.

"I got something to eat at a place called the Mustang Lounge. Did you know they have a yellow propeller on the wall, I guess in case someone needs an extra, and they have great fried green beans and they play euchre. Haven't played since college. Won ten bucks and two beers."

"You're hustling the locals?"

"Did I mention the three Manhattans, and hey, they started it — I just finished it. Never mess with a woman wearing Chanel. I'm going to lie down, they wore me out. Oh, and Evie dear, what happens here stays here." Mother thought about that for a second. "Or maybe not. Maybe it's time that Carmen visits Chicago."

Like Chicago didn't have enough problems. Was it something in the water? A full moon? People take a ten-minute ferry ride, land here and their inner crazy comes out.

Five people wanted to rent the rose bikes for tomorrow, meaning I had to paint more, and four wanted dibs on the jazz bike, and the chef bike got rented for the whole weekend. I promised Lily Harmon I'd paint her a Barbie bike and promised her mother I'd tone down the pointy boobs.

I checked on my own mother, who was sprawled across the bed upstairs, head drooped off one side, feet dangling over the other. I grabbed a shower, then started off for SeeFar to return Angelo's lock-picking tools as a Speedster zoomed by, probably heading for the great carb pig-out down at Goodfellows. I agreed with Ed that there was something going on with Speed and Bunny. Ed's pictures missing off his dining room table underscored the fact even more.

So why would Speed take them? What was the big deal about him and Bunny and his bike?

I still had the lock-picking tools and Speed was not home for dinner. I told Ed I'd poke around, and now was as good a time as any. And I was so out of time.

A damp chill hung over the island, night closing in. I passed Trayser's Trading Post and Thunderbird Gifts, both shut up tight, and I took the side alley by the Speed Shop. It was dark inside except for a blue neon bicycle glowing over the checkout desk. Outside stairs led up to the apartment. Flashlight clamped between my teeth, I slid the hook thing, then the pick, into the lock.

"What are you doing here?" Mother's voice said from behind me.

"Yikes!" I flipped the tools in the air and spun around, my heart in my stomach. "What are *you* doing here?"

"Thought you might be going out for a drink and I was starting to sober up and I really wasn't ready for that yet, so I thought I'd follow along. What's this all about?"

Subtracting ten years from my life and giving me a heart attack? "Would you believe I forgot my key to my boyfriend's place?"

"Worst liar ever." Mother snatched the lock pick and wrench thing off the stoop, and I waited for all hell to break loose. "Well?" she asked.

"Well what?"

"Well, move aside so we can get in, unless you like standing out here in the rain where people can see us." Mother fiddled with the lock.

"You . . . You know how to do this?"

"Had a client accused of industrial espionage a few years ago and we had time to kill while waiting for the jury to come back."

"How'd it go?"

"He got off, and you should see me with a deadbolt."

27

The lock sprang open. "Piece of cake." She looked me in the eyes. "You want to tell me why we're doing this?"

"The guy who owns Rudy's Rides is accused of murder and he didn't do it and this guy might have."

"Got it." She turned the doorknob and I put my hand over hers.

"Wait a minute. Just like that you believe me? We could go to jail, you know."

"Evie, we are not going to jail. I'm an attorney; a good one. Of course I believe you, you're my daughter, and like I just said, you're the worst liar ever. So what are we looking for?" Mother asked as we went inside, my flashlight aimed at the floor and showing the way.

"He owns the cycle shop below and he wants to take over Rudy's place 'cause it's a better location and to cut out the competition. He and the person murdered were once friends, then enemies. Knocking her off and framing Rudy takes care of both problems. Plus, he's a dick."

The flashlight picked out a bedroom in the back, a kitchen to the side, a leather couch, two matching chairs, a flat-screen TV and a closed laptop on a desk. Mother parked herself at the desk. "A friend who becomes an enemy is all about betrayal. She's the one dead, so either she did something to him or she *could* do something to him. Since you don't know what it is, that means we're looking for a secret, and if you think he's the killer, it's a big secret. Intelligent people don't kill unless they have to."

"That's brilliant."

Mother fluffed her hair. "They don't pay me the big bucks for nothing, chickie." She gave a lopsided grin. "Did I really call you chickie? Must have been the Carmen in me sneaking out." Mother opened the laptop.

"Probably password-protected," I offered.

"Busy people don't shut down their computers when they're working; takes too much time to fire them back up. And unless you're the CIA or that Bieber kid, no one really cares what you're doing." She hit the space bar to bring the computer to life, and a calendar of events popped up.

"Your guy's a hard worker; lots of speaking engagements, appearances, and luncheons from one end of Michigan to the other. I'd hire him." She clicked on a folder marked *finances.*

"I know some of these people. They're investing in the Speed Challenge?"

"It's all about cycle racing in Michigan. Speed intends to make the headquarters on the island. I think that's because there's a lot of money here and Speed spent summers here."

"Okay, so this woman knew him when he was young, they were friendly and maybe shared confidences." Mother tapped her finger against her lips. "My best guess is she had him by the shorthairs for some youthful indiscretion and was probably blackmailing him. If this secret got out, it would ruin his fund-raising." Mother clicked back to the calendar, then closed the computer. "No wonder she's dead."

"He stole some photos of them together, and a news article too. They might be here, but I don't know if it means anything."

"If they've gone missing, it's important. Thing's don't just disappear unless they've got a reason to." Mother headed for the bedroom. "I'll take the dresser; you take the closet."

"He's got more shoes than you do," I offered, stepping over three shoe trees.

"If you come across red satin ones, we've got our secret. He has some really expensive briefs here. Nice tushy?"

"Women drool."

"Good to know."

There was a lot more Carmen in Mother than I had ever imagined. "Look at this," I said, dragging the framed *Sports Illustrated* picture from the back of Speed's closet. "Speed got this thing as an award just the other night, and here it is buried in the back of his closet."

Mother parked her hands on hips and stared at the picture. "It's the Tour of Texas, and he won. I'm guessing it's a big deal since it's in *SI.*"

"Why hide it in the closet?"

"Why indeed. We should get out of here."

"The local police might get cranky?"

"If this Speed guy is the killer, two more bodies won't make a hill of beans worth of difference." Mother watched as I slid the picture back in the closet. "So what's with you and this cop?" she asked as I made sure Speed's shoes were neat and tidy like I found them. "I get the feeling he's a little more hard-boiled than your average island officer."

"He's from Detroit, and we drive each

other nuts."

Mother laughed as we headed out. "In more ways than one, from what I see."

"Mother, he's old."

"What, forty-something, I'm guessing? One foot in the grave to be sure."

I locked the door and we crept down the steps, the rain falling harder, streetlights and shop lights reflecting off the wet pavement and sidewalks, fog rolling in off the lake. Mother zipped her black fleece and I realized it was just like the one I had on except hers was newer and accented with a terrific pink scarf she'd probably picked up on the Champs-Élysées. She'd cut her hair and lightened it, and with us being nearly the same size, looking at Mother was looking at myself twenty-five years from now. Lucky me.

"What's this?" Mother asked, taking down a note tacked to the front door of Rudy's. *"Arnold's dock. 9. Donna,"* she read aloud. "Don't you text around here?"

"Cell phone service is tricky, and with the rain, it's worse. Donna is Irish Donna, and she probably needs help . . . loading bags of flour. She owns the Blarney Scone up on Market Street, the pastries are terrific, we'll go there for breakfast tomorrow, you'll love it."

I was babbling, but I sure wasn't about to tell Mother we had a local hit man and that he was also a murder suspect and could very well be making a run for it. Donna knew him better than anyone else. As a distraction from my latest attempt at lying that probably sucked, I pulled out the gold shamrock hanging around my neck. "Donna lent me this to ward off a black cloud that she says is causing all my problems."

"She sounds like a good friend, and I guess the cloud is one explanation why Timmy-boy ran off with my World Series tickets. It's almost nine, dear; we should go."

Mother started off, and I blocked her path. "*Your* World Series tickets?"

"*The* tickets, just *the* tickets. It's late, I'm tired, slip of the tongue, and —"

"What did you do, Mother?"

She let out a deep breath and gave me the *guilty as charged* shoulder roll, just like the time I'd caught her red-handed hiding a package of Oreos behind the ficus plant when I was ten. I had the feeling this was a little more serious.

"All right, all right," she said. "You'll find out sooner or later anyway. I made it look like Tim won those tickets."

"You set him up?"

"And he took the bait. End of story. We're running short on time, dear, and shut your mouth before something flies in and makes a home."

"You sabotaged my wedding?"

"Altered it a little." Mother took the scarf from her jacket and wrapped it around my neck. She kissed me on the forehead. "Tim Whitlock is a jerk — always was, always will be — and not near good enough for you, though you certainly weren't hearing any of it six months ago. Now let's help your friend, though I'm sure it has nothing to do with picking up flour. We need to get a move on now."

"You sabotaged my wedding?"

"One day you'll thank me." She grabbed my hand. "It's almost nine."

"But I loved my wedding dress. It had a train. I lost ten pounds to get into that thing."

"It was all lovely, dear, except for the groom, and once we knew he wasn't showing up, we did enjoy ourselves ever so much more. The band was amazing."

"I . . . I don't remember."

"Two shots of Jack Daniel's and a half bottle of champagne will do that to a body, but we have pictures, the raspberry swirl cheesecake was divine, now let's step on it, there's a killer out there."

"Why do you care so much about this killer?"

"Because you care, and finding the bad guy beats sitting home alone licking my wounds from Peter Bloomfield kicking me to the curb for a two-bit French floozy with no shirt, big boobs and feathers stuck in her hair and pasted to her firm little bottom."

By the time we got to the docks, I was still upset about the wedding, but now mostly because I felt bad that Mother'd had to rescue me and that I couldn't remember the cheesecake. The rain had slowed to a drizzle, a golden halo of water droplets surrounding the dock lights. A foghorn moaned out in the harbor.

"Do you see Donna?" Mother asked me, the big white ferryboat gliding toward us out of a thick bank of clouds, engines doing the slow reverse growl to bring it to a stop. All hands stood alert on deck to toss lines, lower the gangplank and usher fudgies on and off so nobody fell in the drink. The procession of weary tourists shuffled down the wharf, floating in and out of the misty swirls. A group of laughing partiers ran full-tilt to make the last ferry of the night.

"I don't see her anywhere," I said to Mother, stepping out of line to get a better look at the crowd, a dockworker giving me the evil eye to get back where I belonged. "She has red hair and is probably wearing her long green coat tonight. I'll take the front; you check the back." I stood on my tiptoes and leaned to the side to get a glimpse of either Donna or Bourne at the front of the line. Something was up, I could feel it and — *"Yikes!"*

I was airborne over the water, arms flailing, feet searching for the dock, and the ferry . . . the really big ferry . . . coming right at me. "Help!"

The cold closed over me, the weight of my clothes pushing me down, down, down into the blackness, some part of my brain screaming, *Swim, Evie, swim.* Then I went up, up, up — and up never felt so good. In a split second I was on the surface, choking and spluttering and gasping for air. A beefy guy with lights blinking on his orange life vest bobbed beside me and slid an orange ring buoy under my arms.

"Don't move," he ordered as walls of white gracefully slid over us, closing out the dock lights. Holy Saint Patrick, it was the boat passing over us, then it stopped.

"Hold on to me and the ring," Beefy said, and he didn't have to ask twice. In a few strokes we were in front of the ferry, a ladder was lowered over the edge of the dock and Beefy was pushing on my butt as hands reached out to haul me up over the edge.

I sprawled facedown on the dock and kissed it. Last time I kissed something around here it was the ground when I got off the horse. In my other life back in Chicago I mostly kissed chocolate cupcakes and occasionally other people.

"Dear God, Evie. Are you okay?" Mother panted, kneeling beside me, her face white against the darkness. She swiped my hair from my cheek. "Say something."

"Crap."

Mother laughed, but it sounded part sob. "You screamed and you were gone and this gentleman went in the water after you. What happened?"

"Pushed."

"That's what everyone says," the wet, beefy guy grumped, towering over me and dripping. He draped a blanket across me, then jabbed his finger at the yellow line on the dock. "You crossed it; I remember your pink scarf. You're not the first drunk fudgie to take a late-night swan dive. Lucky for you we're running the cat tonight and it just slid right over the top."

"Cat?" Mother asked, helping me to sit.

"Catamaran. Two-side hulls. A regular

334

boat would have just run right over you. Go home, get dry, stay the heck off our docks and don't get drunk."

"Not drunk. Pushed." And this was the second time since I'd gotten to this place. At least I now knew who pushed me the first time and why.

I wobbled to my feet with Mother's help and I hugged Beefy, wet clothes and all. "Thank you for saving my ass."

He gave me a sly grin. "Nice ass to save — but don't do it again. You were lucky this time."

Mother gave Beefy another hug, in case he didn't get how appreciative we were. She put her arm around me, and we squished our way up the dock.

"I really was pushed," I said to Mother.

"I know you were, dear. Your friend Donna was not on that dock tonight, meaning someone had plans for us, and not nice ones."

Us? I looked at the dripping pink scarf around my neck and thought of what the dockworker said about remembering me and remembering the scarf. The thing is, this wasn't my scarf, it was Mother's scarf; her obviously expensive lovely pink silk scarf that anyone would notice. A shiver snaked up my spine, going clear through to my bones, but I wasn't cold now — I was gut-crampingly, heart-poundingly furious.

"You know how to get back to Rudy's shop on your own, right? It's just a block away."

Eyes huge, Mother stopped in the middle of the sidewalk. "What do you mean *on my own;* you can't go someplace right now? You have to go home and get a hot shower and . . . and be safe. You're soaking wet, you need to change, you're freezing and you're shaking. I'm shaking."

"I need to talk to someone."

"Evie."

I kissed Mother on the cheek. "I'll be back in five minutes. Ten, tops. Rudy keeps decent bourbon in the kitchen cabinet. Drink it."

28

Soaked to the bone, I banged on the back door of Sutter's house, and if he didn't answer in one more second, I'd break a blasted window, climb through and beat him to a pulp till he listened to me. I banged again.

"What?" Sutter growled when he opened the door, eyes widening as he took me in. "What happened now?"

I grabbed the front of his shirt with both hands. "The killer, the *real* one, tried to murder my mother tonight. *My mother!*" I punched Sutter's chest to get his attention and because I needed to punch something and he was handy.

"They pushed me off Arnold's pier thinking it was her." I yanked at the soaked pink scarf. "If they thought going after my mother would get me to back off looking for them, they were wrong . . . dead wrong. I started tracking Bunny's killer to save my job, but it's gone way beyond that. Rudy's being framed, my mother's in danger and I'm pissed." I punched his chest again. "Really, really, really pissed."

I turned to leave and Sutter grabbed my arm. "Don't do anything stupid, Chicago. I'll look into this."

I tried to yank my arm away, but Sutter held fast. "I mean it."

"Dutchy played your mother, took advantage of her being alone, stole her fudge recipes and is driving her out of business."

His lips thinned, jaw tightening, a steely, cold look in his eyes.

"There it is. Now you get it."

"Are you okay?"

"No, I'm not okay. I'm going to leave here, have a good cry on the way home then help finish off a bottle of Jim Beam. I've got plenty of practice with both."

"There's a lot more going on here than getting rid of Bunny because she was a pain in the butt."

"The one thing we agree on."

Sutter stilled for a second, the only sound in the kitchen my ragged breathing and the eerie foghorn echoing over the island. Sutter tucked a strand of straggly hair behind my left ear, his fingers lingering at my neck, his touch warm and steady, and I really needed warm and steady right now. My toes curled into my soggy shoes.

"You sure you're okay?"

"Terrific, and I'm going to stay terrific, and the next time I have raspberry swirl cheesecake I'm going to remember it." I pulled my arm free and ran out the door.

When I got back to Rudy's, I grabbed a hot shower and met mother in her jammies at the kitchen table. I take that back — Mother had loungewear. I had jammie pants and a Chicago Cubs T-shirt that I gave to Timmy-boy, then took back when I moved out of our love nest. Mother passed me a glass of bourbon. "How's Nate Sutter?"

"How'd you know I went to see him?"

"He's a cop, he thinks Rudy's guilty and now you have proof that he's not. What did he say?"

I tossed back the bourbon, choking and coughing as it burned a path down my throat. "That he'd look into it," I wheezed. "How are you doing?"

Mother added more Jim Beam to my glass, then clinked hers against it. "The cats and I are bonding."

I took Mother's hand across the table and looked into her steady, intelligent, caring brown eyes. "You were the target of my late-night swim off the docks. Someone thought

I was you. I had on your scarf, the one you wore around town all day. You need to be on the first ferry out of here in the morning."

"That is so sweet." Mother's eyes weren't quite focusing.

"I'm not sweet; I'm trying to keep you alive. Trevor and Lindsey will bury me in the backyard if something happens to you."

"First of all, dear, Carmen bought a really slutty dress and shoes today and she has a hot date with an even hotter Italian."

"Mother, this is serious."

"And I've got a rendezvous in the Woods. Been a long time since I had one of those. And I'm definitely not leaving you here alone with a killer on the loose."

"He might come after you again."

"He won't, dear, that's the whole point." Mother held my hand a little tighter, her eyes dark, serious and completely sober. "You're the target now, not me."

Penny, knock, knock, knock jarred me awake at seven and, considering I hadn't fallen asleep till five, this promised to be a really long day. The slow, steady *clop, clop, clop* of the taxis and drays drifted in from the street and, except for Bambino and Cleveland purring on my back, there was no other sound. No cars squealing to a stop, no motorcycles, no ambulance, no sirens, no growling buses, no trains to rattle the windowpanes.

After a day of *husband does the hussy* and *daughter in the drink,* Mother needed to sleep in. I pulled on jeans and a sweatshirt, did the hair and teeth thing, fed the cats and started coffee. I sat at the little kitchen table, watching morning come to Mackinac and trying to figure out what demonic cretin had pushed me in the water. There was something I wasn't getting, and it was right in front of me. Heck, it had to be right in front of me — the island wasn't that big.

I opened the double doors to Rudy's Rides to start the day and noticed lights on in the back of the Good Stuff. If the killer went after Mother, he might have Rudy or even Irma on the list too.

I peeked in the back window to make sure I wasn't interrupting. Fudge simmered on the stove, ringlets of steam trailing off into the room. A yellow coffeepot and a plate of bagels and strawberries sat on the little table, but Rudy and Irma weren't staring adoringly into each other's eyes. They were staring at the murder board that was really the murder cupboard that Irma started a few days ago.

"Really? A mustache on Bunny?" I said as I walked in, the aroma of rich chocolate laced with whiskey washing over me.

"She had it coming." Rudy poured another cup of coffee and handed it over. "Heard you took a late-night swim."

"Those docks can be tricky," Irma chimed in. "Especially in the fog. Last year a half-tanked fudgie rode a bike right off the end of the pier. When they fished him out, he was still pedaling and wanting to know which way to the Grand. Why were you on the docks at that time of night?"

"Got a note from Irish Donna that wasn't from Irish Donna and I was pushed off that dock," I said, studying the suspect side of the cupboard. "I'm getting close if the killer's coming after me."

Munching a strawberry, I went over to facial-hair Bunny tacked to one side and the usual suspects on the other, with yellow flowered dishes, cups and saucers on the cupboard shelves in between.

"I know Smithy's out — he's got more important things going on right now." I took down Smithy's picture. "So who gets your vote? Huffy, Dwight, Speed or Jason Bourne?" I turned back to Irma and Rudy, both of them staring at me wide-eyed, mouths gaping. "What?"

"Pushed?" Rudy shook his head. "Again? How does this keep happening? The good news is Sutter's got to see once and for all I'm not the killer."

"If it were only that simple," Nate said, coming through the back door.

Nate kissed his mother on the cheek, but he didn't look happy. He didn't look much of anything — he had on his cop face, and the cop face was never good news. "Mira Brindle was watching in that telescope of hers, the one Herman got to keep an eye on Jeannette Holloway's bedroom. She saw you cut the cable on Bunny's bike. She wasn't going to say anything because she didn't like Bunny and she does like Rudy, but Helen Levine convinced her she had to, seems they belong to the garden club and got to talking. You need to come with me to the police station," Nate said to Rudy. "I won't make a formal arrest till Tuesday so the fudgies don't leave and the business community doesn't go ballistic and stick my head on a spear outside the fort. But I can't have a known killer walking the streets."

"Except that's exactly what you *are* doing," Irma said, spreading her hands wide. "The real killer's still out there, Nate."

"And you can't for one minute think Rudy pushed me in the water last night," I added,

343

trickles of fear and frustration crawling up my spine.

Sutter folded his arms, looking every inch the unwavering cop. "Your late-night dip and Bunny being dead aren't necessarily related. Rudy got fed up with Bunny trying to close him down and her antics with the town council. Someone else got fed up with you sticking your nose where it doesn't belong."

"A lot of people wanted Bunny dead," I tried to reason. "Why can't you see that and . . . and I'm going to tell my mother on you, Nate Sutter, then you'll be sorry." Did that sound as bad as I think it did?

Nate gave me a half smile. "I gotta say I haven't heard that one in a while."

"My mother's an attorney, a good one. She can fix this."

Rudy put his arm around me and sat me down in a chair. "I don't see us getting out of this one, Evie Bloomfield. We've had one foot on a banana peel all along and now there's Mira. Helen never did like me and Ed being friends. I'm sure she was happy as a pig in clover when she heard Mira's story. I want you to have Rudy's Rides if things go bad. If we make it through this somehow, we're partners. You're onto something with painting the bikes the way you do, and I bet

344

you're happier here than working for Abigail. You tried so hard to find the killer and help me, it's the least I can do."

"I can't even ride a bike." My voice cracked.

Rudy kissed me on top of my head. "You don't have to ride 'em, Chicago, just rent 'em. And you know advertising. You're good at it even if my daughter's too thick-headed to see it."

"It's going to be okay, Rudy," I said, trying to keep the panic out of my voice as he and Irma followed Sutter out the door. "We'll find the killer, I swear we will, this isn't over."

Nate let the two go on ahead, then looked back to me. "Keep out of this, Chicago."

"Eat dirt and die, Detroit." I slammed the door in Sutter's face and kicked a chair across the kitchen. How could things go from happy to harrowing in under a minute?

I doused the fire under the fudge cooking on the stove then cut across the backyard to the bike shop. I was mad and disgusted and frustrated and had the overwhelming need to break something. Since Sutter wasn't around to tear limb from limb and that stupid broken step was right in front of me, I kicked it. Cussing a blue streak, I yanked and pulled on it till the darn thing finally broke loose, sending me sprawling flat on my butt. I picked up the pieces to toss in the garbage, my gaze zeroing in on the break that wasn't a break, least not all the way. It was sawed through from underneath. No wonder Rudy broke his leg — whoever put this step on used bad wood or . . . or someone wanted Rudy to break his leg and sawed the step on purpose. That was nuts. Who'd want to do a thing like that? Why would they want Rudy laid up?

I walked through the kitchen, told Cleveland and Bambino not to panic, and took the stairs. "Mother, wake up," I said, plopping down on the side of her bed. "I have a problem."

She bolted straight up. "You're pregnant? Wonderful!" She hugged me tight. "I knew there was something going on with you and Nate Sutter. I wanna be called Nana. Nana Carmen. I love it."

"Forget Sutter and not that kind of problem and where the heck did this *Nana* thing come from?"

Mother dove under her pillow. "If it's not good news, it's bad news. Don't admit to anything and call me in the morning."

"It is morning and there's an eyewitness who says Rudy's the killer."

Mother peeked out. "What kind of eyewitness?"

"A woman with a telescope."

Mother sat up again and finger-combed her hair, her eyes clearing. "Telescope means a career busybody, the worst kind. Gossip is their life, and they usually get it right on who's doing what. Where's Rudy now?"

"Police station. Sutter just picked him up. Rudy gave me Rudy's Rides if he goes to jail, and we're partners if he gets out. I can't believe this is happening — he didn't kill Bunny. He's got to get out. What should we do other than beat up Nate Sutter?"

"You stay here. I don't want you going after Sutter on his home turf or I'll have two clients behind bars. I don't have a Michigan license to practice law, but I can ask the right questions, irritate the heck out of everyone and maybe get Rudy released just to get rid of me. Or maybe we should leave Rudy where he is; look what happened to you last night. Rudy could be in danger. Who found this eyewitness, anyway?"

"Someone who doesn't like Rudy."

"That's interesting. Why are we just hearing about this now?"

Mother was cleaned, pressed, fed and out the door in under thirty minutes. As I got the shop ready for business, Irish Donna came in. "Blessed be Saint Patrick, I hear that me shamrock's working overtime just keeping you sucking air."

"By any chance, you didn't leave a note to meet at the docks last night, did you?"

"And be missing *America's Got Talent*? Can't even imagine such a thing."

"Well, Sutter's got Rudy over at the police station and there's an eyewitness who saw him cut Bunny's brake cable. What the heck's going on?"

Not looking one bit surprised, Donna leaned against the pool table and let out an audible sigh. "Mira just couldn't be keeping her mouth shut, could she? I told her she must be mistaken, but she said she saw Rudy right there under the streetlight big as you please. He's a man hard to miss with wild gray hair, wrinkled jacket, that crutch and smoking a cigar of all things."

"But with a broken leg, how could he possibly hunker down to cut the cable?"

"Mira's a lot of things, she is," Donna went on, "but I can't see her lying about something so important as this. What should we be doing to help Rudy?"

A woman came into the shop to return a lilac bike she had rented, but wanted to rent it again on Saturday afternoon. I wrote the woman's name on the workbench because I didn't have paper handy. Two more ladies came in to rent the rose bikes. I took the money and information and watched them pedal off. "This is terrible," I said to Donna.

"That you have customers?"

"That Rudy's not here to see it. I've got to fix this. What do you know about Speed and Bunny? I think she might have been blackmailing him. Something that would hurt his chances of raising money for the Speed Challenge and a reason to get rid of her."

Donna leaned closer. "Blackmail? Are ye sure? Her family has money."

"Had money. Dwight was bleeding her dry, the stock market's not what it used to be and she hadn't done anything to SeeFar in years. Then suddenly she puts a new roof on the place and was starting to get the inside painted all within a few months. Where'd that money come from? And she's got that new yellow bike."

"Ye be thinking Speed gave it to her? I like it, I do. I got scone deliveries to be making and can ask around if Bunny's been spending money like a drunken sailor."

"Keep it casual." I looked Donna square in the eyes. "I didn't fall in the lake last night. I was pushed."

"Stands to reason you were, dear, 'tis the black cloud and that ye got a meddling way about ya that genuinely ticks everyone off to no end. I'd be staying away from the cliffs if I were you."

Donna took off as three floral bikes were returned, then rented right back out again. A husband wanted a bike that could carry fishing gear and another wanted a cart to hold his golf clubs. Like he said, taxis made stops, and he wasn't into stops. He wanted to get where he wanted to go and he wanted to haul — a guy's gotta haul, even if it's on a bike.

By three Rudy and Irma still weren't home, Mother wasn't picking up her phone and I was trying to figure out how Mira saw Rudy cut Bunny's cable when he didn't. To keep busy and not panic, I'd painted a bike with a fly-fishing theme that I named The Angler and another with a golf motif that I named Tiger Woods. If the Grand could have the Dolly Madison suite and the Lady Astor suite, I could name my bikes.

Sheldon had bars, so using the last of my credit card limit, I ordered three tall, skinny golf club/fishing rod two-wheel carts that snapped onto the back of the bikes and that looked easy to pull. I started on a Martha Stewart bike with cookbooks and whisks and spatulas and a plate of spaghetti — I'd kill for a plate of spaghetti right now — as Mother came through the door.

I rushed up to her and hugged her. "I thought maybe Sutter locked you up too." I sniffed. "Wine? Really? I've been worrying myself into a stupor and you're having wine?"

"Angelo took me to lunch at the Gatehouse and we shared a nice pinot. He loves it so much here on the island that he talked his Family into coming up for a team-building symposium at the Grand next spring during the Lilac Festival. Not exactly sure who or what his Family is, but it seems some of *the boys* aren't working together like they should and aren't getting along. He thinks a team-building week would do them all good."

"Uh, what kind of team are we talking about?"

"Thought it best not to ask. Sounds like a family reunion with attitude — I wonder how that's going to work out. He wants to know if I'm coming back and, you know, I think I am." Mother gazed around the shop. "I can set up an office here. Flying between Chicago and the island is a short hop." She batted her eyes. "That will make Angelo happy. It makes me happy. I'll need an office; something in town with a lake view would be nice." She pointed out the window. "If Rudy moves in with Irma, we could convert the deck in the back into a terrific office. I think I need a sailboat. Call it *Carmen's Clubhouse.*"

"Mother, what about Rudy?"

"Oh, I definitely think he and Irma are an item. A nice spring wedding and —"

"I mean how is Rudy right now?"

"When I left him, he and Irma were playing Scrabble. After an hour of my being a raving legal lunatic, Sutter still wouldn't let Rudy go, but I did wangle Irma unlimited visiting privileges and a candlelit dinner from the Yankee Rebel that should be delivered anytime now."

"You are good."

Mother batted her eyes and fluffed her hair, something way more Carmen than Ann Louise. "I have my moments. After the third glass of wine, Angelo and I decided the eyewitness is a setup just like you and me going to the dock last night was a setup. Doesn't take much to put on a gray wig and get a crutch. Everyone knows about Mira and her telescope. Going to be hard to dig up proof of who's involved with Sutter watching us. And you already had one close call."

"So let's go for another one. I'll spread a rumor that I know who the killer is. That will draw him out, and we'll be ready this time."

"We're trying to find the killer for one murder, not cause another. You finish up here. The bikes look great, by the way, no wonder Rudy made you a partner, its a good business decision for him. You're an entrepreneur like your Grandpa Frank, and that Chicago job you have sucks even if you do get that promotion you want."

"How . . . how did you know about me needing a promotion?"

She kissed me on the cheek. "I know everything, dear. Now I have to get dressed. Angelo is picking me up early. There's a terrific jazz group playing in Marquette Park this evening." Mother started for the steps, then came back. "You should come with us."

"And sit between you and Angelo? A dream come true for any daughter. I'll stay out of trouble, promise."

Mother held out her hand. "Then cough it up."

29

"Cough what up? That doesn't sound very ladylike."

"Forget ladylike. You know what."

I fished the lock-picking set out of my pocket and gave it to Mother. "Happy?"

"Delighted beyond words."

"Now go get Carmen all slutted up and have fun." Never imagined I'd be saying that to my own mother. At one time the thought of having Mother here on the island, even part-time, would give me an ulcer and make me break out in hives. Carmen . . . not so much.

I finished Martha Stewart, parked her on the sidewalk and rented her out in fifteen minutes flat. I started in on Babe Ruth . . . a baseball bike, not the candy bar . . . well, maybe a little candy bar on the back fender, as Angelo pranced inside.

"You sure clean up good. Nice suit."

"Do you believe it?" Angelo said. "I'm

driving a freaking horse. It's an automatic, one flick of the reins is go, two flicks is stop, and she gets twenty miles per bag of oats. If the guys in Motown could see me now, they'd laugh so hard they'd split a gut."

"You look dashing."

"What's going to look dashing is Carmen on that seat beside me. I got a blanket for us to sit on and some wine and nice hors d'oeuvre things to eat that I ordered up over at that Gatehouse place." Angelo stood straight and smoothed his jacket. "You should know my intentions with your mother are completely honorable. She's some dish, I'll tell ya. How'd a bum like me get so lucky to have a gal like that on my arm?"

"She's pretty lucky to have found you too; we both are. She has your lock equipment. She confiscated it; she's afraid I'll get into trouble."

"Smart lady. Always listen to your mother." Angelo leaned close. "But if you get in a jam, cookie, a fingernail file and a bobby pin can do more than make a gal look good, if you get my drift."

"How's Dwight working out for you?" I asked, adding a bat and catcher's mitt to the rear fender of Babe Ruth.

"Lousy cook, worse gambler. Only reason

he didn't lose SeeFar in some backroom game before we got it is I was having him watched 'cause he owed us a bundle. We moved fast when we got the word on Bunny, otherwise some guy from Vegas would be living up on that hill."

I put down my brush. "Watched as in twenty-four/seven watched? Like if Dwight cut the brake cables on Bunny's bike to get her money, you would have known about it?"

"Hey, Dwight's a putz, and not exactly the milk-and-cookies type, but even he wouldn't do in his own ma — and yeah, I would know. I only hire the best."

Angelo pulled in a deep breath, his eyes focusing beyond me. "Va-va-voom," he said with an appreciative sigh as Carmen sashayed into the room in a black dress with touches of red lace at the neck and hem. "Those are some shoes. Give a grown man a heart attack."

"You don't look too bad yourself, mister," Carmen purred. My mother purred? Yeah, she really did.

I waved Carmen and Angelo off to their carriage as a perfect evening set over the island. The first notes of some sultry jazz piece floated my way from the park across the street. This wasn't Paris, and I was sure

Mother wasn't over Dad and his French floozie, but she was coping, and if Angelo and Carmen made the coping a little easier, why the heck not.

The good news was that I could cross Dwight off my suspect list; the bad news was I still had three to go — Huffy, Speed and Bourne. Donna was gathering intel on Speed and who knows what she'd dig up and . . . and holy moly! Right here in front of me on the sidewalk with a blanket tucked under his arm and wearing jeans and a white polo shirt was Jason Bourne, sans silver briefcase, heading for the park.

He stopped in front of the shop to look at Tiger Woods and a birds-r-us bike that had the cutest woodpecker, then came inside. "Could you possibly make up a bike with a music theme? Maybe some instruments and notes? Piano keys would be a nice touch. I love music, and I should start riding more, get some exercise."

I guess pulling a trigger didn't burn many calories, not that I said that out loud. "I have one that's a music theme, but it's rented out. I can do another." If he'd asked for dancing pigs twirling batons, I would have said yes to that too.

"I'm headed over to the park for that jazz group that's playing. I hear they're sensational. Sure is a lovely night."

Bourne left and I puffed out a deep breath. Music, scones and murder — Bourne was a man of varied tastes, and . . . and if he was at the concert, he wasn't at his house. Oh, I could not pass this up.

I locked the shop, stuck my nail file, bobby pin and flashlight in my pocket, headed out the side door and knocked right into . . . "Fiona?"

"Bourne's at the concert," she panted. She held up a crowbar. "We can use this to get into that room."

"Not very subtle."

"Screw subtle. Rudy's in the slammer. We'll be less conspicuous if we walk. Do you still have Angelo's lock-picking stuff?"

I held up the file and bobby pin and we took off. We crept along the back edge of Marquette Park, keeping in the bushes till we got to the beloved steps. Foot and carriage traffic on the bluff was light, with most people taking advantage of the concert below. Moonlight sliced through the Mackinaw Bridge, and Bourne's house was dark and deserted.

"How are we going to get to the second floor?" Fiona whispered as we slunk around to the back. "We don't have Angelo to boost us up." She pointed to the side of the house.

"The trellis."

"How many leaves does it have?"

"This is no time for botany." Fiona hooked the crowbar into the waistband of her shorts, the weight nearly pulling them clean off her skinny butt. She started up and I followed. The crowbar slipped, hitting me and falling to the ground.

"Are you okay back there?" Fiona called back to me.

"It hit my head."

"You're still talking, you're fine." We toppled onto the porch in a heap, I handed Fiona the flashlight, stuck the file into the lock and the door opened all by itself. Fiona and I exchanged *yippee* smiles at our good luck, and we headed for the locked room.

"You should have practiced," Fiona said as I stuck the file in the lock.

"You could have practiced, you know."

"Don't be silly, I already know how to hold the flashlight," she laughed.

I fished around for the lever with the wide end of the file and after two tries flipped it open.

"Dang, girl, you're 007 with boobs. Look." Fiona pointed to a chair as we walked into the room. "Bourne has one of those expensive mesh jobs that fit your body like a glove."

I sat at the desk and flipped open the computer.

"Wonder what Bourne's password is? Bull's-eye?"

"Do you password-protect your computer?"

"Never turn it off."

"No one else does either." I hit the space bar to bring the computer to life and Fiona read, *"Her heaving bosom glistened in the silvery moonlight as he slowly slid himself over her."*

Fiona and I exchanged wide-eyed looks as a voice saying, *"Getawayfromthat,"* came from behind us.

We spun around to Jason Bourne, his silhouette framed in the doorway, a flashlight in one hand and something that was definitely not a scone in the other.

30

"What are you doing here?" I yelped as Bourne shone his flashlight in our eyes.

"This is my house."

"You're supposed to be at the . . ." Fiona started then stopped. "You set us up."

"You came to the shop so I'd think you wouldn't be here, that the house would be empty. The open door was a nice touch."

Bourne walked into the room. "I was supposed to double back and be waiting when you got here."

"How'd you know I'd come?"

"You're looking for Bunny's killer, everyone knows that. You were here before — the powdered sugar up the stairs that led to the porch door, the missing scone. You really suck at breaking and entering. You think I killed Bunny. You didn't find any proof the first time, so I figured you'd come back if I made it easy for you. I wanted it on my terms so I could scare the crap out of you and make sure you'd never come back again. Except I got held up by Irish Donna asking a bunch of stupid questions about Speed as if he and I were buddies — yeah, right. You beat me here. And I really didn't want you in . . . here of all places." He nodded at the computer.

"If it makes you feel better," Fiona said. "The scaring the crap part's working great. I mean, you are a hit man."

I looked back to the computer and the heaving bosom and the silvery moonlight. "Except you're not a hit man."

"Of course he is," Fiona said in a *how stupid can you be* tone. "He's got that silver briefcase and he wears a disguise."

I pushed on, trying to make sense of everything I knew or at least thought I knew. "Bunny wasn't blackmailing you because she caught you in the act of knocking someone off in New York, she was blackmailing you because she caught you at your publisher. The books." I pointed to the computer. "You're Sophia Lovelace. Bunny was going to tell everyone that Sophia Lovelace was a middle-aged man living on Mackinac Island eating scones."

"Secret lovers, secret author, secret encounters, hot sex," Bourne said. "It works really well and sells a lot of books. Bunny was in New York drumming up interest in her family history manuscript and saw me coming out of my publisher's building. She knew my disguise and followed me the next time I left the island with the briefcase handcuffed to my wrist. I was always afraid of losing it in a cab or something."

"Good grief, your book is in the silver briefcase," Fiona offered.

"You know what the Internet service is like around here," Bourne said. "And I didn't want my books out there; too many people trying to figure out who I am. I put on a disguise and delivered my books in person. The hit man gossip took over here, so I went with it and Jason Bourne. It was kind of fun, and everyone left me alone, till the Chicago hurricane came along."

"And Bunny," Fiona added.

"Yeah, and Bunny the busybody. She even bought my books to remind me she had the upper hand. When you and I met in her closet," Bourne said to me. "I was looking for the pictures she had of me in New York. She was shaking me down for a lot of money, but I didn't kill her. I'm not Bourne; at heart, I'm Lovelace."

"How do we know you're not just BSing us?" Fiona folded her arms.

"I'm a writer. If I wanted to kill Bunny,

there're many better ways than cutting a bike cable. We have water here, deep water — a cement block at the head and feet and the body's down for the count. 'Course a few puncture wounds to the lungs and stomach keep the gasses from building up and the body floating if the blocks break loose. Whoever did in Bunny wanted the body to be found. Rudy being accused could have been part of the plan to kill Bunny or just someone who didn't like Rudy."

"Sounds like you'd be good at writing murder mysteries," Fiona said.

"Hate murder mysteries. I'm more of a *make love, not war* kind of guy. So, are you two going to blackmail me too?"

"I'm more of a *paint the bike* kind of girl, and Fiona's all about smiling pictures."

"And there's that *cement block and gasses* scenario you just told us about to consider," Fiona said with a shudder. "Besides, every island needs a hit man. Good local color. But if I were you, I'd get better locks and update the mustache."

"And maybe you could give us a book once in a while," I threw in.

"So," Fiona asked me as we left the house and headed for town. "Is he Bourne or Lovelace?"

"Probably always be Bourne to me, and we can cross him off our Bunny Festival list. That leaves Huffy and Speed. I don't know about you but I'm in serious need of a beer."

"The Clarkstons are celebrating their fiftieth anniversary and having a big to-do down at Mission Resort. If I don't get pictures and put it in the *Crier,* they'll lynch me."

"The *Town Crier* is not the *New York Times.*"

"Girl, around here it is. I'll catch up with you tomorrow." Fiona promised she'd get me a piece of anniversary cake and went to the newspaper office to get her camera. I continued on to the Stang, the watering hole for locals. Heck, I'd been here nearly a week, so I was entitled.

The place was jammed, "Boot-Scootin' Boogie" was blaring from the jukebox and Dwight was dancing with some hot-looking girl in a low-cut top and high-cut shorts who was not Huffy. It wouldn't be a problem if it were one of those *I'm here, you're here, let's shake it* kind of dances. This was more *let me buy you a drink, baby, and let's get a room.*

I found a place to stand at the bar and got a Bud Light to offset the calories from the

365

order of fried green beans. "If Huffy gets wind of this, there's going to be hell to pay," Sutter said, coming up behind me, his breath hot on my neck, making me nearly bite the top right off my beer.

"Shouldn't you be back at the ranch minding the felons?"

"Mother's there. She's ready to shoot me with my own gun. It's safer here. Find anything out on the three-seventy-five building?" He snagged one of my beans and popped it in his mouth.

"Jason Bourne didn't kill Bunny, and you're doing it again. You distract me and then you eat all my green beans."

He grinned. "Maybe. And I know Bourne didn't do in Bunny, 'cause Rudy did."

"No wonder Irma wants to shoot you."

Sutter took a drink of my beer and I gave him a hard look, noticing how he favored one leg, his left shoulder sagging slightly, a hint of pain etched in his face. "Then again, I'm guessing somebody already beat her to it. Detroit ain't Disney World, is it, cowboy?"

"You ask a lot of questions. When did you say you were heading back to Chicago? Tomorrow? Good idea." Someone knocked into Sutter and he stumbled against me, my hands against his chest, the heat from his body washing over me, my heart skipping a beat, my brain fading to crumpled sheets on a bed.

"Rudy and I are going to be partners in the bike shop," I said to fill the void. "So I'm not going anywhere. What do you think of that?"

Sutter closed his eyes for a second and let out a long breath. "Dang," he said in a low voice smooth as the bourbon behind the bar. His hand trailed down my arm, his eyes black with a flash of summer lightning, my toes curling into my shoes. His fingers twined slowly into my hair, his palm pressed against the small of my back, and he kissed me full on the mouth right there in front of God and half the population of Mackinac Island. Then he headed for the door.

"Vodka," the bartender said, shoving a shot glass in my hand and pouring one for himself. "After that, we both need a drink."

I downed the booze, the jolt snapping me back to the real world, which wasn't nearly as mind-blowing as the one I'd just been in with Sutter. I turned for the door as Huffy came barreling through, almost knocking me over. "You no-good bastard."

Usually that didn't refer to a woman, but I'd been called worse. "What did I do now?"

"Not you," Huffy huffed, pushing me out of the way. "Him!" She pointed to Dwight and Dance Girl, who were sitting at a table engaged in a rousing game of tonsil hockey. Everyone backed away, Dwight doing the *cool dude* bit.

"We have a plan," Huffy snarled, hands on hips as she came up to Dwight. "Bunny's gone, and that means you and I are together."

"*You* have a plan," Dwight said in an even tone, taking a swig of beer. "Fact is, I think this was all your plan. You knocked off my mother to get the house, to get the money, to get *me*." Dwight did *cool dude kicked up a notch.* "You framed Rudy for what you did."

"That's crazy."

"Is it? Everyone knows you've been after me forever. Well, I don't want you, and I sure as heck never signed up for baby duty." Dwight kissed Dance Girl, then said to Huffy, "You're on your own, Huffy."

"You're not getting away with this," Huffy yelled, her face red.

"You're the one not getting away. In fact, you're going to prison, and I'm going to help put you there."

"Go to hell, Dwight."

"You first."

Huffy snatched a tray of beers and crashed it over Dwight's head. Dance Girl jumped out of the line of fire as Dwight sprawled onto the floor. Huffy peered down at him. "You led me on, got what you wanted from me all these years and then when it finally happens, you run."

Huffy turned to Dance Girl. "Stay away from him." She jabbed her finger at the floor. "That piece of slime-sucking crud's mine and going to stay mine, or he's not going to belong to anybody — you get what I'm talking about?"

Huffy stormed out the door, and the bartender helped Dwight to his feet and dusted him off. "You owe me thirty-seven fifty for the beers, Romeo. Try and stay alive till you write me a check."

I headed back to the bike shop determined to think less about Sutter and the kiss and more about the Stang, Huffy and the beers. One got me in a lot of trouble; the other got Rudy out of a lot of trouble. Did Huffy plan the whole Bunny thing, or was Dwight shooting off his mouth to get out of being Papa Dwight? By the time I got back to the shop, all I wanted was for this day to end. I fed Bambino and Cleveland, promised them Rudy would be back soon and told them a Twain story that was really another one from the back of a cereal box — but the cats weren't buying it for a minute. As I took out the trash, someone grabbed me from behind.

Speed spun me around and pinned me against the deck railing. His eyes blazed and his hands were around my throat. "You mess up my life, I end yours. I warned you once; you should have listened."

Black dots danced in front of my eyes, and breathing was tough. *Think, Evie, think!* Shaking, I pulled the nail file from my pocket and jabbed it at Speed's middle.

"Ouch!" Speed yelped, stumbling back, looking down at my file sticking out of his black jacket, which had taken most of the impact. "You stabbed me."

"You choked me," I wheezed, collapsing against the back wall of the shop. I plopped down on the floor beside the blue paint smear from when Angelo had scared the heck out of me. I seriously needed to stay off this deck.

Speed tossed down the file and slid up his shirt. "I'm bleeding."

"And not nearly enough," Mother growled, running out onto the deck. "Evie, get a kitchen knife, we need to do a better job." She gave me a *follow my lead* look, then grabbed Speed by his jacket. "You tried to kill my daughter just like you killed Bunny."

"I wasn't going to kill your daughter, and I didn't do anything to Bunny," Speed said, trying to back away from Mother, a touch of fear in his eyes. "She was the one blackmailing me."

"For what?" I asked, my brain cells starting to function. "Paying off a racing judge? Taking a shortcut? Cheating in a race, like the Tour of Texas maybe? That's why you didn't look thrilled when you got the picture of you in *Sports Illustrated,* and that's why you shoved it in the back of your closet."

"How'd you know about the closet?"

Best defense was a scary offense. "You were doping?"

"Heck no. I didn't cheat in that race or in any other. I used to tell Bunny I took my super vitamins and that's why I was so *speedy.* It was a running joke between us till she threatened to tell the press it was for real that I was taking stuff. Any hint of scandal, true or not, would cut me off at the knees for raising money, and she knew it."

"So that's why you killed her."

"It was easier for me to keep paying Bunny, least for now. Once I got the Speed Challenge off the ground, I would have made my move, and no one would have ever found the body."

"Sounds good except that finding Bunny's body framed Rudy for the murder and you wanted his shop. You even came to me to get Rudy to sell it to you."

"I wanted to make sure I got the place and not Huffy. It was already going under; I didn't have to frame Rudy to get it. A dead body attracts the wrong kind of attention, and I don't need that — something you, Granny Scone and Foxy Mamma here need to remember. Just stay out of my life, will ya?"

Hunched over, Speed trotted down the back alley. I picked up my file from the deck and turned to Mother. "So what do you think, Carmen? Is he our killer?"

"Dear, he called me Foxy Mamma; I'm biased and proud of it. But even if I weren't, Speed didn't do in Bunny. He's right about the body thing. He would have gotten rid of it; any killer would have, unless . . . unless finding the body was necessary for whatever reason."

"Like securing an inheritance?"

"That would work. Got somebody in mind?"

31

I was out the door and heading for the police station before Mother was up and the first ferry of the day zoomed across the lake. I truly wanted to avoid Sutter because of the kiss, and I had no idea what to do about it, but I wanted to get Rudy out of jail more. Sutter and I needed to chat. I pulled an organic strawberry smoothie out of my bag and handed it to the desk clerk, Molly. "Is Sutter here?"

"Pissed and in his office."

I pulled out a chocolate doughnut. One can only take so much healthy food.

Molly's eyes brightened. "He got a call from the Detroit PD. Seems he was doing more than writing parking tickets back there, and some bad guys are looking for him."

I headed down the hall, Molly yelling halfheartedly between smoothie slurps and doughnut chomps how I couldn't go back there. It wasn't that I liked Huffy all that much — actually, I didn't like her at all — but she'd been messed over by a crappy guy and I'd been messed over by a crappy guy, so we belonged to the same crappy club and I felt bad for her. Plus I thought she was innocent. She was a mamma and her baby came first. She wouldn't chance jail.

"Oh good, now you show up, my day's complete," Sutter said when I walked in. Huffy was sitting in a chair across from him.

"I don't think she did it," I said.

"Thank you, Sherlock Holmes, now you can leave."

Sutter took my arm, hauling me toward the door as I said, "Can you really see Huffy here knocking off her kid's grandma, even if it meant she'd get the man of her dreams, who's actually turning out to be the man of her nightmares?"

"Kid?" Sutter stopped and looked to Huffy as she made the rounded belly sign over her stomach.

Sutter pointed to a plastic bag on his desk. "We found this gray curly wig and crutch in her apartment. She cut Bunny's bike cable, then dressed up like Rudy to frame him."

"Let me guess." I held up my hands. "An anonymous tip put you onto the wig and crutch?"

"This is all Dwight," Huffy said. "You gotta see that he planted those things to make it look like knocking off Bunny was all my idea and to frame Rudy for it. It's him getting rid of me and the baby. He wants us out of his life so he can carouse and carry on like he always has. I say we neuter him."

I was just about to tell Huffy to count me in when the captain barged into the room. "I did it. I'm guilty. I knocked off Bunny and framed Rudy. Sorry about Rudy, but I'm glad Bunny kicked the bucket."

The captain held out his hands. "Put on the cuffs and let my daughter go. This is no place for the mother of my grandchild."

A big, sappy smile slid over the captain's face and he reached in his back pocket and pulled out a baby captain's hat. "Got this on eBay for ten bucks and it's just like mine. Cutest thing I ever saw. Draw up anything, Sutter, I'll sign it. Which way to the cells?"

He turned to me. "By the way, that other bike Rudy ordered came in yesterday and I dropped it at the bike shop on my way here. The bikes you've painted look great. If you do one on the ferries, can you put me in? Maybe my hat?"

"You got it," I said. "Congrats on the baby."

"That's it." Sutter stood up. "I've heard that pregnancy makes people crazy; I just didn't expect it to be contagious. Everybody get out. The Mackinaw Bridge walk starts in one hour and I've got to be there. I swear if any of you come near me, I'm throwing you in the lake."

We all trooped down the hall as Irma came in the station, bandana over her nose and mouth, squirt gun in hand.

Nate asked, "Is there an outbreak of something besides insanity that I should know about, Mother?"

She waved her squirt gun. "It's a jailbreak, dear." She held up a basket. "I'm taking Rudy for a picnic. It's beautiful outside and I'm sure it's against the law on this particular island to keep someone in jail over a holiday." She shot Nate, a stream of water splattering across his front. "I'm getting pretty good with this thing, so don't give me any sass."

Nate held up his hands. "This isn't over. Somebody killed Bunny."

Irma patted his cheek. "Of course they did, dear. But it's not Rudy; we all know that."

When I got back to the bike shop, Mother had left a note saying that she and Angelo were doing the bridge walk. In Chicago the

376

only bridge Mother ever mentioned was her bridge club and walking was boring exercise on a machine.

Abigail sent me a text asking about my Labor Day celebration plans on the island and that she was thinking about visiting, making me think the girl was having a breakdown. I hadn't even been sure she knew what a weekend was. That she said she wanted to visit nearly gave me a heart attack. To try and keep her in Chicago, I sent her an All is terrific here text and a picture of the bikes I had painted. Just when I thought I'd have her out of my life, she wasn't? What was going on with Rudy's daughter?

I opened the shop to get ready for the day. I rented out all my themed bikes before noon. I needed to sketch up more ideas and get painting. Maybe Rudy's Rides could sponsor a bike parade next year and tie it in with the Lilac Festival. Great promo. Maybe I should tell Abigail that and she'd see I was on top of things and she'd stay the heck away?

I unboxed the folding bike that the captain had dropped off and screwed on the pedals and seat. Sutter was right about one thing — someone did knock off Bunny. The problem was I had no idea who, and Rudy was still suspect number one, with the cutters found in his kitchen.

Someone was playing me, and I was falling for it. Speed, maybe? He gave me that no-body spiel, but I wasn't buying it. He hated Bunny, he had a lot to lose if she blabbed and he wanted Rudy's Rides. Then again, Bourne had a lot to lose if Bunny blabbed, and disguise was his specialty. He could have easily dressed up like Rudy to do the deed.

Fiona dropped off anniversary strawberry cream cake from the Clarkstons' party, along with the latest on her old boss, Peephole Perry, who had apparently peeped on the wrong person and was now on the lam. As long as he didn't lam here, Fiona didn't care what happened to the sleazebag. I draped two bike locks over the handlebars as a little present for Ed and his new purchases so the bikes wouldn't get stolen when he and Helen the horrible took them out. I put a *Be back in thirty* sign on the front door and headed for the docks. I wrangled with the dock master again about making a delivery and not robbing everyone, then made my way to *Helen's Heaven.* Boats? I took a steadying breath, willed myself not to lose my lunch, then lifted the bike on board. I started to leave, then spotted a bank of angry clouds off to the west. It probably wouldn't rain till the evening, but I had no idea if Ed would visit his boat today or not, and I didn't want to leave a new bike in the rain. I had on the same jeans from last night, so I pulled out my handy-dandy file and bobby pin and unlocked the cabin door. I was getting pretty good at this, even on a queasy stomach.

The inside of the boat was as pristine as the outside . . . if you liked boats. There was a spotless white sofa, cobalt blue club chairs, a white kitchen area and a coral dining area. Helen had expensive taste. I parked the bike in the kitchen, grabbed paper from the drawer to write Ed a note saying that I hoped he would enjoy the folding bike — and stopped dead. Right there next to the pens was a packet of cigars — cheap cigars, with one missing. Ed hated cigars. And there was a wig jammed in beside it. Maybe it was to tease Rudy? Except I'd never seen Ed tease Rudy. They were pals, but not joke-around kind of pals. They were buddies . . . or were they?

Barely breathing, my stomach rolling for more reasons than seasickness, I opened one, two then three closets and found a crutch leaning against the side, a crumpled white suit jacket hung next to it, a saw on the floor.

"Running off to Tahiti?" Sutter said, clambering down the steps as I came back into the main room. "The dock master called and said somebody was picking a lock on one of his boats and the last time she was here, she was covered in white paint and . . . Whoa, this time you're green."

I took Sutter's hand and led him to the drawer with the wig and the cigars. "There's a crutch and white wrinkled suit jacket in the bedroom. What is going on? Or maybe nothing's going on and it's me overreacting? We both know I do that sometimes, well, maybe a lot of the time, and you already found a wig and crutch at Huffy's, except we know Huffy didn't kill Bunny. But why would Ed frame Rudy for murder?"

The step creaked, and Ed and Helen were framed in the doorway, a gun in Ed's hand. "Don't do it," he said to Nate as he reached for his own gun. "You might be faster than me, but I bet I can put a bullet in Chicago here before you get one off. Put your gun on the floor real easy and kick it over to me, and don't dirty the carpet, we just had it cleaned. The dock master called and said someone was breaking into our boat and that you were here too. We figured you were up to no good."

"That dock master knows we're all out here," Sutter said in a low, even voice, like someone who'd had a gun pointed at him before.

Helen smirked. "Four of us go out for a little sail and two come back. Everyone knows how you and this girl here are always at each other. A little shoving match and you just happened to fall overboard and we couldn't save you."

"Hold on," I said in a high, shrill voice, like someone who'd never had a gun pointed at her. "This is crazy. Why frame Rudy for Bunny's death?" I turned to Ed. "He's your best friend." My eyes shot wide open, my stomach doing a double flip. "And you're going to make this boat move?" I felt light-headed and gagged and stumbled against the wall, knocking off a row of family pictures of *Helen's Heaven,* the good times.

Nate grabbed my arm. "Take a deep breath."

I stared at the floor, trying not to lose my lunch. My head cleared, and I picked up one of the pictures. "I . . . I know this guy from Chicago. He runs an ad agency — one of Abigail's competitors. In fact, he and Abigail are both pitching to a client next week. That's why she sent me here and she didn't come and . . . and . . ."

"And this has nothing to do with Bunny or Rudy," Nate said. "This is about money and business, isn't it, Ed?"

Ed scowled. "This is about family. Ed Junior needs this next contract — *we* need it — and the only way for that to happen is to get Abigail out of Chicago. All of our money is tied up in the agency and Junior is running it into the ground. No one pitches a project like Abigail. She worked for me — I taught her all she knows."

"And she's kicking Junior's butt," I said, starting to put it all together. "You're the one who cut Rudy's step when you were acting like you were doing repairs. You wanted him to break his leg, thinking that would get Abigail here."

"And instead, you showed up with paint cans," Ed hissed.

"So you upped the stakes and killed Bunny and pinned it on Rudy," Sutter said. "For sure that would get his daughter to come."

"That nosy Bunny saw Ed cutting the step and started to blackmail him," Helen added. "We had to put an end to that, and framing Rudy for the murder knowing Mira and her telescope would see the whole thing was a perfect fit. Even if Rudy is Ed's friend, it couldn't be helped. Bunny would be gone and Abigail would come to the island, and by all rights it should have worked," Helen fumed. "Whoever heard of putting a body on ice for a week? It's indecent. And then Chicago here bonded with Rudy and started hunting for the murderer. You're not very good, you know."

"Couldn't be too bad," I said. "You pushed me in the lake to get rid of me." I drew in a sharp breath. "That was supposed to be Mother."

"We figured her sharing space with Bunny might dampen your enthusiasm a bit."

I jumped up, ready to commit murder of my own, and Sutter pulled me down. "Easy, girl." He gave me a hard look. "I sure could use some of your fried green beans about now."

"We're dying, and you're thinking food? Men! And did you have to mention fried?" I burped.

"Fried green beans that I steal from you all the time by . . ." Sutter jabbed me in the ribs.

By distracting me and getting my attention on something else, I finished to myself.

"Shut up, you two." Helen turned to Ed. "We'll tie them up and get going before that dock master comes over here to see what's going on."

"I'm going to be sick." I stood up, leaning over the white couch. "Those blueberries for breakfast didn't sit too well." I gagged.

"Blueberries?" Helen shrieked. "For God's sake, move."

I hunched my shoulders, gagged and didn't budge. Helen rushed for me, Sutter dove for Ed, pinning him against the wall, and I tackled Helen to the floor. I picked up a framed picture of Ed Junior, the happy years, and whacked her over the head. "That's for Mother," I yelled at Helen. Then I whacked her again.

Sutter snagged me by the back of my shirt, bringing me beside him, gun in hand. "Well done, Evie Bloomfield."

"I wasn't kidding about the blueberries." I headed for the steps, then turned back. "Say it. After all this time, I gotta hear it."

I got a half smile from Sutter. "Rudy didn't kill Bunny."

And that made me smile. "So, are you staying around here or leaving?"

"Does it matter to you?"

"Yeah, I think it does, actually. By any chance, do you like cheesecake?"

The employees of Thorndike Press hope you have enjoyed this Large Print book. All our Thorndike, Wheeler, and Kennebec Large Print titles are designed for easy reading, and all our books are made to last. Other Thorndike Press Large Print books are available at your library, through selected bookstores, or directly from us.

For information about titles, please call:
   (800) 223-1244

or visit our Web site at:
   http://gale.cengage.com/thorndike

To share your comments, please write:
Publisher
Thorndike Press
10 Water St., Suite 310
Waterville, ME 04901